book three

RED
DICE

Text copyright © 1994 Christopher Pike

First published in the USA in 1994 and 1996 as two separate paperbacks
by Pocket Books, a division of Simon & Schuster Inc.

The Last Vampire: Red Dice first published in Great Britain in 1995
by Hodder Children's Books

The Last Vampire: Phantom first published in Great Britain in 1996
by Hodder Children's Books

This bind-up edition published in Great Britain in 2010
by Hodder Children's Books

4

ISBN-13: 978 1 444 90051 4

Typeset in New Baskerville by Avon DataSet Ltd,
Bidford-on-Avon, Warwickshire

Printed in Great Britain by
Clays Ltd, St Ives plc

The paper and board used in this paperback by Hodder Children's Books are
natural recyclable products made from wood grown in sustainable forests.
The manufacturing processes conform to the environmental regulations of
the country of origin.

Hodder Children's Books
a division of Hachette Children's Books
338 Euston Road, London NW1 3BH
An Hachette UK company
www.hachette.co.uk

For Rene

1 ➤～

I am a vampire. Blood does not bother me. I like blood. Even seeing my own blood does not frighten me. But what my blood can do to others – to the whole world for that matter – terrifies me. Once God made me take a vow to create no more vampires. Once I believed in God. But my belief, like my vow, has been shattered too many times in my long life. I am Alisa Perne, the now-forgotten Sita, child of a demon. I am the oldest living creature on earth.

I awake in a living room smelling of death. I watch as my blood trickles through a thin plastic tube into the arm of Special Agent Joel Drake, FBI. He now lives as a vampire instead of the human being he was when he closed his eyes. I have broken my promise to Lord

Krishna – Joel did not ask me to make him a vampire. Indeed, he told me not to, to let him die in peace. But I did not listen. Therefore, Krishna's protection, his grace, no longer applies to me. Perhaps it is good. Perhaps I will die soon. Perhaps not.

I do not die easily.

I remove the tubing from my arm and stand. At my feet lies the body of Mrs Fender, mother of Eddie Fender, who also lies dead, in a freezer at the end of the hall. Eddie had been a vampire, a very powerful one, before I cut off his head. I step over his mother's body to search for a clock. Somehow, fighting the forces of darkness, I have misplaced my watch. A clock ticks in the kitchen above the stove. Ten minutes to twelve. It is dark outside.

I have been unconscious for almost twenty-four hours.

Joel will awaken soon, I know, and then we must go. But I do not wish to leave the evidence of my struggle with Eddie for the FBI to examine. Having seen how Eddie stole and used the blood of my creator, Yaksha, I know I must vaporize this sick house. My sense of smell is acute, as is my hearing. The pump that cools the large freezer in the back is not electric but powered by gasoline. I smell large amounts of fuel on the back porch. After I toss the gasoline all over the house, and wake Joel, I will strike a match. Fire pleases me, although it has the power to destroy me. Had I not been a vampire, I might have become a pyromaniac.

The gasoline is stored in two twenty-gallon steel

tanks. Because I have the strength of many men, I have no trouble lifting them both at once. Yet even I am surprised by how light they feel. Before I passed out, I was like Joel, on the verge of death. Now I am stronger than I can ever remember being. There is a reason. Yaksha gave me what blood he had left in his veins before I buried him in the sea. He gave me his power, and I never realized how great it was until this moment. It is a wonder I was able to defeat Eddie, who also drank from Yaksha. Perhaps Krishna came to my aid, one last time.

I take the drums into the living room. From the freezer, I remove Eddie's body, severed head, and even the hard blood on the freezer floor. I pick them all up and place them on my living room barbecue. Next I begin to break up the couch and tables into easy-to-burn pieces. The noise causes Joel to stir but he does not waken. Newborn vampires sleep deep and wake up hungry. I wonder if Joel will be like my beloved Ray, reluctant to drink from the living. I hope not. I loved Ray above all things, but as a vampire, he was a pain in the ass.

I think of Ray.

He has been dead less than two days.

'My love,' I whisper. 'My sorrow.'

There is no time for grief; there never is. There is no time for joy, I think bitterly. Only for life, pain, death. God did not plan this creation. It was a joke to him, a dream. Once, in a dream, Krishna told me many

3

secrets. But he may have lied to me. It would have been like him.

I am almost done throwing the fuel around and tearing up the house when I hear the sound of approaching cars. There are no sirens but I know these are police cruisers. Police drive differently from normal people, worse actually. They drive faster and the officers in these squad cars are anxious to get here. I have incredibly sensitive hearing – I count at least twenty vehicles. What brings them here?

I glance at Joel.

'Are they coming for Eddie?' I ask him. 'Or for me? What did you tell your superiors?'

But perhaps I am too quick to judge, too harsh. Los Angeles has seen many strange sights lately, many bodies killed by superhumans. Perhaps Joel has not betrayed me, at least not intentionally. Perhaps I have betrayed myself. I have gotten sloppy in my old age. I hurry to Joel's side and shake him roughly.

'Wake up,' I say. 'We have to get out of here.'

He opens his drowsy eyes. 'You look different,' he whispers.

'Your eyes are different.'

Realization crosses his face. 'Did you change me?'

'Yes.'

He swallows weakly. 'Am I still human?'

I sigh. 'You're a vampire.'

'Sita.'

I put a finger to his lips. 'Later. We must leave here

quickly. Many cops are coming.' I pull him to his feet and he groans. 'You will feel stronger in a few minutes. Stronger than you have ever felt before.'

I find a Bic lighter in the kitchen, and we head for the front door. But before we can reach it I hear three cruisers skid to a halt outside. We hurry to the back, but the situation is the same. Cops, weapons drawn, have jumped out of their cars with whirling blue and red lights cutting paths in the night sky. More vehicles appear, armored monstrosities with SWAT teams inside. Searchlights flash on and light up the house. We are surrounded. I do not do well in such situations, or else, one might say, I do very well – for a vampire. What I mean is, being trapped brings out my most vicious side. I push aside my recently acquired revulsion for violence. Once, in the Middle Ages, surrounded by an angry mob, I killed over a hundred men and women.

Of course, they didn't have guns.

A bullet in the head could probably kill me, I think.

'Am I really a vampire?' Joel asks, still trying to catch up with reality.

'You're not an FBI agent anymore,' I mutter.

He shakes himself as he straightens up. 'But I am. Or at least they think I am. Let me talk to them.'

'Wait.' I stop him, thinking. 'I can't have them examine Eddie's remains. I don't trust what will happen to his blood. I don't trust what his blood can still do. I must destroy it, and to do that I must burn down this house.'

Outside, through a bullhorn, a gruff-voiced man calls for us to come out with our hands in the air. Such an unimaginative way of asking us to surrender.

Joel knew what Eddie had been capable of. 'I was wondering why everything smelled like gasoline,' he remarks. 'You light the place on fire – I have no problem with that. But then what are you going to do? You can't fight this army.'

'Can't I?' I peer out the front window and raise my eyes to the rhythmic thrumming in the sky. They have a helicopter. Why? All to catch the feared serial killer? Yes, such a beast would demand heavy forces. Yet I sense a curious undercurrent in the assembled men and women. It reminds me of when Slim, Yaksha's assassin, came looking for me. Slim's people had been warned that I was not normal. As a result, I barely escaped. In the same way, these people know that there is something unusual about me.

I can almost read their thoughts.

This strikes me as strange.

I have always been able to sense emotions. Now, can I read thoughts, too?

What power has Yaksha's blood given me?

'Alisa,' Joel says, calling me by my modern name. 'Even you cannot break free of this circle.' He notices I'm lost in thought. 'Alisa?'

'They think there is a monster in here,' I whisper. 'I *hear* their minds.' I grip Joel. 'What did you tell them about me?'

He shakes his head. 'Some things.'

'Did you tell them I was powerful? Fast?'

He hesitates, then sighs. 'I told them too much. But they don't know you're a vampire.' He, too, peers through the curtains. 'They were getting suspicious about how the others died, torn to pieces. They had my file on Eddie Fender, including where his mother lived. They must have tracked us here that way.'

I shake my head. 'I cannot surrender. It is against my nature.'

He takes my hands. 'You can't fight them all. You'll die.'

I have to smile. 'More of them would die.' I lose my smile. 'But if I do make a stand here, you will die also.' I am indecisive. His advice is logical. Yet my heart betrays me. I feel doom closing in. I speak reluctantly. 'Talk to them. Say what you think best. But I tell you – I will not leave this house without setting it ablaze. There will be no more Eddie Fenders.'

'I understand.' He turns for the door, then stops. He speaks with his back to me. 'I understand why you did it.'

'Do you forgive me?'

'Would I have died?' he asks.

'Yes.'

He smiles gently, not turning to look at me. I feel the smile. 'Then I must forgive you,' he says. He raises his hands above his head and reaches for the doorknob. 'I hope my boss is out there.'

Through a crack in the curtains I follow his progress.

Joel calls out his identity and a group of FBI agents step forward. I can tell they're FBI by their suits. Joel is one of them. He looks the same as he did yesterday. Yet they don't greet him as a friend. In an instant I grasp the full extent of their suspicions. They know that whatever plague of death has been sweeping L.A. is communicable. Eddie and I left too many bodies behind. Also, I remember the cop I freed. The one whose blood I sampled. The one I told I was a vampire. The authorities may not have believed that man, but they will think I am some kind of demon from hell.

Joel is handcuffed and dragged into an armored vehicle. He casts me a despairing glance before he vanishes. I curse the fact that I listened to him. Now I, too, must be taken into the vehicle. Above all, I must stay close to Joel. I don't know what he'll tell them. I don't know what they'll do with his blood.

Many of them are going to die, I realize.

The SWAT team cocks their weapons.

They call again for me to surrender.

I twirl the striker on the lighter and touch it to the wood I have gathered around Eddie's body. I say goodbye to his ugly head. Hope the Popsicles you suck in hell cool your cracked and bleeding lips. Casually, while the inferno spreads behind me, I step out the front door.

They are on me in an instant. Before I can reach the curb, my arms are pulled behind me and I am handcuffed. They don't even read me my rights. You have the right to a pint of blood. If you cannot afford one, the court will bleed a little for you. Yeah, I think sarcastically as they shove me into the back of the armored vehicle where they threw Joel, I will be given all my rights as an American citizen. Behind me I see them trying to put out the fire. Too bad they brought the firepower but forgot the fire engines. The house is a funeral pyre. Eddie Fender will leave no legacy to haunt mankind.

But what about me? Joel?

Our legs are chained to the floor of the vehicle. Three men with automatic weapons and ghostly faces lit from a single overhead light sit on a metal bench across from us, weapons trained on us. No one speaks. Another two armed men sit up front, beside the driver. One carries a shotgun, the other a machine gun. They are separated from us by what I know is bulletproof glass. It also acts as soundproofing. I can break it with my little finger.

But what about the miniature army around us? They won't break so easily. As the door is closed and we roll forward, I hear a dozen cars move into position around us. The chopper follows overhead, a spotlight aimed down on our car. Their precautions border on the fanatical. They know I am capable of extraordinary feats of strength. This realization sinks deep into my consciousness. For five thousand years, except for a few isolated incidents, I have moved unknown through human history. Now I am exposed. Now I am the enemy. No matter what happens, whether we escape or die trying, my life will never be the same.

I'll have to tear up my credit cards.

'Where are you taking us?' I ask.

'You are to remain silent,' the middle one says. He has the face of a drill sergeant, leathery skin, deeply etched lines cut in from years of barking commands. Like his partners, he wears a flak jacket. I think I would look nice in one. I catch his eye and smile faintly.

'What's the matter?' I ask. 'Are you afraid of a young woman?'

'Silence,' he snaps, shaking his weapon, shifting uncomfortably. My stare is strong medicine. It can burn holes in brain neurons. My voice is hypnotic, when I wish it to be. I could sing a grizzly to sleep. I let my smile widen.

'May I have a cigarette?' I ask.

'No,' he says flatly.

I lean forward as far as I can. These men, for all their plans, have not come as well prepared as Slim's people did. Yaksha had them bring cuffs made of a special alloy that I could not break. I can snap these like paper. Yet they are seated close together, these SWAT experts, and they have three separate weapons leveled directly at me. They could conceivably kill me before I could take out all of them. For that reason I have to take a subtle approach.

Relatively speaking.

'I don't know what you've been told about me,' I

continue. 'But I think it's way out of line. I have done nothing wrong. Also, my friend here is an FBI agent. He shouldn't be treated this way. You should let him go.' I stare deep into the man's eyes, and I know all he sees is my widening black pupils, growing as large as the dark sides of twin moons. I speak softly, 'You should let him go *now*.'

The man reaches for his keys, then hesitates. The hesitation is a problem. Pushing a person's will is always a hit-or-miss proposition. His partners are watching him now, afraid to look at me. The youngest one rises half off his bench. He is suddenly scared and threatens me with his weapon.

'You shut your goddamn mouth!' he yells.

I lean back and chuckle. As I do, I catch his eye. Fear has made him vulnerable; he is an easy mark. 'What are you afraid of?' I ask. 'That your commander will let me go? Or that you'll turn around and shoot him?' I bore my gaze into his head. 'Yeah, you could shoot him. Yeah, that might be fun.'

'Alisa,' Joel whispers, not enjoying my game.

The young man and the commander exchange worried glances. The third guy has sat up, panting, not really understanding what is happening. Out of the corner of my eye, I see Joel shaking his head. Let him see me at my worst, I think. It is the best way to begin our new relationship, without illusions. My eyes dart from the commander to the young one. The temperature inside their craniums is increasing. Ever so

11

slightly, each weapon begins to veer toward the other man's chest. Yet I know I'll have to push them a lot harder to get them to let me go or kill each other. It is not necessary. I can do it on my own. Really, I just want to distract them a bit—

Before I break them in two.

With their guns aimed away from me, they are vulnerable when I suddenly shoot my legs up, snapping my ankle chains. The third man, the one I have left untouched, reacts quickly, by human standards. But he is moving in slow motion compared to a five-thousand-year-old vampire. As he reaches for the trigger on his gun, my right foot lashes out and my big toe crushes his flak jacket, his breastbone, and the beating heart beneath the two. The heart beats no more. The man crumples and falls into a pitiful ball.

'Should have given me the cigarette,' I say to the commander as I snap my handcuffs and reach over to take his head between my palms. His eyes grow round. His lips move. He wants to tell me something, maybe apologize. I'm not in the mood. He is putty in my hands, Silly Putty once I squeeze my palms together and crack his skull. Now his mouth falls open as his eyes slowly close. His brains leak out the back, over his starched collar. I don't want his flak jacket.

I glance over at the young one.

He's more scared than before.

I just stare at him. He has forgotten his weapon.

'Die,' I whisper intently. My will is poisonous, when I

am mad, and now, with Yaksha's blood in my veins, the poison is worse than the venom of a cobra. The young man falls to the floor.

His breathing stops.

Joel looks as if he will be sick.

'Kill me,' he swears. 'I cannot stand this.'

'I am what I am.' I break his chains. 'You will become what I am.'

He is bitter. He has no illusions. 'Never.'

I nod. 'I said the same thing to Yaksha.' I soften, touch his arm. 'I cannot let them take you or me into custody. We could have a thousand Eddies running around.'

'They just want to talk to us,' he says.

I shake my head as I glance at the men up front, unaware, so far, of what has happened to their comrades. 'They know we are not normal,' I whisper.

Joel pleads. 'You can escape far more easily without me. Fewer people will have to die. Leave me behind. Let them catch me in a shower of bullets. My blood will soak the pavement, nothing more.'

'You are a brave man, Joel Drake.'

He grimaces as he glances at what I have done to the others. 'I have spent my life trying to help people. Not destroy them.'

I stare softly into his eyes. 'I can't just let you die. You don't know what I have sacrificed to keep you alive.'

He pauses. 'What did you sacrifice?'

I sigh. 'The love of God.' I turn toward the men at the front. 'We will discuss this later.'

Joel stops me one last time. 'Don't kill when you don't have to.'

'I will do what I can,' I promise.

The bulletproof glass is two inches thick. Although the ceiling of the van forces me to crouch, I am able to leap far enough off the floor to plant two swift kicks onto the barrier. I have exceptionally strong legs. The glass shatters into thousands of little pellets. Before the two armed men can turn, I reach forward and knock their heads together. They collapse in a mangled heap. They are unconscious, not dead. I remove the revolver from the hip holster of the driver and place the barrel to his head.

'The men in the back are dead,' I whisper in his ear. 'If you glance in your rearview mirror you will see it is true. But I have allowed your partners up front to live. That is because I am a nice girl. I am nice and I am nasty. If you tell me where we are headed, I will be nice to you. If you don't, if you try to alert your partners on the road ahead of us or behind us, I will tear out your eyes and swallow them.' I pause. 'Where are you taking us?'

He has trouble speaking. 'C-Fourteen.'

'Is that a police station?'

'No.'

'What is it? Quickly!'

He coughs, frightened. 'A high-security facility.'

'Who runs it?'

He swallows. 'The government.'

'Are there labs there?'

'I don't know. I've only heard stories. I think so.'

'Interesting.' I tap his head lightly with his gun. 'What's your name?'

'Lenny Treber.' He throws me a nervous glance. Sweat pours off him in a river. 'What's your name?'

'I have many names, Lenny. We are in a tight fix here. You and I and my friend. How do we get out of it?'

He can't stop shaking. 'I don't understand.'

'I don't want to go to C-Fourteen. I want you to help me escape this dragnet. It is to your advantage to help, and to the advantage of your fellow cops. I don't want to leave several dozen women widowed.' I pause. 'Are you married, Lenny?'

He tries to calm himself with deep breaths. 'Yes.'

'Do you have children?'

'Yes.'

'You don't want your children to grow up without a father, do you?'

'No.'

'What can you do to help me and my friend?'

It is hard for him to concentrate. 'I don't know.'

'You will have to do better than that. What happens if you radio ahead and say you need to take a bathroom break?'

'They won't believe it. They'll know you have escaped.'

'Is this van bulletproof?'

'Yes.'

'What did they tell you about me?'

'That you were dangerous.'

'Anything else?' I ask.

He is near tears. 'They said you can kill with your bare hands.' He catches a clear view of the brain tissue dripping out of the commander's skull. It is a gruesome sight, even by my flexible standards. A shudder runs through Lenny's body. 'Oh God,' he gasps.

I pat him sweetly on the back. 'I do have my bad side,' I admit. 'But you cannot judge me by a few dead bodies. I don't want to kill you, Lenny, now that we're on a first-name basis. Think of another way for us to escape the escorts.'

He struggles. 'There isn't one. This job has the highest security imaginable. They'll open fire if I try to get away from them.'

'Those were the orders?'

'Yes. Under no circumstances were you to be allowed to escape.'

I ponder this. They must know me, even better than Lenny thinks. How's that possible? Have I left that much evidence behind? I think of the Coliseum, the necks I broke, the javelins I threw. It's possible, I suppose.

'I am going to escape,' I tell Lenny, picking up the dropped machine gun and shotgun from the front seats. I also yank a flak jacket off one of the men. 'One way or the other.'

'They'll open fire,' Lenny protests.

'Let them.' I take ammunition for both weapons

from the unconscious men. I gesture to Joel, who is still getting adjusted to his vampire senses. He's staring around the interior of the van as if he's stoned. 'Put on one of those flak jackets,' I tell him.

'Does there have to be shooting?' he asks.

'There will be a lot of shooting.' I speak to Lenny. 'What's the top speed of this van?'

'Eighty miles an hour.'

I groan. 'I need a cop car.'

'There are a lot of them behind and in front of us,' Lenny says.

I peer at the chopper in the sky. 'They hang close to the ground.'

'They're heavily armed,' Lenny says. 'They won't let you escape.'

I climb in the front seat beside him, shoving the men aside. The flak jacket is a little large on me. 'You think I should surrender?'

'Yes.' He adds quickly, 'That's just my opinion.'

'You just follow my orders if you want to live,' I say, studying the cruisers in front, in back. Sixteen altogether – two officers in each, I know. Plus there are at least three unmarked cars – FBI agents. It continues to amaze me how quickly they took Joel into custody. They hardly gave him a chance to speak. I call back to him, 'Come up here. We're going to switch vehicles in a few minutes.'

Joel pokes his head close to my shoulder, flak jacket in place. 'The chopper is a problem,' he says. 'It doesn't matter how good a driver you are or how many cop cars you disable. It'll stay with us, lighting us up.'

'Maybe. Put on a seat belt.' I brace a foot on the dashboard and point to an approaching alley. 'There, Lenny, I want you to take a hard left. Floor it as soon as you come out of the turn.'

Lenny sweats. 'OK.'

I start to hand Joel Lenny's revolver. 'Don't be afraid to cover my back.' I pause and catch his eye. 'You are on my side, aren't you?'

Joel hesitates. 'I won't kill anybody.'

'Will you try to kill me?'

'No.'

I give him the revolver. 'All right.' The alley closes. 'Get ready, Lenny. No tricks. Just put as much distance between us and the procession as you can.'

Lenny veers to the left. The alley is narrow; the van shoots through it at high speed, knocking over garbage cans and crates. The response from the cops is immediate. Half the cars jam into the alley in pursuit. But half is better than all, and locked in behind us as they are, the cops can't fire at us so easily.

Unfortunately, the alley crosses several streets. Fortunately, it's midnight, with almost no traffic. At the first street we're lucky. But we lose two police cars to a collision. At the second crossing we're also fortunate. But as we drive into the third cross street we smash sideways into the only vehicle on the street, an open produce truck loaded with oranges. The fruit spills over the van. Lenny has bumped his head on the steering wheel and appears to be dazed. He gets another bump on his head when a squad car smashes into us from behind. This is what I wanted – a pileup.

'Come on!' I call to Joel.

I jump out of the side of the van and raise the machine gun and fire a spray of bullets at the cars piled up behind us. They are pinned down, but I know it won't be long before a herd of fresh cars comes around the block. The suddenness of my attack causes them to scramble from their vehicles. Overhead, the chopper swoops dangerously low, the spotlight momentarily focused straight on me. I look through the glare of the light and see a marksman stand in the open doorway and raise a high-powered rifle. Pumping the shotgun, I take aim at him and pull the trigger.

The man loses the top of his head.

His lifeless body falls onto the roof of a nearby building.

I am not finished.

My next shot takes out the spotlight. My third hits the small vertical rotor at the rear. The blade sputters but continues to spin. Pumping the shotgun, I put another round in it, and this time the propeller dies. It is the vertical rotor that prevents fuselage rotation and also provides rudder control. In other words, it gives stability to the helicopter. Immediately the flying machine veers out of control. To the horror of the watching police officers, it crash-lands in the midst of their line of cars. The explosion is violent, crushing several officers, setting a few ablaze. I use the distraction to reach in and pull Joel out of the van. We run down the block, faster than any human could.

All this has happened in ten seconds.

So far, not a single shot has been fired at us.

A second line of cop cars comes around the block.

I jump into the middle of the street and pour two shotgun rounds into the window of the first one, killing both officers inside. The vehicle loses control and crashes into a parked car. The police cars behind it slam on their brakes. A spray of bullets from my machine gun makes them scramble out of their vehicles in search of cover. I run toward the second car, shielding Joel with my body. To the police, I know, my movements appear as nothing more than a blur. They can't get a lock on me. Nevertheless, they do open fire and a hail of bullets flies around me. My flak jacket takes several rounds, causing no damage. But one bullet catches me in the leg above my left knee and I stumble, although I don't fall. Another shot hits me in my right upper arm. Somehow, I reach the second police car and shove Joel inside. I want to drive. I am bleeding, and the pain is intense, but I am in too much of a hurry to acknowledge it.

'Keep your head down!' I snap at Joel as I throw the car in gear. Peeling out, we are treated to another shower of bullets. I take my own advice and duck. Both the front and rear windshields shatter. Glass pellets litter my long blond hair. It will take a special brand of shampoo to get them out.

We escape, but are a marked couple in a highly visible car. I jump on the Harbor Freeway, heading north, hoping to put as much distance between us and our pursuers as quickly as possible. I keep the accelerator floored, weaving in and out of the few cars. But I have two police cars on my tail. Worse, another helicopter has appeared in the sky. This pilot has learned from his predecessor. He keeps the chopper up high, but not so high that he can't track us.

'We can't hide from a chopper,' Joel says again.

'This is a big city,' I reply. 'There are many places to hide.'

He sees I am bloody. 'How bad are your injuries?'

It is an interesting question because already – in the space of a few minutes – they have completely healed. Yaksha's blood – it is an amazing potion.

'I am all right,' I say. 'Are you injured?'

'No.' He pauses. 'How many men have died since this started?'

'At least ten. Try not to count.'

'Is that what you did after a few thousand years? You stopped counting?'

'I stopped thinking.'

I have a goal. Because I know we cannot stay on the freeway long, I decide that the only way we can escape the helicopters is to get into one ourselves. Atop several of the high-rises in downtown Los Angeles there are helicopter pads with choppers waiting to whisk executives to high-level meetings. I can fly a helicopter. I can operate any piece of machinery humankind has developed.

I exit the freeway on Third Street. By now I have ten black-and-whites on my tail. Coming down the off ramp, I see several cop cars struggling to block the road in front of me. Switching to the wrong side of the street, I bypass them and head east in the direction of the tallest buildings. But my way is quickly blocked by another set of black-and-whites. We must have half the LAPD after us. I am forced to swerve into the basement garage of a building I don't know. A wooden bar swings down to block my way, but I don't stop to press the green button and collect my ticket. Nor does the herd of law enforcement behind me. We all barrel through the barricade. A sign for an elevator calls my attention and I slam the car to a halt inches from the door. We jump out and push the button. While we wait for our ride to higher floors, I open fire on our pursuers. More people die. I lied to Joel. I do count – three men and a woman take bullets in the face. I am a very good shot.

The elevator comes and we pile inside.

I press the top button. Number twenty-nine.

'Can they halt the elevator from the basement?' I ask as I reload.

'Yes. But it'll take them a few minutes to figure out how to do it.' He shrugs. 'But does it matter? They'll surround this building with an army. We're trapped.'

'You're wrong,' I say.

We exit onto the top floor. Here there are expensive suites, for law firms, plastic surgeons, and investment counselors. But there is too much high-priced real estate in Los Angeles – several of the suites are empty. Kicking in the door of the nearest vacancy, I stride up and down beside the wide windows, studying the neighbouring buildings. I will have to cross the block and move over a few buildings to reach a high-rise that has a helicopter pad. I curse the fact that I am not a mythic vampire from films, capable of flying.

Yet I am able to leap tall buildings in a single bound.

Joel moves to my side. Below us, we watch the forces of righteousness gather. Two more helicopters have appeared in the night sky. Their bright beams rake the sides of the building.

'They won't come up the elevator after us,' Joel says. 'They will only come when they have us surrounded top and bottom.' He pauses. 'What are we going to do?'

'*I* am going to set a new Olympic record.' I point to the building across the street. Its roof is only three stories below where we are. 'I am going to jump over to it.'

He is impressed. 'That's far. Can you really do it?'

'If I get a running start. I'll come back for you in a few minutes, in a helicopter. I will land it on the roof of this building. Be waiting for me.'

'What if you miss the roof of that building?'

I shrug. 'It's a long way down.'

'Could you survive the fall?'

'I think so. But it would take me time to recover.'

'You shouldn't come back for me,' Joel says. 'Steal a helicopter and escape.'

'That is not a consideration.'

He speaks seriously. 'Too many people have died. Even if we escape, I can't live with this slaughter on my conscience.'

I am impatient. 'Don't you see how dangerous you are to the human race? Even dead. They could take your blood, inject it into animals, into themselves – just as Eddie did. And they will do that, after witnessing what we can do. Believe me, I only kill tonight so that the world can wake safely in the morning.'

'Is that true, Sita? You would die to save all these men and women?'

I turn away. 'I would die to save you.'

He speaks gently. 'What did you sacrifice to keep me alive?'

I would weep, I think, if I could. 'I told you.'

'I didn't understand.'

'It doesn't matter. It's done.' I turn back to him. 'There will be time later for these discussions.'

He touches my hair – pieces of glass fall to the floor. 'You miss him.'

'Yes.'

'I didn't know what he meant to you when I watched him die.'

I smile sadly. 'Nothing is really known about a person until he or she is gone.'

'I cannot take his place.'

I nod weakly. 'I know.' Then I shake my head. 'I need to go.'

He wants to hug me. 'This could be goodbye.'

'It is not over yet.'

Before launching my daring leap, I kick out the window that blocks my way. This alerts the buzzing choppers but I don't give them time to zero in on me. I back away from the windows, taking only the shotgun with me, giving the machine gun to Joel.

'Are you afraid of heights?' he asks.

I kiss him. 'You don't know me. I am afraid of nothing.'

Taking a deep breath, I begin my hard approach. I can accelerate sharply and be at full speed in less than ten strides. My balance and ability to judge distance are flawless. I hit the shattered bottom edge of the window perfectly and all at once I am airborne.

The flight across the gap between the buildings is breathtaking, even for me. It seems as if I'll float forever, moving horizontally, in defiance of gravity. The searchlights on the helicopters are too slow to catch me. I soar in darkness, a huge bat, the cool air on my face. Below, the tiny figures raise their heads skyward, blinking at the impossible. I almost laugh. They thought they had me trapped, silly mortals. They thought wrong.

My landing is not entirely smooth because I have such momentum. I am forced into a roll as I skitter across the rooftop. I am bleeding as I finally come to a halt and jump up. Overhead the choppers are frantically manoeuvering to open fire. I am not given a chance to catch my breath before moving. Leaping for the next rooftop, I watch as a line of bullets rips a path in front of me.

The ensuing jumps between buildings are all on the same side of the street and not so dramatic as the first one. Yet the last leap, to the skyscraper with the helicopter pad, is to be the most dramatic of all. Because I cannot jump to the top of a building twenty stories up, I do not plan to land on top of the skyscraper. I will jump *into* it, through its wall of windows. I only hope that I don't hit the steel and concrete between floors.

Once again, the choppers approach, their machine guns blasting.

Once again, I take a running start.

The windows of the skyscraper rush toward me like a hard black wall. An instant before contact, I lean back and kick out with my feet. My timing is perfect; the glass shatters around the lower part of my body, sparing my face and arms. Unfortunately, I land awkwardly on a row of secretarial desks. The shock is incredible, even for me. Coming to a halt in a pile of ruined PCs and paper clips, I lie still for a whole minute, trying to catch my breath. I am now covered with blood from head to toe. Yet even as I grimace in pain my flesh wounds begin to close and my broken bones begin to mend.

I have company on the outside. One of the helicopter pilots has taken it upon himself to come level with the hole I have punched into the side of the skyscraper. The chopper floats just outside the shattered window, scanning the office with its bright searchlight. There are three men, including the pilot, aboard the craft. Peering through the wreckage, I notice that the machine gunner has an itchy finger. I think to myself how much more I would prefer to have a police chopper than a civilian one. But the pilot is not reckless. He keeps the chopper constantly moving a little from side to side. For me to try to leap onto it would be risky. I opt for the more conservative plan.

I get up slowly, limping. My right shinbone is still fractured, but it will be all right in another minute – God bless Yaksha's blood. Ducking behind the desks, the beam from the searchlight stretching long, stark shadows across the office, I move away from the broken window. The helicopter swoops in a narrow arc, sometimes onto the far side of the hole, sometimes closer to where I'm hidden. The windows are tinted; it is easier for me to follow their movements than for them to follow mine, unless their light were to hit me directly. Yet they seem obsessed with the space just beyond the hole. They must feel that I am in the wreckage somewhere near it, injured and dying.

'Come to me baby,' I whisper.

On their third swing toward my side, I punch out the window in front of me and open fire. I take out the machine gunner first; I don't like his looks. The searchlight goes next. I take aim on the fuel tank. As I said, I enjoy fireworks, wicked explosions. When I pull the trigger on the shotgun, the chopper detonates in a huge fireball. The pilot screams, the flames engulfing his body. The other man is blown out the side door, in pieces. The life goes out of the machine and it sinks to the ground. Far below I hear people crying. Far above, to my right, I hear the other two helicopters veer away. They have lost enthusiasm for the fight.

On the way to the elevator, I pass a custodian. He hardly looks up. Despite my blood and artillery, he wishes me a good evening. I smile at him.

'You have a good night,' I say.

The elevator takes me to the top floor, and from there it is not hard to find a private access ladder onto the roof. Not one but two helicopters wait to fly us to freedom. Both are jet powered and I am pleased. They will at least be as fast as the cops' choppers, if not faster. Unfortunately there's a security guard on duty. An old guy, obviously working the night shift to supplement a meager retirement, he takes one look at me and hurries over. He has a handgun but doesn't draw it. His glasses are remarkably thick; he squints through the lenses as he looks me up and down.

'Are you a cop?' he asks.

I don't have the heart to lie to him. 'No. I'm the bad guy. I'm the one who just blew that chopper out of the sky.'

He is awestruck. 'I watched you jumping from building to building. How do you do that?'

'Steroids.'

He slaps his leg. 'I knew it! The drugs young people are taking these days. What do you want? One of these choppers?'

I point my shotgun at him. 'Yes. Please give me the keys. I don't want to have to kill you.'

He quickly raises his hands. 'You don't have to do that. The keys are in the ignitions. Do you know how to fly a helicopter?'

I turn my weapon aside. 'Yes. I've been taking lessons. Don't worry about me.'

He walks me to the closest chopper, a Bell 230. 'This baby has a range of over three hundred miles. You want to get far out of town. The radio and TV are babbling about you, calling you a band of Arab terrorists.'

I laugh as I climb into the cockpit. 'You do nothing to destroy their illusions. Just tell them you were overwhelmed by superior forces. You don't want people to know a young woman stole a helicopter out from under your nose.'

'And a blond one at that,' he agrees. 'You take care!'

He closes the door for me and I'm off.

Picking up Joel proves to be the easiest part of the night. The police helicopters are holding back – over a mile away. They aren't used to being blown out of the sky. The fire from the last downed chopper spreads over the front of the skyscraper. In the distance I see smoke from the first chopper. Joel shakes his head as he climbs in.

'They'll never stop hunting us after this,' he says.

'I don't know,' I jest. 'They might be afraid to come after me.'

We head northeast. I'm anxious to get out of the suburban sprawl and into the wild, somewhere we can disappear. The nearby mountains are a possibility. Our chopper is fast, capable of going two hundred miles an hour. To my surprise, the police helicopters don't really pursue us. It's not just because we're faster than they are − a fact I have to question. They allow the gap to grow between us to at least twenty miles. The length of the space doesn't reassure me because I know they still have us under visual observation. Nothing will be gained by plunging low to the ground, below the radar. They are waiting for something, biding their time.

'Reinforcements,' I mutter as we swoop over the sleeping city at an elevation of a thousand feet.

Joel nods. 'They've called for bigger guns.'

'Army helicopters?'

'Probably.'

'Which direction will they come from?'

'There is a large base south of here. You might want to head north.'

'I was planning to do so after I reached the Cajon Pass.' The pass cuts into the desert, also a nice place to hide. Highway 15 runs through the pass, and if followed far enough, leads to Las Vegas.

'You might not want to wait that long,' Joel advises.

'I understand.' Yet the temptation to put more

distance between us and our pursuers is great. It gives me the illusion of safety, a dangerous illusion. But the farther we go, the more the desert beckons me. Being winter, the mountains are covered with snow, and even though I am highly resistant to cold, I don't like it. At our present speed Cajon Pass is not far ahead. Once over it, we will be clear of the city, able to roam free.

I ask the question I have been waiting to ask.

'Are you thirsty?'

He is guarded. 'What do you mean?'

I glance over. 'How do you feel?'

He takes a deep breath. 'Feverish. Cramping.'

I nod. 'You need blood.'

He takes time to absorb my words. 'Do you really drink people's blood? Like in the stories?'

'The stories have germs of truth in them, but can't be taken literally. As a vampire, you do need blood to survive. Yet you do not need to kill the person you drink from, and your contact with them will not change them into vampires. You can also live off the blood of animals, although you will find it unsatisfying.'

'Do I need blood every day?'

'No. Every few days. But at first, you will crave it every day.'

'What happens if I don't drink it?'

'You will die horribly,' I say.

'Oh. Do I still need to eat regular food?'

'Yes. You will get hungry as before. But if need be, you will be able to survive for a long time without food.

You will also be able to hold your breath for incredible lengths of time.'

'But what about the sun? You sat out in the sun with me.'

'Yes. But that is not something you want to try yet. The sun won't kill you, but it will irritate you, at least for the first few centuries. Even now, after five thousand years, I'm not nearly so strong while the sun is up. But forget everything else you've heard about vampires. Crucifixes and white roses and running water – none of those will bother you. Bram Stoker was just spicing up his novel when he wrote that stuff.' I pause. 'Did you know I met him once?'

'Did you tell him you were a vampire?'

'No, but he knew there was something special about me. He autographed my copy of *Dracula* and tried to get my address. But I didn't give it to him.' I raise my wrist to my mouth. 'I am going to open my vein. I want you to suck my blood for a few minutes.'

He fidgets. 'Sounds kinky.'

'You'll enjoy it. I taste wonderful.'

A moment later Joel reluctantly accepts my bleeding wrist, but he is no Ray. He has seen plenty of blood in his line of work and it doesn't make him sick to his stomach. Indeed, after a couple of minutes he is sucking hungrily on my wrist. I have to stop him before he is sated. I cannot allow my strength to wane.

'How do you feel?' I ask as I take back my arm.

'Powerful. Aroused.'

I have to laugh. 'Not every girl you meet will be able to do that for you.'

'Can we be killed with a stake through the heart?'

The laughter dies in my throat. His question brings back the agony of the wound I suffered when my house exploded and Yaksha supposedly died. The chest pain is still there – yet, since drinking Yaksha's blood, it has receded. I wonder what Yaksha would think of me now that I have broken Krishna's vow against creating more vampires. After I have killed so many innocent people. No doubt he would say I am damned.

I miss Yaksha. And Ray. And Krishna.

'You can be killed that way,' I say quietly.

Ten minutes later we reach the gap in the mountains and I veer north, climbing in altitude. The pass is almost a mile above sea level. The police helicopters are now thirty miles behind us, blinking red and white dots in the night sky. We have at most four hours of night left. Before then, I must find shelter for Joel and a place to sit quietly and plot my next moves. Scanning left and right, I consider dumping the helicopter. The cliffs of the pass offer more hiding places than the desert will. Yet I don't want to set down so soon. Another idea has come to me, one that may throw our pursuers off.

What if I were to crash the helicopter into a lake?

It would sink and hopefully leave no sign behind.

The plan is a good one. Fuel dictates I choose the closest lake, Big Bear or Arrowhead. But once again I resist heading into the snowy mountains. As a new born, Joel will not fare well there. I remember how sensitive I was to the cold after Yaksha changed me. Vampires, serpents, the offspring of yakshinis – we prefer warmth.

I need a sand dune oasis with a lake in the center of it.

We plunge over the pass and into the desert.

The bleak landscape sweeps beneath us.

Time passes. I cannot see anyone following.

'We can't stay up here forever,' Joel says finally.

'I know.'

'What are you waiting for?'

'Lake Mead.' Hoover Dam – it is only twenty minutes away, I estimate.

But I have waited too long.

Five minutes later I catch sight of two military helicopters, coming at us from the west, not the south. Because my eyes are so sharp, I see them far off – sixty miles away. I feel it is still possible to reach the lake. Yet I know they have spotted us, that they are tracking us on their radar. When I alter course slightly, they do likewise. Joel sees my concern but doesn't understand it at first. Even changed, his sight is no match for mine.

'What is it?' he asks.

'We have company,' I say.

He looks around. 'Can we reach the lake?'

'Possibly.' I ask in jest, 'Can we fight two Apache helicopters?'

'No way.'

I guess at the type of craft that pursues us, but a few minutes later I see that I was right. My knowledge of the Apache isn't extensive, but I have read enough to know that we are facing the most lethal attack helicopter on earth. The two choppers move close to each other, on a direct intercept course with us. Black as the desert sky, with wide hypnotic propellers – they are clearly faster than we are. Their machine-gun turret and rocket launchers hang from the sides like dangerous fists. They sweep toward us for a knockout punch. Joel sees them.

'Maybe we should surrender,' he suggests.

'I never surrender.'

They catch us three miles short of the lake. The wide flat expanse of water is clearly visible, but it could be on the other side of the moon for all the good it can do us now. That's what I think at first. Yet the Apaches do not immediately lock on their weapons. They swoop above and below us, dangerously close, ordering us to land.

'Somebody has told them to take us alive,' Joel observes.

'Who?'

Joel shrugs. 'The order could have come from the President of the United States. But I suspect the commander of the base where these helicopters originated has given the order.'

'We only need to get to the water,' I say. 'They couldn't imagine that we'd try to vanish underwater.'

'I can't imagine it. Can we really hold our breath a long time?'

'I can go an hour.'

'But what about me?'

I pat his leg. 'Have faith. We should have died a dozen times tonight and we're still alive. Maybe Krishna hasn't deserted us after all.'

'If they open fire in the next minute we might have a chance to ask him directly,' Joel says dryly.

The Apaches buzz us a couple of times more, then grow tired of the cat-and-mouse game. They lay down a stream of bullets across our path and I have to slow sharply to avoid being torn to shreds. Still, they could blow us out of the sky whenever they wish. Yet they hold back, although they don't want me flying above the lake. They try blocking our path and I have to go into a steep dive to stay on course. We come within several feet of the ground and Joel almost has a heart attack.

'You are one mean pilot,' he says when he catches his breath.

'I'm pretty good in bed as well,' I reply.

'Of that I have no doubt.'

These military men are not like the LAPD. They expect their orders to be obeyed. They may have instructions to take us alive, but they also have orders to prevent us from escaping. A quarter mile from the water, they open fire with surgical precision and suddenly our rotor blades are not a hundred percent intact. Our copter falters in the air, but stays up. The noise above us is deafening. Yet I continue on toward the lake. I have no choice.

'Get ready to jump,' I tell Joel.

'I'm not leaving till you leave.'

'Nice line. But you have to jump as soon as we cross over the water. Swim for the far shore, not the near one. Stay under water as long as possible.'

Joel hesitates. 'I don't know how to swim.'

'What?'

'I said I don't know how to swim.'

I can't believe it. 'Why didn't you tell me that earlier?'

'I didn't know what you had planned. You didn't tell me.'

'Joel!'

'Sita!'

I pound the chopper dashboard. 'Damn! Damn! Well, you're just going to have to learn how to swim. You're a vampire. All vampires can swim.'

'Says who?'

'Says me, and I'm the only authority on the subject. Now stop arguing with me and prepare to jump.'

'You jump with me.'

'No. I have to wait until they fire their lethal blow – that way they'll think I'm dead.'

'That's crazy. You will be dead.'

'Shut up and crack your door slightly. When you reach the far shore, run into the hills and hide. I'll find you. I can hear a vampire breathing ten miles away.'

The Apaches are still determined to prevent us from reaching the water. One swoops overhead and literally drops itself directly into our path. I have to go into another steep dive to avoid it, which is easy to do because the craft is ready to crash anyway. The water is now only a hundred yards away. The Apache behind us opens fire. They mimic my earlier strategy. They blow off our tail rotor. I immediately lose control. We spin madly to the left. Yet the water is suddenly below us.

'Jump!' I scream at Joel.

He casts me one last glance – his expression curiously sad.

Then he is gone.

Pulling back hard on the steering bar, I try to gain altitude, partly to distract them from Joel and partly to stay alive. It is my hope they didn't see him jump. My chopper swings farther out over the water. A mile away I see Hoover Dam. There is no way I can make it that far. The chopper bucks like a hyperactive horse on speed. Cracking my door, I take hold of the shotgun and blast at one of the Apaches as it swings nearby. I hit the top blades, but these suckers are tough. The military chopper banks sharply. Then the two helicopters regroup, hovering behind me, twin hornets studying a wounded butterfly. Over my shoulder I see one pilot nod to his gunner. The man reaches for a fresh set of controls, no doubt the firing mechanism for the rockets. As I throw my door open wide, an orange tongue of flame leaps out from the side of the Apache.

My reflexes are fast, blinding by human standards, but even I cannot out-run a missile. I am barely free of my seat when the rocket hits.

My chopper vaporizes in midair.

The shock from the explosion hits with the power of an iron fist. A fragment of burning metal cuts into my skull above my hairline, sending waves of searing pain through my whole system. I topple like a helicopter without a stabilizing propeller. Blood pours over my face and I am blinded. I do not see the cold water of the lake approaching, but I feel it when it slaps my broken side. The molten shrapnel in my head shudders as it contacts the dark liquid. A burst of steam almost causes my skull to explode. I feel myself spiraling down into a forsaken abyss. Consciousness flickers in and out. The lake is bottomless, my soul as empty as dice without numbers. As I start to black out, I wish that I didn't have to die this way – without Krishna's grace. How I would love to see him on the other side – his divine blue eyes. God forgive me, how I love him.

2

I awake with a pale wash of light panning across my face. Opening my eyes, I see it is the searchlights of hovering helicopters pointing down on me. Only they are high in the air, and I am many feet underwater, on my back, on the bottom of the lake. Even though unconscious, my mind must have had the wisdom to halt my breathing. I don't know how long I have been out. My head still hurts but the pain is bearable. It is obvious that the personnel in the helicopters cannot see me.

I wonder how Joel is, if he escaped.

My left leg is pinned under the wreckage of my chopper. It is good because otherwise I would be floating on the surface, probably with many bullet holes in me. Pulling my leg free, I roll over on my belly and begin to swim away from the lights, not sure at first if I am moving deeper into the lake or closer to the shore. My desire for breath is strong but not overwhelming. I know I can swim a long way before I'll have to surface. They can't scan every square inch of the lake. I am going to escape.

Yet there will be no freedom for me if Joel is not free.

Ten minutes later, when the lights are far behind me, I allow myself to swim to the surface and peek. I am far out in the center of the lake. Behind me, near the shore where my chopper was blown out of the sky, the helicopters still circle, their beams still focused on the water. Close to this spot, on the shore, are several trucks, many uniformed people, some cops, some army personnel. Joel stands in the middle of them, a dozen guns pointed at his head.

'Damn,' I whisper. 'He really couldn't swim.'

I cannot rush in to save him. I know this yet I have to stop myself from making the attempt. It is my nature to act quickly. Patience has not come to me over the centuries. Floating in the center of the black lake, it seems to me the years have only brought grief.

Joel is ushered into an armoured truck. Men on the shore are donning scuba gear. They want my body, they want to see it before they can rest. I know that I must act quickly if I am to track Joel. Yet I also know I have to stop killing. They'll be looking for any suspicious deaths in the area as a way to confirm I am still alive. A

41

throbbing sensation in my forehead draws my attention. I reach up and pull away a chunk of shrapnel that has been working its way out of my skull. Before the infusion of Yaksha's blood, such an injury would have killed me.

I swim for the shore where Joel is being held, but a mile to the left, away from him and the dam. I am a better swimmer than most dolphins and reach land in a few minutes. No one sees me as I slip out of the water and dash into the rocky hills. My first impulse is to creep closer to the armed assembly. Yet I cannot steal one of their vehicles to follow Joel. Fretting about the growing gap between us, I turn away from the small army and run toward the campgrounds. Even in the winter, families come to Lake Mead to enjoy the nature. Overhead, an almost full moon shines down on me. Just what I don't need. If an Apache spots me again, I swear, I am going to jump up and grab its skids and take it over. My turn to fire the rockets.

The thoughts are idle, the mental chatter of a natural born predator.

I find a family of three asleep in a tent on the outskirts of the campground, their shiny new Ford Bronco parked nearby and waiting for me to steal. Silently, I break the lock and slip in behind the steering wheel. It takes me all of two seconds to hot-wire the vehicle. Then I am off, the window down.

Throughout my long life, hearing has always been my best sense. I can hear snowflakes as they emerge

from a cloud two miles overhead. Indeed, I have no
trouble hearing the army's motor parade start their
engines and pull away from the lake. Probably the
commander thinks he should get Joel to a secure place,
even before the body of the blond witch is found. I use
my ears to follow them as they move onto a road that
leads away from the lake. Yet, with my nose in the air, it
is my sense of smell that is the most acute. It startles me.
I can smell Joel – even in the midst of the others –
clearly, in fact. I suspect this is another gift of Yaksha,
master yakshini, born of a demonic race of serpents.
Snakes always have exceptional senses of smell.

I am grateful for this newfound sense because I can
accurately trail the military parade from a great
distance. These people are not stupid – they will check
to see if they are being followed. Once again I am struck
by my ability to sense their thoughts. I have always been
able to discern emotions in mortals, but never ideas.
Yaksha must have been an outright mind reader. He
never told me. I know for sure the people up ahead are
checking their backs. I allow the distance between us to
grow to as much as fifteen miles. Naturally I drive with
the lights out.

At first the group heads in the direction of Las Vegas.
Then, five miles outside the City of Sin, they turn east
onto a narrow paved road. The column stretches out
and I have to stay even farther back. There are many
signs: RESTRICTED AREA. I believe we are headed to some
sort of government base.

My hunch is confirmed less than an hour later. Approximately fifty miles outside of Las Vegas, the armoured vehicle carrying Joel disappears into an elaborately defended camp. I speed up and take my Bronco off the road, parking it behind a hill a mile from both the road and the camp. On foot, I scamper toward the installation, growing more amazed with every step at how complex and impenetrable it appears. The surrounding fence is over a hundred feet high, topped with billowy coils of barbed wire. Ordinarily I could jump such a barrier without breaking a sweat. Unfortunately, the place has manned towers equipped with machine guns and grenade launchers every two hundred feet. That's a lot of towers. The compound is huge, at least a half mile across. In addition to the towers and fence, there is a densely packed maze of three-foot high electronic devices – they resemble metal baseball bats – stretched along the perimeter. I suspect that if tripped they emit a paralyzing field. Vampires are sensitive to electricity. I was once hit by a bolt of lightning and spent the next three days recovering in a coffin. My boyfriend at the time wanted to bury me.

One side of the compound is devoted almost exclusively to a concrete runway. I remember reading about a top-secret government installation in the desert outside of Las Vegas that supposedly tests advanced fighter craft, nuclear weapons, and biological weapons. I have a sneaking suspicion that I am looking at it.

The compound backs into a large barren hill, and I believe the military has mined deep into the natural slope to perform experiments best hidden from the eyes of spy satellites.

There are Sherman tanks and Apache helicopters parked close to barrack-like structures. No doubt the weapons can be manned in ten seconds. One thing is immediately clear to me.

I will not be able to break into the compound.

Not and get out alive.

The armoured vehicle carrying Joel has halted near the centre of the compound. Armed soldiers scurry to line up around it, their weapons drawn and leveled. A cruel-faced general with a single star on his shoulder and death in his eyes approaches the vehicle. Behind him is a group of white-clad scientists – just what I don't want to see. The general signals to somebody out of view and the side door on the armoured vehicle swings open. Heavily chained, his shoulders bowed down, Joel is brought into the open. The general approaches him, strangely unafraid, and searches him. Then he glances over his shoulder. Several of the scientists seem to nod. I don't understand the exchange. What are they approving? That Joel is a genuine vampire? They don't know about vampires.

'Or do they?' I whisper.

But it's not possible. For the last two thousand years or more, Yaksha and I were the only vampires on earth. Recently there have been others, of course. But Ray's conversion was short-lived, Eddie was a psychotic aberration, and I destroyed all of Eddie's offspring.

Or did I?

This general wanted us taken alive, I realize. He's the one who gave the order to the Apache pilots. They waited a long time before they used their rockets, and then only when they were forced to. In fact, the general is probably angry that they used them at all. The way he's studying Joel – it's almost as if he's gloating. The general wants something from Joel, and he knows what it is.

Joel is taken inside a building.

The general confers with one scientist and then they, too, go inside.

I sit back and groan. 'Damn.'

My objective is clear. I have to get Joel out of the compound before they can perform extensive tests on him – more specifically, before they can analyze his blood. I'm not even sure what they will find, but whatever they discover, it won't bode well for the long-term survival of the human race.

But I cannot force my way inside. Therefore, I must sneak in. How do I do that? Make friends with the guards? Seduce Mr Machine Gun Mike? The idea may not be as farfetched as it seems with my magnetic personality and hypnotic eyes. But from what I can see, all the men live at the compound. This is unfortunate.

I glance in the direction of Las Vegas, neon fallout on the horizon.

'But the boys must leave the compound and go out on the town now and then,' I mutter.

It is two hours before dawn. While I study the compound with my powerful eyes, searching for a vulnerable spot, I see the scientist whom the general conferred with climb into an ordinary car. He stops at a checkpoint before exiting the compound. By then I am running for my Bronco.

I want to talk to this scientist.

As I climb in my stolen vehicle, I notice that my arms and hands are glowing with a faint white light. The effect stuns me. My face is also glowing! In fact, all my exposed skin shines with the same iridescence as the full moon, which hangs low in the sky in the direction of Las Vegas.

'What kind of radiation are they fooling with out here?' I mutter.

I decide to worry about it later.

The scientist is a speed demon. He drives close to a hundred all the way to Las Vegas, or at least until he hits the public highway, five miles outside the town. I push the Bronco to keep up. I suppose no cop will give him a ticket on a government road. It is my hope he lives in Vegas, but when he goes straight to the Mirage Hotel, my hopes sink. He's probably just out for a few hours of fun.

I park near him in the lot and prepare to follow him inside.

Then I remember what I am wearing.

A ripped flak jacket and bloody clothes.

I do not panic. The people I stole the Bronco from are on vacation. They will have, I'm sure, ladies' clothes somewhere in the vehicle. Lo and behold, in the back I find a pair of blue jeans, two sizes too big, and a black Mickey Mouse sweatshirt that fits like a wet suit. Luckily, the blood and glass washed out of my hair while I slept beneath Lake Mead. Standing in a dark corner of the parking lot, I change quickly.

I find the scientist inside at the dice table.

He is an attractive man, perhaps forty-five, with thick black hair and large sensual lips. His face is sun dried, tanned and lined, yet on him the effect is not unpleasant. He looks like a man who has weathered many storms and come out ahead. His gray eyes are deep set, very alert, focused. He has discarded his white lab coat for a nicely tailored sports coat. He is holding a pair of red dice as I enter, and it seems to me that he is secretly willing them to obey his commands, as so many other gamblers do.

He fails to throw a pass, a seven, or an eleven. He loses his bet and the dice pass to another player. I note that he had a hundred-dollar chip on the table, not a small bet for a scientist on the government payroll. I am surprised when he lays down another hundred dollars. He loses that as well.

I observe the man for forty-five minutes. He is a regular – one of the pit bosses calls him Mr Kane, another, Andy. Andrew Kane, I think. Because Andy continues to lose, at an alarming rate, he is forced to sign a slip to get more chips when the cash in his pockets is gone. But these black honeybees vanish rapidly, and his eagerness turns to frustration. I have been counting. Two thousand dollars gone – just like that. Sighing, he leaves the table and, after a double scotch at the bar, leaves the casino.

I follow him home. The place is modest.

He goes inside and prepares for bed. As the morning sun splashes the eastern sky, he turns out his own light. Obviously he works the night shift. Or else the general had called Andy into work because of Joel. I wonder if he will be working long hours in the days to come. Memorizing his address, I drive back toward the Mirage. If it is Andy's favourite hangout, it'll be mine as well.

I have no credit cards, money, or identification, but the woman at the reservation desk hands me a key to a luxury suite after staring hard into my beautiful blue eyes. Inside my room, I place a call to my primary business manager in New York City. His voice is unaffected – the government has not gotten to him yet. We do not talk long.

'Code red,' I say. 'Have the package delivered to the Mirage Hotel, Las Vegas. Room Two-One-Three-Four. Immediately.'

'Understood,' he says and hangs up.

The package will include everything I need to start a

new life: passport, driver's license, cash, and credit cards. It will arrive at my door in the next hour. There will also be an elaborate makeup kit inside, wigs and different-coloured contacts. Over the last fifty centuries, I have prepared for every eventuality, including this one. Tomorrow I will look like someone else, and Andrew Kane will meet a mysterious young woman, and fall in love.

3 ～〜

The following evening a demure redhead with short bangs and green eyes waits outside Andrew Kane's house. Actually, I have been in the front seat of my newly purchased Jeep since noon, but the mad scientist has been fast asleep, as most normal people would be after staying up all night. I came to his house early because I am anxious to go through his things, learn exactly what he does before I make a move on him. The one fact that guides me as to his importance is that the general spoke only to him after Joel was brought inside the compound. Yet intuitively I sense Andy's value. There is something fascinating in his grey eyes, even though he is a degenerate gambler. This quality does not bother me, however, because I might be able to use his obvious casino debt against him. Of course, I plan to use Andy to get into the compound to rescue Joel.

Quickly. I feel the pressure of each passing hour.

Joel will be thirsty already, unless they happen to feed him.

A newborn's thirst is agonizing.

The papers are shouting about the barbaric terrorist attack in Los Angeles. Authorities estimate that there were at least three dozen Islamic fanatics involved, and that the local police were overwhelmed by superior forces and military equipment. The mayor has vowed that the city officials will not rest until the murderers are brought to justice.

When in doubt, blame it on the Arabs.

The hot sun is draining for me after such an intense night. Yet I bear it better than I would have before drinking Yaksha's blood. I suspect, after five thousand years, the sun had no effect on Yaksha. I sure could use his power now. I pray he is finally at peace, in Krishna's blue abode. How often I pray to Krishna. How curious, since I am supposed to hate him. Oh well, the heart of a vampire is unfathomable. No wonder superstitious people are always trying to drive stakes through our hearts.

It is five in the evening before Andrew Kane emerges from his house and climbs in his car. He has no time for the casinos now. No doubt the general waits for him. Andy drives the five miles on Highway 15, then turns onto the government road, once again pushing his speed up to near a hundred. My Jeep has a powerful engine – I cruise five comfortable miles behind him. Actually, it is probably something of a waste to follow him all the way into work. He'll just drive inside and disappear into one of the buildings. But I want to see how long it takes him to pass through security, how many checks he goes through. Close to the compound, I veer off the road and tear across the desert, parking near the hill I hid behind before. On the seat beside me are high-powered binoculars. Even my supernatural sight can be improved by mechanical aids.

I am not given a chance to reach my vantage point before Andy gets to the front gate of the compound. Still, I can see well enough. He is stopped, naturally, but the guards know him well. He hardly has to flash his badge. The guards do not search his trunk. He parks his car in the same spot and enters the building where Joel was taken, the largest, most modern building in the whole complex. Chemical smells drift out from the building. It definitely has a lab inside.

I would like to examine the compound further but night is the time to do it. Plus I am anxious to get into Andy's house. I tear back to Las Vegas, not passing anyone on the road. I wonder if the scuba divers are still searching the bottom of Lake Mead for my body. I wonder if the general suspects I will try to rescue Joel. I doubt it.

Andy's house is a three-bedroom affair at the end of a quiet cul-de-sac. This being Las Vegas, there is the obligatory pool in the backyard. Leaving my Jeep on the adjoining street, I climb his wall and pick his back door lock. Inside it is cool; he left the air conditioning on. I shut the door and stand listening for a moment, smelling. Many aromas come to me then. They tell me much about the man, even though we have never been formally introduced.

He is a vegetarian. There is no smell of animal flesh. He doesn't smoke, but he does drink. I see as well as smell the bottles of liquor in a walnut cabinet. He does not use cologne, but there is a faint odor of various makeup products. Our Mr Andrew Kane resents middle age.

He is a bachelor, there are no pictures of a wife or kids on the walls. I step into the kitchen. He eats out mostly; there is little food in the refrigerator. I rifle through his bills on the kitchen counter. There are a couple of envelopes from banks. He is up to his limit on three credit cards.

I walk into the bedroom he uses as an office.

I almost faint.

On his desk is a black and white and red plastic model of the double helix DNA molecule. That is not what staggers me. Beside it is a much more complex model of a different kind of DNA – one that has twelve strands of encoded information instead of two. It is not the first time I have seen it. Seven hundred years ago, the great Italian alchemist, Arturo Evola, created a similar model after spending six months in my company.

'It's not possible,' I whisper.

Andrew Kane has already begun to crack the DNA of the vampire.

4 ～～

Italy, during the thirteenth century, embodied all that was wonderful and horrible about the Middle Ages. The Catholic Church was the supreme power. Monarchs came and went. Kings and queens fought and died. But the Roman Pope wielded the true power over life and death.

Art was the gift of the Church to the people in those days. This was above and beyond the gift of their strict theology, which did nothing for the poor masses except keep them confused until the day they died. I say that with well-deserved bitterness. It would have been impossible to live in those days and not become angry at the Church. Today, however, I think the Church does much that is good, and much that is questionable. No religion is perfect, not after man gets through with it.

I lived in Florence from 1212 till 1245 and spent many months touring the churches where the finest paintings and sculptures were displayed. The Renaissance was, of course, a long way off, and Michelangelo and Da Vinci had yet to be born. Still, these earlier days were remarkable for their creativity. I remember well Bonaventura Berlinghieri's radiant *St Francis* and Niccola Pisano's hypnotic sculpture *Annunciation to the Shepherds.*

The Inquisition was another gift of the Church. The boon of the devil in the minds of most people in those days. Two informants, whose identities could remain unknown to the victim, were all that was necessary to charge someone with being a heretic. The informants could be heretics themselves, or witches – not pleasant titles to earn in old Italy. A confession was necessary to convict anyone of being a heretic. A little stretching of the limbs, or burning with live coals, or torturing the victim on the *strappado* – the dreaded vertical rack – was usually enough to get an innocent person to confess. I remember going to the central city courtyard to watch the victims being burned alive at the stake. I used to think back over the barbarism of the Emperors of the Roman Empire, the Mongolian hordes, the Japanese shoguns – and yet their forms of torture all paled compared to the pain caused by the Church because the people who lit the pyres wore crosses. They chanted prayers while their victims screamed and died.

I observed only a few executions before I lost the stomach for them. Yet I thwarted the Inquisition in my own way, by secretly killing many of the inquisitors. I usually left their bodies in compromised places – houses of prostitution and the like – to discourage thorough investigations. As I drained the inquisitors' blood, sucking their large neck veins and arteries, I whispered in their ears that I was an angel of mercy. None of them died easily.

Yet the Church was bigger than a single vampire, the Inquisition an infection that spread and multiplied through its own mysterious madness. It could not be easily stopped. It cast a gloom over my stay in Florence, over my joy in the resurgence of mankind's creativity. I have hunted humans throughout time, and yet I am proud of them as well, when they do something bold, something unexpected. The best art always comes unbidden.

Arturo Evola was not known as an alchemist or else he would not have lasted a day in medieval Florence. He was a twenty-one-year-old Franciscan priest, and a devout one at that. He had entered the priesthood at the age of sixteen, which was not unusual at that time, because the easiest way to obtain the finest education was to become a priest. He was a brilliant man, undoubtedly the most inspired intellect of the thirteenth century. Yet history does not know him. Only I do, and my memories of him are filled with sorrow.

I met him after Mass one day. I despised the Church, but enjoyed the actual service. All the chanting, the choirs, and I loved to hear the early organs played. Often I would go to communion, after attending confession. It was difficult for me to keep a straight face while I told of my sins. Once, for fun, I told a priest the *whole* truth of what I had done in my life. But he was drunk and just said to do five Hail Marys and to behave myself. I didn't have to kill him.

I received the Holy Eucharist from Arturo and met him after the service. I could tell he was attracted to me. In those days many priests had mistresses. I had gone out of my way to see Arturo because a gypsy healer had told me about him. He was an alchemist, she said, who could turn stone into gold, sunlight into ideas, moonlight into lust. The gypsy had a high opinion of Arturo. She warned me to approach him cautiously because his real work had to be kept from the Church. I understood.

Commonly, an alchemist is known as an esoteric chemist who attempts to convert base metals into gold. This is a crude understanding. Alchemy is a comprehensive physical and metaphysical system embracing cosmology as much as anthropology. Everything natural and supernatural can be found in it. The goal of alchemy is to experience the totality of the organism. It is a path of enlightenment. The gypsy said Arturo was a born alchemist. Knowledge came to him from inside. No one had to teach him his art.

'The only trouble with him is he's a Catholic,' she said. 'A fanatic.'

'How does he merge the two disciplines?' I asked.

The gypsy blessed herself. She was superstitious of the Church as well. 'God only knows,' she said.

Arturo did not strike me as a fanatic when we first met. His demeanor was soft, like his lovely eyes. He had a special ability to listen totally to a person, a rare gift. His large hands were exceptionally fine; when he brushed my arm with his fingers I felt he was capable of touching my heart. And he was so young! That first afternoon we talked about astronomy – a midway subject, in my mind, to alchemy. He was delighted with my knowledge of the heavens. He invited me to share a meal and afterward we went for a walk around the city. When we said goodbye that night, I knew he was in love with me.

Why did I pursue him? For the same reason I have done many things in my life – I was curious. But that was only my initial reason. Soon I, too, was in love with him. I must say, the feeling was present before I began to probe his knowledge of alchemy. Before going that deep into his secret world, I knew he was unlike other priests of his day. He was a virgin, and his vow of celibacy was important to him.

I did not just spring the questions on him one day. Can you turn copper into gold? Can you heal lepers? Can you live forever? I showed him a glimpse of my knowledge first, to inspire him to share his. My understanding of the medical properties of herbs is extensive. An old friar in Arturo's church became ill with a lung infection, and it seemed as if he'd die. I brought Arturo an herb concoction of echinacea and goldenseal and told him to give it to his superior. The friar recovered within twenty-four hours and Arturo wanted to know who had taught me how to make tea.

I laughed and told him about my Greek friend, Cleo, failing to mention how many centuries ago he had died. Arturo was impressed. It was only then he began to talk about his crystals and magnets and copper sheets – the secret elements of alchemy that have now passed from human understanding. That very day Arturo confessed his mission in life to me. To discover the elixirs of holiness and immortality – as if searching for the secret to one of these conditions was not enough. Arturo always thought big. He was determined to re-create nothing less than the blood of Jesus Christ.

'What makes you think you can do it?' I asked, shocked.

His eyes shone as he explained. Not with a mad light, but with a brilliance I had never seen before or since in a mortal man.

'Because I have found the spirit of man,' he said. 'I have proven that it exists. I can show you how to experience it, how to remove the veil of darkness that covers it.'

Sounded interesting to me. Arturo took me to a secret chamber beneath the church where he lived. Apparently the elderly friar whose life I had saved knew of Arturo's hobby and looked the other way. He was the only one who knew of the master alchemist, besides the gypsy. I asked Arturo about her. Apparently she had nursed him back to health when he had fallen from a horse while riding in the countryside. They had shared many intimate conversations over late-night fires. Arturo was surprised, and a bit angry, that she had told me about him.

'Don't blame her,' I said. 'I can be most persuasive.' It was true that I had used the power of my eyes on her, when I saw she was hiding something important.

Arturo took me down into his secret room and lit many candles. He asked me to lie on a huge copper sheet, as thin as modern paper. On adjacent shelves, I noted his collection of quartz crystals, amethysts, and precious stones – rubies, diamonds, and sapphires. He also had several powerful magnets, each cut into the shape of a cross. I had never seen a magnetic cross before.

'What are you going to do?' I asked as I lay down on the copper.

'You have heard of the human aura?' he asked.

'Yes. It is the energy field that surrounds the body.'

'Very good. It is spoken of in ancient mythology and is present in art. We see the halos in paintings above the heads of members of the holy family, and in drawings of saints. Still, most people don't believe in the aura because they don't experience it. They are only conscious of their physical bodies. What I am going to do to you now is draw out your aura, allow your consciousness to expand into it, so that your spiritual body becomes the focus of your attention, and not the physical body.'

'Do you not like my physical body?' I asked. I often flirted with him.

He paused and stared down at me. 'It's very lovely,' he whispered.

He told me to close my eyes. He didn't want me to see how he set up the crystals and magnets. I peeked, of course, and saw that crystals were placed above my head and magnets below my body, at angles. He was creating a grid of some kind, one that transmitted unseen energies. He prayed as he worked, Hail Marys and Our Fathers. I have always enjoyed those prayers. But for me, of course, they reminded me of Radha and Krishna.

When Arturo was done, he told me to keep my eyes closed and breathe naturally through my nose. The breath was important, he said. It was one of the secrets of experiencing the soul.

For the first few minutes not much happened. But then, slowly, I felt an energy rise from my body, from the base of my spine to the top of my head. Simultaneously, I felt my mind expand. I became as big as the secret chamber. A curious floating sensation enveloped me, a warm peacefulness. My breath went in and out, sometimes fast, sometimes slow. I had no control over it and wanted none. Time passed. I wasn't entirely awake, but I wasn't asleep either. It was a mystical experience.

When Arturo spoke next, he sounded many miles away. He wanted me to sit up, to come out of the state. I resisted – I liked where I was. But he took my arm and forced me to sit up, breaking the spell. I opened my eyes and gazed at him.

'Why did you stop it?' I asked.

He was perspiring. 'You can get too much energy at once.' He stared at me; he seemed out of breath. 'You have an amazing aura.'

I smiled. 'What is special about it?'

He shook his head. 'It is so powerful.'

The experiment in consciousness raising was interesting, but I failed to see how his technique would allow him to transform human blood into Christ's blood. I quizzed him about it at length but he would divulge no more secrets. The power of my aura continued to puzzle him. As we said good night, I saw fear in his eyes, and deep fascination. He knew I was no ordinary woman. That was all right, I thought. No harm done. He would learn no more about my special qualities.

But that was not to be.

He was to learn everything about me.

Perhaps even more than I knew myself.

There was an altar boy, Ralphe, who lived with the priests. Twelve years old and possessed of an exceptional wit, he was a favourite of Arturo's. Often the two would go for long hikes in the hills outside Florence. I was fond of Ralphe myself. The three of us had picnics in the woods and I would teach Ralphe the flute, for which he had a talent. The instrument had been a favourite of mine since the day I met Krishna. Arturo used to love to watch us play together. But sometimes I would get carried away and weave a melody of love, of romantic enchantment and lost dreams, which would always leave Arturo quiet and shaken. How long we could go on like this, chaste and virtuous, I didn't know. My alchemist stirred ancient longings inside me. I wondered about the energies his crystals invoked.

One day while I was helping Ralphe repair a hole in the church roof, the boy decided to amuse me by doing a silly dance on the edge of the stone tiles. I told him to be careful but he never listened. He was having too much fun. That is the mysterious thing about tragedy – it often strikes at the happiest moment.

Ralphe slipped and fell. It was over a hundred feet to the ground. He fell on the base of his spine, crushing it. When I reached him, he was writhing in agony. I was shaken to the core, I who had seen so much pain in my life. But centuries of time have not made me insensitive. One moment he had been a vibrant young man, and now he would be crippled for the rest of his days, and those would not be long.

I loved Ralphe very much. He was like a son to me.

I suppose that's why I did what I did.

I did not need to make him a vampire to help him.

I opened the veins on my right wrist and let the blood splash where his shattered spinal column had pierced his skin. The wound closed quickly, the bones mended. It seemed he would make a complete recovery. Best of all, he appeared unaware of why he had recovered so quickly. He thought he'd just been lucky.

But there is good luck and bad luck.

Arturo saw what I did for Ralphe. He saw everything.

He wanted to know who I was. What I was.

I find it hard to lie to those I love.

I told him everything. Even what Krishna had told me. The tale took an entire night. Arturo understood when I was through why I preferred to tell the story in the dark. But he didn't recoil in horror as I spoke. He was an enlightened priest, an alchemist who sought the answer to why God had created us in the first place. Indeed, he thought he knew the answer to that profound question. We were here to become like God. To live like his blessed son. We just needed a few pints of Christ's blood to do it.

Arturo believed Krishna had let me live for a purpose. So that my blood could save mankind from itself.

From the start, I worried about him mixing Christ and vampires.

'But I will make no more vampires,' I protested.

He eagerly took my hands and stared into my eyes. A fever burned in his brain; I could feel the heat of it. On his fingertips, in his breath. Whose soul did I experience then? Mine or his? It seemed in that moment as if the two of us had merged. For that reason, his next words sounded inevitable to me.

'We will make no more vampires,' he said. 'I understand why Krishna made you take such a vow. What we will create with your blood is a new man. A hybrid of a human and a vampire. A being who can live forever, in the glory of light instead of the shadow of darkness.' His eyes strayed to the wooden crucifix hung above his bed. 'An immortal being.'

He spoke with such power. And he was not insane.

I had to listen. To consider his words.

'Is it possible?' I whispered.

'Yes.' He hugged me. 'There is a secret I haven't told you. It is extraordinary. It is the secret to permanent transformation. If I have the right materials – your blood, for example – I can transform anything. If you wish, you can become such a hybrid. I can even make you human again.' He paused, perhaps thinking of my ancient grief over the loss of Lalita, my daughter. He knew my sterile condition was the curse of my unending life. He must have known, since he added, 'You could have a child, Sita.'

5 ~~~~~

Around midnight I return to the compound, determined to learn its layout from the outside. Dressed totally in black, I have an Uzi strung over my back, a high-powered pair of binoculars in one hand, a Geiger counter in the other. The momentary phenomenon of my glowing skin continues to haunt me. I wonder if they are doing something weird to Joel – using radiation on him.

I have decided the ideal vantage point from which to study the compound is the top of the hill in which the base is dug. To get to it I have to take a long walk. Here the terrain is even too rough for my new Jeep. I move swiftly, my head down, like the mystical serpent I embody. A deep desire to plant my teeth in that general

I saw the past night stays with me. He reminds me of Eddie – not of the psycho's warped nature but of his delusions of grandeur. I can tell a lot by a man's face. Perhaps I read his mind a little as well. The general wants to use Joel to get ahead in the world, maybe take it over. I don't know where the Pentagon gets these people.

At the top of the hill I scan each square foot of the compound. Once again I am stunned by the level of security. It is as if they are set up to ward off an attack from an alien race. While I watch, a sleek jet with the lines of a rocket lands on the runway. It is like no jet I have ever seen before, and I suspect it can do Mach 10 – ten times the speed of sound – and that Congress has never heard of it.

My Geiger counter indicates the radiation here is three times what is normal, but still well within safety limits. I'm puzzled. Radiation couldn't have been responsible for my luminous skin. Yet the fact that the level is high confirms that there are nuclear warheads in the vicinity. I suspect I am sitting above them, that they are stored in the caves the military has dug into this hill. The caves are now an established fact. I watch as men and equipment ride a miniature rail-road beneath me into and out of the hill. This is how the human race gets into trouble. The danger of renegade vampires is nothing compared to the folly of handing unlimited sums of money over to people who like to keep 'secrets.' Who have on their payroll physicists and chemists and genetic engineers who, as children, rooted for Pandora to open her box of evils.

How Andrew Kane has partially managed to duplicate Arturo Evola's work continues to preoccupy me. I cannot imagine an explanation.

A black cart rides beneath me into the hill. Soldiers sit on it, smoking cigarettes and talking about babes. My Geiger counter momentarily jumps. The level is not high enough to harm the human body, but it does confirm that the boys in uniform are sitting next to a thermonuclear device. I know the famed fail-safe system is a joke, as do most people in the government. The President of the United States is not the only one who can order an American-made nuclear device to explode. In West Germany, before the Wall came down, the authority to fire a miniature neutron bomb was often in the hands of a lieutenant. Currently, *all* the nuclear submarine captains in the U.S. Navy have the authority to launch their missiles without the required presidential black box and secret codes. It is argued that the captains must have this authority because if the country is attacked the President would most likely be one of the first to die.

Still, it makes me nervous.

The general must have the authority to trigger these bombs if he wishes.

It is good to know.

I have finished my study of the compound and am walking back to my Jeep when I notice that my legs are glowing again, as are my hands and arms. Once more, every square inch of my exposed skin is faintly shining with the whiteness of the moon – not good here at a top-secret camp. It makes me that much more visible. I hurry to my Jeep, climb inside, and drive away.

But long before I reach Las Vegas, I pull over, far off the road.

A bizarre idea has occurred to me.

The problem is not radiation. It is not man-made.

Climbing out of the Jeep, I remove all my clothing and stand naked with my arms outstretched to the moon, as if I were worshipping the astronomical satellite, bowing to it, drinking up her rays. Slowly the skin on my chest and thighs begins to take on the milky radiance. And it seems the more I invite the moonlight onto my skin, *into* my heart, the brighter it becomes. Because if I will it to stop, my skin returns to normal.

'What does it mean, Yaksha?' I whisper to my dead creator.

My right arm, as the moonlight floods in, shines particularly bright. Holding it close to my eyes, *I can see through it!* I can actually see the ground through my flesh!

I put my clothes back on.

I can't look like a Christmas light when I try to seduce Andrew Kane.

6 ∼

I am Lara Adams as I enter the casino later that night and stand beside Andrew Kane at the dice table. I'm still a redhead, with a soft southern accent and a prim and proper smile. The name is not new to me. I used it to enroll at Mayfair High in Oregon, where I met Ray and Seymour. It's hard to believe that was less than two months ago. How life can change when you're a vampire on the run.

Andy glances over at me and smiles. He has the dice in his hands. He has been in the casino five minutes but already he's had a couple of drinks.

'Do you want to place a bet?' he asks.

I smile. 'Do you feel hot?'

He shakes the dice in his palm. 'I *am* hot.'

I remove a stack of black hundred-dollar chips from my bag and place one on the pass line, his favourite bet – seven or eleven. Andy rolls the dice. They dance over the green felt. Coming to a halt, the numbers four and three smile up at us.

'Lucky seven,' the croupier says and pays off our bets. Andy flashes me another smile.

'You must be good luck,' he says.

I double my bet. 'I have a feeling this is my night,' I say.

By the time the dice come to me, Andy and I have lost a combined total of eight hundred dollars. That is about to change. With my supernatural balance and reflexes, with practice, I can roll any number I desire. I have been practicing in my suite since I returned from the compound. Carefully I set the dice upright in my left palm in the configuration: five and six. In a blur, I toss them out. They bounce happily, seemingly randomly to human eyes. But they come to a halt in the same position they started out. Andy and I each win a hundred dollars on the number eleven. Since I threw a pass, I am invited to throw another – which I do. The people at the table like me. Most bet on the pass line.

I throw ten passes in a row before I let the dice go. We mustn't get greedy. Andy appreciates my style.

'What's your name?' he asks.

'Lara Adams. What's yours?'

'Andrew Kane. Are you here alone?'

I pout. 'I did come with a friend. But it seems I'll be

going home alone.'

Andy chuckles. 'Not necessarily. The night's still young.'

'It's five in the morning,' I remind him.

He nods at the glass of water I sip. 'Can I get you something stronger?'

I lean against the table. 'I think I need something stronger.'

We continue to play craps, winning better than honest wages when I am throwing the dice. The people at the table don't want me to surrender the designated high roller position, but I am careful not to appear superhuman, just damn lucky. Andy bets heavily and wins back all the money he lost the night before, and then some. We both drink too much. I have four margaritas, Andy five Scotches and water, on top of what he had drunk before I entered. The alcohol has no effect on me. My liver neutralizes it almost the instant it enters my system. I can take in all kinds of poisons and remain undisturbed. Andy, however, is now drunk, just the way the casinos like people. He is betting five hundred dollars a roll when I pull him away from the table.

'What's the matter?' he protests. 'We're winning.'

'You can be winning and courting disaster at the same time. Come on, let's have some coffee. I'm buying.'

He stumbles as he walks beside me. 'I've been at work all night. I'd like a steak.'

'You shall have whatever you want.'

The Mirage coffee shop is open twenty-four hours a day. The menu is flexible – Andy is able to get his steak. He orders it medium rare with a baked potato. He wants a beer, but I insist he have a glass of milk.

'You're going to destroy your stomach,' I say as we wait for our food. I do have favourite foods, besides blood. I have ordered roast chicken with rice and vegetables. Surprisingly, for a vampire, I eat plenty of vegetables. Nothing is as good for the body as those fresh greens, except, perhaps, those dripping reds. Sitting with Andy, I become thirsty for blood as well. Before I rest, I will grab some male tourist off the streets, show him a good time. That is, if I don't spend the night – the day – sleeping beside Andy. His eyes shine as he looks me over.

'I can always have it removed,' he replies.

'Why not just drink less?'

'I'm on vacation.'

'Where are you from?'

He chuckles. 'Here!' He is serious for a moment. 'You know you are one beautiful young woman. But I suppose you know that.'

'It's always nice to hear.'

'Where are you from?'

'The South – Florida. I came with a boyfriend for a few days, but he got angry with me.'

'Why?'

'I told him I wanted to break up.' I add, 'He's got a nasty temper.' I sip my milk, wishing I could squeeze our waitress's veins into it, add a little flavor. 'What about you? What do you do?'

'I'm a mad scientist.'

'Really? What are you mad about?'

'You mean, what kind of scientist am I?'

'Yes. And do you work around here?'

His voice takes on a guarded note, even though he is still quite drunk. 'I'm a genetic engineer. I work for the government. They have a lab – in town.'

I mock him playfully. 'Is it a top-secret lab?'

He sits back and shrugs. 'They would like to keep it that way. They don't feel comfortable unless we're working outside the reach of mainstream scientists.'

'Do I detect a note of resentment in your tone?'

'Not resentment – that's too strong a word. I love my job. It has provided me opportunities I couldn't get in the normal business world. I think what you sense is frustration. The opportunities presented in our lab are not being fully exploited. We need people of many disciplines involved, from all over the world.'

'You would like the lab to be more open?'

'Precisely. But that doesn't mean I don't appreciate the need for security.' He pauses. 'Especially as of late.'

'Interesting things are happening?'

He looks away and chuckles, but there is a note of sorrow in his voice. 'Very interesting things.' He turns back to me. 'May I ask you a personal question, Lara?'

'By all means.'

'How old are you?'

I flirt. 'How old do you think I am?'

He is genuinely puzzled. 'I don't know. When we were at the table, you seemed about thirty. But now that we're alone together you seem much younger.'

I have designed my makeup and dress to appear older. My longish white dress is conservative; I have a strand of pearls around my neck. My lipstick is glossy, overdone. I wear a red scarf to match my red wig.

'I'm twenty-nine,' I say, which is the age on my new driver's license and passport. 'I appreciate your compliment, however. I take care of myself.' I pause. How old are you?'

He laughs, picking up his glass of milk. 'Let's just say my liver would be a lot younger if this was all I drank.'

'"Milk does a body good."'

He sets the glass down and stares into it. 'So do other things.'

'Andy?'

He shakes his head. 'Just something that's going on at work. I can't talk about it. It would bore you anyway.' He changes the subject. 'Where did you learn to throw dice like that?'

'Like what?'

'Come on. You always throw them the same way, resting the number you want to come up on your open palm. How do you do it? I've never seen anyone who could control the bounce of the dice.'

I realize I went too far. He is a smart man, I remind myself. His powers of observation are keen, even when he is intoxicated. Yet, at the same time I don't mind that he sees something special in me. I have no time to cultivate his interest slowly. I must have him under my thumb by tomorrow night. It is then I plan to rescue Joel.

I answer his question carefully. 'I have had many interesting teachers. Perhaps I could tell you about them sometime.'

'How about now, tonight?'

'Tonight? The sun will be up in an hour.'

'I don't have to be at work until it goes down.' He reaches across the table and takes my hand. 'I like you, Lara. I mean that.' He pauses. 'I feel like I've met you before.'

I shake my head, wondering if he senses the similarities between Joel and myself. 'We have never met,' I tell him.

7 ~~

We go back to his place. He offers me a drink. When I decline, he has one himself – a Scotch on the rocks. The food in his stomach has sobered him up somewhat, but he quickly proceeds to get drunk again. He has a real problem, and now it is my problem as well. Granted, his intoxicated state makes his tongue loose and he tells me far more about his work than he should, although he has yet to mention Joel or vampires. Still, I will need him clear headed to help me. I have no time to repair his wounded psyche. I wonder what makes him drink so much. He lied when he said he didn't resent his boss. Obviously he hates the general. But I cannot read his mind, probably because he keeps it scrambled with booze. I sense only deep emotional conflicts, coupled with intellectual excitement. He is grateful to be working on Joel, analyzing his blood, and yet it bothers him that he is directly involved in the project. I have no doubt of this.

We sit on the couch in the living room. He rifles through his mail and then throws it on the floor. 'Bills,' he mutters, sipping his drink. 'The hardest reality of life, besides death.'

'The way you gamble, I hope the government pays you well.'

He snorts softly, staring at the eastern sky, which has begun to brighten. 'They don't pay me what I'm worth, that's for sure.' He glances at my strand of pearls. 'You look like you don't have to worry about money.'

'Daddy made millions in oil before he died.' I shrug. 'I was his only child.'

'He left it all to you?'

'Every last penny.'

'Must be nice.'

'It is very nice.' I move closer to him on the sofa, touch his knee. I have an alluring touch. I swear sometimes I could seduce an evangelist's wife as easily as I could a horny Marine. Sex holds no mystery for me, and I have no scruples. I use my body as easily as any other weapon. I add, 'What exactly do you do at your lab?'

He gestures to his office. 'It's in there.'

'What's in there?'

He takes another swallow of Scotch. 'My greatest

discovery. I keep a model of it at home to inspire me.' He burps. 'But right now a fat raise would inspire me more.'

Even though I know what's in his office, I walk over and have a peep at the two models of the DNA, the human one and the vampiric molecule. 'What are they?' I ask.

He is enjoying his drink too much to get up. 'Have you heard of DNA?'

'Yes, of course. I graduated from college.'

'What school did you go to?'

'Florida State.' I return to my place on the couch, closer to him than before. 'I graduated with honours.'

'What was your major?'

'English lit, but I took several biology classes. I know that DNA is a double helix molecule that encodes all the information necessary for life to exist.' I pause. 'Are those models of human DNA?'

He sets his drink down. 'One of them is.'

'What's the other one?'

He stretches and yawns. 'A project my partners and I have been working on for the last month.'

My blood turns cold. It was in the last month that Eddie began to produce his horde of vampiric gangbangers. Andy has been able to duplicate Arturo's visions of vampire DNA because he has been analyzing the molecules for a while, long before Joel was captured. That can only mean one of Eddie's offspring escaped my slaughter.

'*I don't know. I destroyed your silly gang.*'

'*You're not sure of that.*'

'*Now I am sure. You see, I can tell when someone lies. It's one of those great gifts I possess that you don't. There is only you left, and we both know it.*'

'*What of it? I can make more whenever I feel the need.*'

Eddie admitted that there were no others. He couldn't have tricked me, yet perhaps he himself was tricked. Maybe one of *his* offspring had made another vampire and didn't tell him. It's the only explanation. That vampire must have been caught by the government and taken to the desert compound. I wonder if the mystery vampire is still in the place. My rescue effort has just been complicated.

I have to wonder if I'm already too late. Andy has – at the least – an outline of the DNA code of the vampire. How long will it be before he and his partners are able to create more bloodsuckers? The only thing that gives me hope is that the general struck me as a man who keeps everything under wraps, until it is time to make his move. Andy has said as much about him. Everything connected to vampires is still probably locked up in the compound.

In response to Andy's comment, I force a chuckle. Boy, do I force it. 'Are you making a modern Frankenstein monster?' I ask, kidding, but not kidding.

My question hits a nerve, for obvious reasons, and Andy sits quietly for a moment, staring at his drink as if it were a crystal ball.

'We are playing a high-stakes game,' he admits. 'Altering the DNA code of any species is like rolling the dice. You can win and you can lose.'

'But it must be exciting to be playing such a game?'

He sighs. 'We have the wrong pit boss in charge.'

I put my hand on his shoulder. 'What's his name?'

'General Havor. He's a hard ass – I don't think his mother gave him a first name. At least I don't know it. We call him "General" or "Sir." He believes in order, performance, sacrifice, discipline, power.' Andy shakes his head. 'He definitely doesn't create an environment for free thinking and loving cooperation.'

I am the understanding girlfriend. 'You should quit then.'

Andy flashes an amused, bitter grin. 'If I quit now I'd be walking away from one of the greatest discoveries of modern time. Plus I need the job. I need the money.'

I caress his hair. My voice is soft and seductive. 'You need to relax, Andy, and not think of this stupid general. Tell you what – when you get off work tomorrow, come straight to my suite. I'm staying at the Mirage, Room Two-One-Three-Four. We can play the tables and have another late dinner together.'

Gently he takes my hand. His eyes momentarily come into focus, and I see his intellect again, feel his warmth. He is a good man, working in a bad place.

'Do you have to go now?' he asks sadly.

I lean over and kiss him on the cheek. 'Yes. But we'll

see each other tomorrow.' I sit back and wink. 'We'll have fun.'

He is pleased. 'You know what I like about you, Lara?'

'What?'

'You have a good heart. I feel I can trust you.'

I nod. 'You can trust me, Andy. You really can.'

8 ~~~

One of the saddest stories told in modern literature, to me at least, is Mary Shelley's *Frankenstein*. Because in a sense I am that monster. Knowingly or unknowingly, to much of history, I am the inspiration of nightmares. I am the primeval fear, something dead come to life, or better yet – and more accurate – something that refuses to die. Yet I consider myself more human than Shelley's creation, more humane than Arturo's offspring. I am a monster, but I can also love deeply. Yet even my love for Arturo could not spare him from plunging us into a nightmare from which there seemed to be no waking.

His secret of transformation was very simple, and profound beyond belief. It is fashionable among New Age adherents to use crystals to develop higher states of consciousness. What most of these people do not know is that a crystal is merely an amplifier, and that it has to be used very carefully. Whatever is present in the aura of the person, in the psychic field, gets magnified. Hate can be boosted as easily as compassion. In fact, cruel emotions expand more easily when given the chance. Arturo had an intuitive sense of the proper crystal to use with each person. Indeed, on most people he refused to use crystals at all. Few, he said, were ready for such high vibrations. How tragic it was that when he had a vial of my blood in his hand, his intuition deserted him. It is a pity his special genius did not leave him as well. It took a genius to take us as far as he did.

A mad one.

Using the magnets and copper sheets, in his secret geometric arrangements, the vibrations from whatever Arturo placed over the person were transmitted into the aura. For example, when he placed a clear quartz crystal above my head, a deep peaceful state settled in my mind. Yet if he used a similar crystal with young Ralphe, the boy would become irritated. Ralphe had too much going on in his mind and was not ready for crystals. Arturo understood that. He was an alchemist in the truest sense of the word. He could transform what could not be changed. Souls as well as bodies.

Arturo did not believe the body created the mind. He felt it was the other way around, and I believe he was correct. When he altered an aura, he changed the person's physiology as well. He just needed the proper materials, he said, to change anything. A flawed human into a glorious god. A sterile vampire into a loving mother.

It was, in the end, the chance to become human again that caused me to give him my blood. To hold *my* daughter in *my* hands again – what ecstasy! I was seduced by ancient griefs. Yaksha had made me pay dearly for my immortality, with the loss of Rama and Lalita. Arturo promised to give me back half of what had been stolen. It had been over four thousand years. Half seemed better than nothing. As I let my blood drip into a gold communion chalice for Arturo, I prayed to Krishna to bless it.

'I am not breaking my vow to you,' I whispered, not believing my own words. 'I am just trying to break this curse.'

I did not know, as I prayed to my God, that Arturo was also praying to his. To allow him to convert human and vampiric blood into the saving fluid of Jesus Christ. Genius may make a person a fanatic, I don't know. But I do know that a fanatic will never listen to anything other than his own dreams. Arturo was soft and kind, warm and loving. Yet he was convinced he had a great destiny. Hitler thought the same. Both wanted something nature had never granted – the perfect being. And I, the ancient monster, just wanted a child. Arturo and I – we should never have met.

But perhaps our meeting was destined.

My blood looked so dark in the chalice.

The sacredness of the chalice did nothing to dispel my gloom.

Arturo wanted to place my blood above the head of select humans. To merge the vibration of my immortal pattern into that of a mortal. If he changed the aura, he said, the body would be transformed. He, of all people, should have known how potent my blood was. He had stared deep into my eyes. He should have known my will would not bend easily to the will of another.

'You will not put the blood in their veins?' I asked as I handed him the chalice. He shook his head.

'Never,' he promised. 'Your God and my God are the same. Your vow will remain unbroken.'

'I'm not fooling myself,' I said quietly. 'I have broken a portion of it.' I moved close to him. 'I do this for you.'

He touched me then – he rarely did, before that night. It was hard for him to feel my flesh and not burn. 'You do this for yourself as well,' he said.

I loved to stare deeply into his eyes. 'That is true. But as I do this – for you as well as for myself – you must do likewise.'

He wanted to draw back but he only came closer. 'What do you mean?'

I kissed him then, for the first time, on the cheek. 'You have to break your vow. You have to make love to me.'

His eyes were round. 'I can't. My life is dedicated to Christ.'

I did not smile. His words were not funny, but tragic.

The seed of all that was to follow was hidden inside them. But I did not see that then, at least not clearly. I just wanted him so badly. I kissed him again, on the lips.

'You believe my blood will lead you to Christ,' I said. 'I do not know about that. But I do know where I can take you.' I set down the bloody chalice and my arms went around him, the wings of the vampire swallowing its prey. 'Pretend I am your God, Arturo, at least for tonight. I will make it easy for you.'

There was one last ingredient in Arturo's technique that I did not witness during my first session. While I was lying on the floor with all the paraphernalia around me, he had set a mirror above the crystals. This mirror was coordinated with an external mirror, which allowed moonlight to shine through the crystals. It was actually the light, altered by its passage through the quartz medium, that set in motion the higher vibration in the aura that altered the body. Arturo never focused the sun directly through the crystals, saying it would be much too powerful. Of course, Arturo understood that the light of the moon was identical to the light of the sun, only softened by cosmic reflection.

Arturo made with his own hands a crystal vial to hold my blood.

His first experiment was with a local child who had been retarded since birth. The boy lived on the streets and existed on the scraps of food tossed to him by strangers. It was my desire that Arturo first work on someone who couldn't turn him over to the Inquisition. Still, Arturo was taking a big risk experimenting on anyone. The Church would have burned him at the stake. How I hated its self-righteous dogma, its hypocrisy. Arturo never knew how many inquisitors I killed – a small detail that I forgot to mention in my confession to him.

I remember well how gently Arturo spoke to the child to get him to relax on the copper sheet. Normally the boy was filthy, but I had given him a bath before the beginning of the experiment. He was naturally distrustful of others, having been abused so many times during his life. But he liked us – I had been feeding him off and on and Arturo had a way with children. Soon enough, he was lying on the copper and breathing comfortably. The reflected moonlight, peering through the dark vial of my blood, cast a haunting red hue over the room. It reminded me of the end of twilight, of the time just before night falls.

'Something is happening,' Arturo whispered as we watched the boy's breathing accelerate. For twenty minutes the child was in a state of hyperventilation, twitching and shaking. We would have stopped the process if the boy's face hadn't looked calm. Plus, we were watching history being made, maybe a miracle.

Finally the boy lay still. Arturo diverted the reflected moonlight and helped the boy to sit up. There was a new strangeness to his eyes – they were bright. He hugged me.

'*Ti amo anch'io*, Sita,' he said. '*I love you, Sita.*' I had never heard him say a whole sentence before. I was so overjoyed that I didn't stop to think I had never told him my real name. In all of Italy, only Arturo and Ralphe knew it. We were both happy for the child, that his brain seemed to be functioning normally. It was one of the few times in my life I cried, tears of water, not tears of blood.

The red tears would come later.

This first successful experiment gave Arturo tremendous confidence and weakened his caution. He had seen a mental change; he wanted to see a physical one. He went looking for a leper, and brought back a woman in her sixties whose toes and fingers had been eaten away by the dread disease. Over the centuries I had found it particularly painful to look upon lepers. In the second century, in Rome, I had a beautiful lover who developed leprosy. Toward the latter stages of his disease, he begged me to kill him, and I did, crushing his skull, with my eyes tightly clenched. Of course, now there is AIDS. Mother Nature gives each age its own special horror. She is like Lord Krishna, full of wicked surprises.

The woman was almost too far gone to notice what we were doing to her. But Arturo was able to get her breathing deeply, and soon the magic was happening again. She began to hyperventilate, twitching worse than the boy had. Yet her eyes and face remained calm. I was not sure what she felt; it was not as if she suddenly sprouted toes and fingers. When she was through, Arturo led her upstairs and had her lie down on a bed. But from the start she did seem stronger, more alert.

A few days later she began to grow toes and fingers.

Two weeks later there was no sign of her leprosy.

Arturo was ecstatic, but I was worried. We told the woman not to tell anyone what we had done for her. Of course she told *everyone*. The rumours started to fly. Wisely, Arturo passed her cure off to the grace of God. Yet, during these days of the Inquisition, it was more dangerous to be a saint than a sinner. A sinner, as long as he or she was not a heretic, could repent and escape with a flogging. A saint might be a witch. Better to burn a possible saint, the Church thought, than let a genuine witch escape. They had a weird sense of justice.

Arturo was not a complete fool, however, He did not heal more lepers, even though dozens came to his door seeking relief. Yet he continued to experiment on a few deaf and dumb people, a few who were actually retarded. Oh, but it was hard to turn away the lepers. The lone woman had given them such hope. Modern-day pundits often talk of the virtue of hope. To me, hope brings grief. The most content people are those who expect nothing, who have ceased to dream.

I had dreamed what it would be like to be Arturo's lover, and now that he was mine, he was unhappy. Oh, he loved to sleep with me, feel me close beside him. But he believed he had sinned and he couldn't stop. The timing of our affair was unfortunate. He was breaking his vow of celibacy just when he was on the verge of fulfilling his destiny. God would not know whether to curse or bless him. I told him not to worry about God. I had met the guy. He did what he wanted when he wanted, no matter how hard you tried. I told Arturo many stories of Krishna, and he listened, fascinated. Still, he would weep after we had sex. I told him to go to confession. But he refused – he would only confess to me. Only I could understand him, he said.

But I didn't understand. Not what he had planned.

He began to have visions during this period. He'd had them before – they didn't alarm me, at least not at first. It was a vision that had given him the mechanics of his transformative technique, long before we met. But now his visions were peculiar. He began to build models. Only seven hundred years later did I realize he was building models of DNA – human DNA, vampiric, and one other form. Yes, it is true, while we watched the people twitch on the floor under the influence of my bloody aura, Arturo saw more deeply than I did. He actually understood the specific molecule whose code defined the body. He saw the molecule in a vision, and he watched it change under the magnets, crystals, copper, and blood. He saw the double helix of normal DNA. He saw the twelve straight strands of my DNA. And he saw how the two could be conjoined.

'We need twelve helix strands,' he confided in me. 'Then we will have our perfect being.'

'But the more people you experiment on, the more

attention you will draw to yourself,' I protested. 'Your Church will not understand. They will kill you.'

He nodded grimly. 'I understand. And I cannot keep working on abnormal people. To make a leap toward the perfect being, I must work with a normal person.'

I sensed what was in his mind. 'You cannot experiment on yourself.'

He turned away. 'What if we try Ralphe?'

'No,' I pleaded. 'We love him the way he is. Let's not change him.'

He continued to stare at the wall, his back to me. 'You changed him, Sita.'

'That was different. I knew what I was doing. I had experience. I healed his wounds. I altered his body, not his soul.'

He turned to me. 'Don't you see it's because I love Ralphe as much as you do that I want to give him this chance? If we can change him from the inside out, transform his blood, he will be like a child of Christ.'

'Christ never knew of vampires,' I warned. 'You should not mix the two in your mind. It's blasphemy – even to me.'

Arturo was passionate. 'How do you know he didn't? You never met him.'

I got angry. 'Now you speak like a fool. If you want to experiment on anyone, use me. You promised me you would when we started this.'

He stiffened. 'I can't change you. Not now.'

I understood what he was saying. Suddenly I felt the

weight of shattered dreams. In my mind I had been playing with a daughter who had never been born, and who probably never would be.

'You need my blood first,' I replied. 'The pure vampire blood.' It was true he had to replenish the blood in the crystal vial, not before each experiment, but often. Old blood did not work – it was too dead. I continued, 'But what if your experiment does work and you do create a perfect being? I cannot give enough blood to alter everyone on this planet.'

He shrugged. 'Perhaps those who are altered can become the new donors.'

'That is a huge *perhaps*. Also, I know people. This will be an exclusive club. It doesn't matter how good your intentions are now.' I turned away and chuckled bitterly. 'Who will be given a chance at perfection? The nobility? The clergy? The most corrupt will feel they are the most deserving. It is the oldest lesson of history. It never changes.'

Arturo hugged me. 'That will not happen, Sita. God has blessed this work. Only good can come from it.'

'No one knows what God has blessed,' I whispered. 'And what he has cursed.'

A few days went by during which Arturo and I hardly spoke. He would stay up late making models of molecules no one had seen, afraid to talk to me, to touch me. I never realized until then how he saw me as both a gift and a test from God. Of course I had given him my immortal perception on the matter, but he had seen me that way from the start. I brought him magic blood *and* delicious sensuality. He was supposed to take one and not the other, he thought. He lost his intuitive sense that kept him from mistakes, I believe, because he no longer thought he was worthy of having it. He stopped praying to God and started muttering to himself about the blood of Jesus Christ. He was more obsessed with blood than I was, and I had it for dinner every few days.

One evening I could find Ralphe nowhere. Arturo said he had no idea where he was. Arturo wasn't lying, but he wasn't telling the whole truth either. I didn't press him. I think I didn't want to know the truth. Yet had I insisted he tell me, I might have stopped the horror, before it got out of hand.

The screams started in the middle of night.

I was out for a walk at the time. It was my custom to go out late, disguised, find a homeless person, drink a pint of blood, whisper in his or her ear, and put the person back to sleep. Except for evil priests, I didn't often kill in those days. The cries that came to me that night chilled me through. I ran toward the sounds as fast as I could.

I found five bodies, horribly mangled, their limbs torn off. Obviously, only a being of supernatural strength could have committed these acts. One person, a woman with an arm lying beside her, was the last one still alive. I cradled her head in my lap.

'What happened?' I asked. 'Who did this to you?'

'The demon,' she whispered.

'What did this demon look like?' I demanded.

She gagged. 'A hungry angel. The blood –' Her eyes strayed to her severed arm and she wept. 'My blood.'

I shook her. 'Tell me what this demon looked like?'

Her eyes rolled up into her head. 'A child,' she whispered with her last breath and died in my arms.

Sick at heart, I knew who the child was.

Far away, on the far side of the town, I heard more screams.

I flew toward them but once again I was too late. There were more shredded bodies, and this time there were witnesses. An angry mob with burning torches was gathering. They had seen the demon child.

'It was heading for the woods!' they cried.

'We have to stop it!' others cried.

'Wait!' I yelled. 'Look how many it has killed. We can't go after it without help.'

'It killed my brother!' one man cried, pulling out a knife. 'I'm going to kill it myself.'

The mob followed the man. I had no choice but to tag along. As we wound through the dark streets, we found still more bodies. A few had had their heads ripped off. What was the mob thinking? I asked myself. They would fare no better against the monster. Of course mobs and rational thought are not complementary. I have seen too many mobs in my day.

When we reached the trees on the edge of town, I

left the rabble to search for the monster myself. I could hear it, two miles ahead, laughing uproariously as it tore off the head of an animal. It was fast and strong, but I was a pure vampire, not a hybrid. It would be no match for me.

I came across it as it ducked from tree to tree, preparing to attack the mob.

'Ralphe,' I whispered as I moved up behind him.

He whirled around, his face covered with blood, a wild light in his eyes. Or I should say, no light shone there. His eyes were snakelike. He was a serpent on the prowl, searching for the eggs of another reptile. Yet he recognized me – a faint flicker of affection crossed his face. If it was not for that, I would have killed him instantly. I had no hope he could be converted back to what he had been. I have intuition of my own. Some things I simply know. Usually the bitterest of things.

'Sita,' he hissed. 'Are you hungry? I am hungry.'

I moved closer, not wanting to alert the mob, which was closing in. Ralphe had left a trail of blood. The stuff dripped off him; it was enough to make even me sick. My heart broke in my chest as he came within arm's reach.

'Ralphe,' I said softly, all the time knowing it was hopeless. 'I have to take you back to Arturo. You need help.'

Terror disfigured his bloody expression. Obviously the transformation had not been pleasant for him. 'I will not go back there!' he shouted. 'He made me hungry!' Ralphe paused to stare down at his sticky hands. A portion of his humanity did indeed remain. His voice faltered on a lump of sorrow in his throat. 'He made me do this.'

'Oh, Ralphe.' I took him in my arms. 'I'm so sorry. This should never have happened.'

'Sita,' he whispered, nuzzling his face into my body. I could not kill him, I told myself. Not for the whole world. But just as I swore the vow inside, I leapt back in pain, barely stifling a cry. He had bitten me! His sorrow had vanished in a lick of his lips. I watched in horror as he chewed down a portion of my right arm, an insane grin on his face. 'I like you, Sita,' he said. 'You taste good!'

'Would you like more?' I asked, offering him my other arm, tears filling my eyes. 'You can have all you want. Come closer, Ralphe. I like you, too.'

'Sita,' he said lustfully as he grabbed my arm and started to take another bite. It was then I spun him around in my arms and gripped his skull from behind. With all the force I could muster and before my tears overwhelmed me, I yanked his head back and to the side. Every bone in his neck broke. His small body went limp in my arms – he had not felt any pain, I told myself.

'My Ralphe,' I whispered, running my hands through his long fine hair.

I should have fled with his body then, buried it in the hills. But the execution was too much, even for a monster like me. The life went out of me and I wanted to collapse. When the mob found me, I was cradling Ralphe's body in my arms, weeping like a common mortal. My ancient daughter, my young son – God had stolen them both from me.

The mob surrounded me.

They wanted to know how I had stopped the demon child.

A few in the mob knew me.

'You take care of this boy!' they cried. 'We saw you and the priest with him!'

I could have killed them right then, all fifty of them. But the night had seen too much death. I let them drag me back to the town, their torches burning in my bleary eyes. They threw me in a dungeon near the centre of town, where the executions took place, taunting me that they were going to get to the bottom of how this abomination was created. Before the sun rose, I knew they would be pounding on Arturo's door, digging into his secret underground chamber, collecting the necessary evidence to show the feared inquisitors. There would be a trial and there would be a judge. The only problem was, there could be only one sentence.

Yet I was Sita, a vampire of incomparable power. Even the hard hand of the Church could not close around my throat unless I allowed it. But what about Arturo? I loved him but could not trust him. If he lived, he would continue his experiments. It was inevitable because he believed it was his destiny. He had enough of my blood left to make another Ralphe, or worse.

A few hours later they threw him in a cell across from me. I begged him to talk to me but he refused. Huddled up in a corner, staring at the wall with eyes as vacant as dusty mirrors, he gave no indication of what was going through his mind. His God did not come to save him. That was left for me to do.

I ended up testifying against him.

The inquisitor told me it was the only way to save my life. Even chained in the middle of the high court with soldiers surrounding me, I could have broken free and destroyed them all. How tempting it was for me to reach out and rip open the throat of the evil-faced priest, who conducted his investigation like a hungry dog on a battlefield searching for fresh meat. Yet I could not kill Arturo with my own hands. It would have been impossible. But I could not have him live and continue his search for the sacred blood of Jesus Christ. Jesus had died twelve hundred years ago, and the search would never end. It was a paradox – the only solution was agonizing. I could not stop Arturo so I had to let others stop him.

'Yes,' I swore on the Holy Bible. 'He created the abomination. I saw him do it with my own eyes. He *changed* that boy. Then he tried to seduce me with the black arts. He is a witch, Father, that fact is indisputable. God strike me down if I lie!'

The old friar at the church also testified against Arturo, although the inquisitor had to first stretch him on the *strappado* to get the words out of his mouth. It broke the friar's heart to condemn Arturo. He was not alone in his guilt.

Arturo never confessed, no matter how much they tortured him. He was too proud, his cause too noble, in his mind. After the trial, we never spoke. Indeed, I never saw him again. I didn't attend his execution. But I heard they burned him at the stake.

Like any witch.

9 ~~~

I sit at a poker table trying to bluff a high roller from Texas into folding. The game has been going on a while. There is one hundred thousand dollars in cash and chips on the table. His hand is better than mine. Yaksha's mind-reading gift has grown more powerful in me – I can now see the man's cards as if viewing them through his eyes. He has three aces, two jacks – a full house. I have three sixes – Satan's favourite number. He has the winning hand.

The Texan wears leather cowboy boots, a five-gallon hat. The smoke from his fat cigar does not irritate my eyes. He blows a smelly cloud my way as if to intimidate me. I smile and match his last bet, then raise him another fifty thousand. We are enjoying a private game, in a luxurious corner of the casino, where only fat cats hang out. Three other men sit with us at the table, but they have since folded. They follow the action closely – they all know each other. The Texan will not like to be humiliated in front of them.

'You must have a royal flush, honey child,' he says. 'Betting the way you do.' He leans across the table. 'Or else you got a sugar daddy paying your bills.'

'Honey and sugar,' I muse aloud. 'Both are sweet – like me.' I add, sharpening my tone, 'But I pay my own bills.'

He laughs and slaps his leg. 'Are you trying to bluff me?'

'Maybe. Match my bet and find out.'

He hesitates a moment, glancing at the pot. 'The action is getting kind of heavy. What do you do, child, to have so much dough? Your daddy must have given it to you.'

He is trying to ascertain how important the money is to me. If it means a lot, in my mind, then I will be betting heavily only if I have an unbeatable hand. Leaning across the table, I stare him in the eye, not strong enough to fry his synapses but hard enough to shake him. I don't like being called a child. I am five thousand years old after all.

'I earned every penny of it,' I tell him. 'The hard way. Where did you get your money, old man?'

He sits back quickly, ruffled by my tone, my laser vision. 'I earned it by honest labour,' he says, lying.

I sit back as well. 'Then lose it honestly. Match my bet or fold. I don't care which. Just quit stalling.'

He flushes. 'I'm not stalling.'

I shrug, cool as ice. 'Whatever you want to call it, old man.'

'Damn you,' he swears, throwing his cards down. 'I fold.'

My arms reach out and rake in the money. They're all staring at me. 'Oh,' I say. 'I bet you're wondering what I had? But you're all too professional to ask, aren't you?' I stand and start to stuff the cash and chips in my purse. 'I think I'll call it a night.'

'Wait right there,' the Texan says, getting up. 'I want to see those cards.'

'Really? I thought you had to pay to see them. Are the rules different for Texans?'

'They are when you've got fifty grand of my money, bitch. Now show me.'

I dislike being called a 'bitch' more than a 'child.'

'Very well,' I say, flipping over my cards. 'You would have won. That's the last time I show a hand you didn't pay to see. Now do you feel better? You were bluffed out of your wrinkled skin, old man.'

He slams the table with his fist. 'Who are you anyway?'

I shake my head. 'You're a sore loser, and I've wasted enough time on you.' I turn away. One of his partners grabs my arm. That is a mistake.

'Hold on now, honey,' he says. The others move closer.

I smile. 'Yes?' Of course I am protected by the casino. I need only raise my voice and these men will be thrown out. But I dislike going to others for help, when I am so capable of taking care of myself. Dinner will be a four-course meal tonight, I think. 'What can I do for you?' I ask.

The man continues to hold on to my arm but doesn't respond. He glances at the Texan, who is clearly the boss. The Texan has regained his smile.

'We would just like to play some more, honey,' he says. 'That's only fair. We need a chance to win our money back.'

My smile widens. 'Why don't I just give you the money back?'

My offer confuses him. The Texan shrugs. 'If you want. I'll be happy to accept it.'

'Good,' I say. 'Meet me at the west end of the hotel parking lot in ten minutes. We'll go for a little drive. You'll get all your money back.' I glance at the others. 'The only condition is you must all come.'

'Why do we have to go anywhere?' the Texan asks. 'Just give it to us now.'

I shake off the other's hold on me. 'Surely you're not afraid of little old me, sugar daddy?' I say sweetly.

The men laugh together, a bit uneasily. The Texan points a finger at me.

'In ten minutes,' he says. 'Don't be late.'

'I never am,' I reply.

* * *

We meet as planned and drive a short distance from town, each in our own cars. Then I lead them off the road and into the desert a few miles, stopping near a low-lying hill. The time is eleven at night, the evening cool and clear, the almost full moon brilliant against the night sky. The men park beside me and climb out. They *are* afraid of me. I can smell their fear. Except for the big boss, they are armed. The bulges beneath their coats are noticeable. I smell the gunpowder in their bullets. They probably figure I am setting them up to be robbed. They study the terrain as they walk toward me, puzzled that I am alone. They are not very subtle. Two of them have their hands thrust in their coat pockets, their fingers wound around their handguns. The Texan steps in front and reaches out to me.

'Give us your bag,' Tex orders.

'All right.' I hand him my bag. The money is inside, much to his pleasure. His eyes are wide as he counts it. I know he had expected to find a gun in the bag. 'Are you satisfied?' I ask.

Tex nods to a partner. I am frisked. Roughly.

'She's cool,' the partner mumbles a moment later, backing away.

Tex stuffs the money in his pockets. 'Yeah, I'm satisfied. But I don't get it. Why did you drag us all the way out here?'

'I'm hungry,' I say.

He grins like the crooked oil baron that he is. 'We would have been happy to have taken you to dinner, honey pie. We still can. What would you like?'

'Prime ribs,' I say.

He slaps his leg again. Must be a nervous gesture with him. 'Goddamn! That's my favourite. Ribs dripping with red juice. We'll take you out and get you some right now.' He adds with a phony wink, 'Then maybe we can have a little fun afterward.'

I shake my head as I take a step toward him. 'We can eat here. We can have a picnic. Just the five of us.'

He glances at my car. 'Did you bring some goodies?'

'No. You did.'

His impatience is never far away. 'What are you talking about?'

I throw my head back and laugh. 'You're such a fake! Your politeness only appears when it is useful to you. Now that you have stolen the money I won fair and square, you want to take me out for dinner.'

Tex is indignant. 'We did not steal this money. You offered to return it to us.'

'After pressure from you. Let's call a spade a spade. You're a crook.'

'No one calls me that and gets away with it!'

'Really? What are you going to do? Kill me?'

He steps forward and slaps me across the face with the back of his hand. 'Bitch! You just be happy I'm not that kind of man.'

I put a hand to my mouth. 'Aren't you that kind of man?' I ask softly. 'I see your heart, Mr Money Bags. You have killed before. It's good we meet tonight, out here in the desert. If you lived, you would probably kill again.'

He turns to leave. 'Let's get out of here, boys.'

'Wait,' I say. 'I have something else to give you.'

He glances over his shoulder. 'What?'

I take another step forward. 'I have to tell you who I really am. You did ask, remember?'

Tex is in a hurry. 'So, who are you? A Hollywood star?'

'Close. I am famous, in certain circles. Why just a few days ago the entire LAPD was chasing me around town. You read about it in the papers?'

A wary note enters his voice. Once again, his men glance around, this time looking for Arab backups. 'You're not connected to that group of terrorists, are you?'

'There were no terrorists. That was just the cops trying to cover their asses. It was just me and my partner. We caused all the ruckus.'

He snorts. 'Right. You and your partner wasted twenty cops. You must be a terminator, huh?'

'Close. I'm a vampire. I'm five thousand years old.'

He snickers. 'You're a psycho, and you're wasting my time.' He turns again. 'Good night.'

I grab him by the back of his collar and yank him close, pressing his cheek next to mine. He is so startled – he hardly reacts. But his men are better trained. Suddenly I have three revolvers pointed at me. Quickly, I shield myself with Tex. My grip on him tightens, cutting off his air. He gags loudly.

'I am in a generous mood,' I say calmly to the others. 'I will give you men a chance to escape. Ordinarily I would not even consider it. But since my cover has been blown, I am not so picky about destroying every shred of evidence.' I pause and catch each of their eyes, no doubt sending a shiver to the base of their spines. 'I suggest you get in your cars and get out of here – out of Las Vegas completely. If you don't, you will die. It is that simple.' I throttle Tex and he moans in pain. My voice takes on a mocking tone, 'You can see how strong I am for a honey child.'

'Shoot her,' Tex gasps as I allow him a little air.

'That is a bad idea,' I say. 'To shoot me they have to shoot you first because you are standing in front of me. Really, Tex, you should think these things out before giving such orders.' I glance at the others. 'If you don't get out of here, I'll have you for dinner as well. I really am a vampire and, for me, prime ribs come in all shapes and forms.' With one hand, I lift Tex two feet off the ground. 'Do you want to see what I do to him? I guarantee it will make you sick to your stomach.'

'God,' one of the men whispers and turns to flee. He doesn't bother with the car. He just runs into the desert, anywhere to get away from me. Another fellow edges toward the periphery. But the remaining man – the guy who grabbed me in the casino, the same one who frisked me – snaps at him.

'She's not a vampire,' he says. 'She's just some kind of freak.'

110

'That's it,' I agree. 'I take steroids.' I glance at the guy who wants to leave. 'Get out of here while you still can. You will see neither of these men alive again. Believe me, you'll hear their screams echoing over the desert.'

My tone is persuasive. The guy leaves, chasing after the first one. Now there are just the three of us. How cozy. In reality, I was not looking forward to having to dodge the bullets fired by three separate men. I allow Tex a little more air, let him say his last words. His tune has not changed.

'Shoot her,' he croaks at his partner.

'You could try it and see what happens,' I remark.

The hired hand is unsure. His gun wavers in the air. 'I can't get a clear shot.'

Tex tries to turn toward me. 'We can make a deal. I have money.'

I shake my head. 'Too late. I don't want your money. I just want your blood.'

Tex sees I am serious. My eyes and voice appear devilishly wicked when I am in the mood, and I'm starving right now. Tex turns deathly pale, matching the colour of the moonlight that pours down on us.

'You can't kill me!' he cries.

I laugh. 'Yes. It will be very easy to kill you. Do you want me to demonstrate?'

He trembles. 'No!'

'I will give you a demonstration anyway.' I call over to Tex's partner, who has begun to perspire heavily. 'What is your name?'

'Go to hell,' he swears, trying to circle around us, to get off a lucky shot.

'That cannot be your name,' I say. 'Your mother would never have called you that. It doesn't matter. You are going to be nobody in a minute. But before I kill you, is there anything you want to say?'

He pauses, angry. 'Say to who?'

I shrug. 'I don't know. God, maybe. Do you believe in God?'

I exasperate him. 'You are one weird bitch.'

I nod solemnly. 'I am weird.' The full power of my gaze locks into his eyes. With me boring into him, he is unable to look away. All he sees, I know, is my fathomless pupils, swelling in size like black holes. I speak very slowly, softly. 'Now my dear man, you are going to take your gun and put it in your mouth.'

The man freezes for a moment.

Then, as if in a dream, he opens his mouth and puts the gun between his lips.

'Chuck!' Tex screams. 'Don't listen to her! She's trying to hypnotize you!'

'Now I want you to grasp the trigger,' I continue in my penetrating voice. 'I want you to place a certain amount of pressure on the trigger. Not enough to fire the bullet, mind you, but almost enough. There, that is perfect, you have done well. You are half an inch from death.' I pause and turn down the power of my eyes. My voice returns to normal. 'How does it feel?'

The man blinks and then notices the barrel in his

mouth. He almost has a heart attack. He is so scared, he actually drops the gun. 'Jesus Christ!' he cries.

'See,' I say. 'You must believe in God. And because I do as well, and I can only drink the blood of one of you at a time, I think I will let you go as well. Quick, join your partners out in the desert, before I change my mind.'

The man nods. 'No problem.' He dashes away.

'Chuck!' Tex screams. 'Come back here!'

'He is not coming back,' I tell Tex seriously. 'You cannot buy that kind of loyalty. You certainly cannot buy me. You can't even buy my dinner.' I pause. 'You must understand by now that you *are* dinner.'

He weeps like a child. 'Please! I don't want to die.'

I pull him closer, whisper my favourite line.

'Then you should never have been born,' I say.

I enjoy my meal.

When I am finished draining the Texan and have buried him far from his car, I go for a walk in the desert. My thirst is satisfied but my mind is restless. Andy will be off work in a few hours. I should be planning how I will convince him to help me, yet I cannot concentrate. I keep thinking I'm missing something important. I contemplate the last few days and somehow I know something is missing – a piece of the puzzle. This piece exists just beyond the edge of my vision. What it is, I cannot grasp.

Arturo's ghost haunts me. The world never knew

what it had lost in him. What greater sorrow could there be? I ask myself how he would have been remembered if there had been no Inquisition. If there had been no Sita and no magical blood to poison his dreams. Perhaps his name would have been uttered in the same breath as that of Leonardo da Vinci, of Einstein. It tortures me to think of the lost possibilities. Arturo the alchemist – the founder of a secret science.

'What did you do to Ralphe?' I whisper aloud. 'Why did you do it? Why did you refuse to talk to me when we were in jail?'

But his ghost has questions of its own.

Why were you so quick to kill Ralphe?

'I had to,' I tell the night.

Why did you betray me, Sita?

'I had to,' I say again. 'You were out of control.'

But I never accused you, Sita. And you were the real witch.

I sigh. 'I know, Arturo. And I was not a good witch.'

I have come far from where I started. A steep hill stands before me and I climb to the top of it. Twenty miles off to my left is Las Vegas, glowing with extravagance and decadence. The almost full moon is high and to my right. The hike has left me hot and sweaty. After shedding my clothes, I once more bow to the lunar goddess. This time I feel the rays enter my body, a tingling coolness that is strangely comforting. My breathing becomes deep and expanded. I feel as if my lungs can draw in the whole atmosphere, as if my skin can soak up the entire night sky. My heart pounds in my chest, now circulating a milky white substance instead of sticky red blood. Without using my eyes, I know I am becoming transparent.

I feel extraordinarily light.

As if I could fly.

The thought comes from an unknown place. It is like a hissed whisper spoken to me from the eternal abyss. Perhaps Yaksha's soul returns to grant me one final lesson.

The soles of my feet leave the top of the hill.

But I have not jumped. No.

I am floating – a few inches above the cool sand.

10 ~~~

When I return to my room, I call Seymour Dorsten, my friend and personal biographer, the young man I cured of AIDS with a few drops of my blood. Seymour is my psychic twin – he often writes about what I am experiencing, without my having to tell him what it is. Lately, I've been *broadcasting* him great material. I wake him up, but as soon as he hears my voice he is instantly alert.

'I knew you'd be calling me soon,' he says. 'Was that you down in Los Angeles?'

'Joel and I.'

He takes a moment to absorb what I am saying. 'Joel is a vampire now?'

'Yes. Eddie roughed him up bad. He was dying. I had no choice.'

'You've broken your vow.'

'Do you need to remind me?'

'Sorry.' He pauses. 'Can I become a vampire?'

'You don't want the headache. Let me tell you what's been happening.'

For the next ninety minutes Seymour listens while I detail everything that has occurred since just before I rescued Yaksha and battled with Eddie. I mention Tex, sleeping in his shallow grave in the desert, and my levitating in the moonlight. Seymour ponders my words for a long time.

'Well?' I ask finally. 'Have you been writing about all of this already?'

He hesitates. 'I was writing a story about you. In it you were an angel.'

'Did I have wings?'

'You were glowing white and flying high above a ruined landscape.'

'Sounds like the end of the world,' I remark.

Seymour is serious. 'It will be the end of the world if you don't get Joel away from these people. You think they really have another vampire in addition to Joel?'

'Yes. Andy has constructed a model of vampire DNA. He wouldn't have had time to do it after Joel was brought to him.'

'How do you know what vampire DNA looks like?'

I haven't told Seymour about Arturo. The story is too painful, and besides, I don't think it applies to the situation.

'Trust me, I have experience in the matter,' I reply. 'Andy's model is accurate. Anyway, whether I have to rescue one or two, my dilemma is the same. I have to get in there and then I have to get three of us out.'

'It sounds like your best bet is Andy. Can't you stare him in the eye and make him do what you want?'

'That can backfire. If I push too hard, I'll scramble his brain, and the others will know there's something wrong with him. But if I'm careful I can plant a few suggestions deep in his mind.'

'Money is a smart angle. Offer him millions. The fact that he hates his boss doesn't hurt either.'

'I agree. But, Seymour, you're supposed to tell me what I'm missing.'

'Do you feel you're missing something?' he asks.

'Yes. I can't explain, but I know it's there. It's just not evident to me.'

Seymour considers. 'I'll tell you a couple things you won't want to hear. When you get inside the compound, you can't go straight for Joel.'

'Why not?'

'You have to get to the general. You have to be able to control him.'

'He might be harder to get to than Joel.'

'I doubt it. Joel will be locked in a cage even you wouldn't be able to escape from. Obviously they know how strong a vampire is.'

'Joel is powerful, no doubt. But he is still a child next to me. They don't know that.'

'They know more than you think, Sita. You're really not looking at the whole picture. They're probably still searching Lake Mead for your body. The fact that they haven't found it tells the general that you're still alive. And for you to have survived what they put you through means that you have to be handled with *extreme* care.' Seymour pauses. 'The general must have figured you'll come for Joel.'

'You sound so certain,' I say. 'I'm not.'

'Look at it logically. You had several chances to leave Joel during your fight with the LAPD – but you didn't. In fact, you showed tremendous loyalty to him. Believe me, they have constructed a psychological profile on you. They know you're coming for him. They'll be waiting for you. That's one of the reasons you have to go after the general first. Control him and his mind and you control the compound.'

'His associates will know something is up.'

'You need only control him for a short time. Also, you have no choice. You need the general for something other than rescue and escape.'

'What?' I ask, knowing what he'll say.

'Samples of vampire blood will be spread all over the compound. I bet they have several labs there, and you won't be able to walk around and find all the samples. On top of that, they'll have the research that they've conducted in their computers. For these reasons the compound has to be completely destroyed. It's the only way. You're going to have to force the general to detonate a nuclear warhead.'

'Just like that? Blow up all those people?'

'You killed plenty of people down in L.A.'

My voice is cool. 'I didn't enjoy that, Seymour.'

He pauses. 'I'm sorry, Sita. I didn't mean to imply that you did. And I don't mean to sound cold and cruel. I'm not, you know. I'm just a high school kid, and a lousy writer on top of that.'

'You're too brilliant to be lousy at anything. Please continue with your analysis. How can I get Joel out alive and blow the place up?'

He hesitates. 'You might not be able to do both.'

I nod to myself. 'This could be a suicide mission. I've thought of that.' I add sadly, 'Won't you miss me?'

He speaks with feeling. 'Yes. Come here tonight. Make me a vampire. I'll help you.'

'You're not vampire material.'

'Why? I'm not sexy enough?'

'Oh, that's not the problem. If you were a vampire, I'm sure you'd be a sex machine. It's just that you're too special to be . . .' My voice falters as I think of Arturo. 'To be contaminated by my blood.'

'Sita? What's wrong?'

I swallow past my pain. 'It's nothing – the past. That's the trouble with living for five thousand years – I have so much past. It's hard to live in the present when all that history is inside you.'

'Your blood saved my life,' Seymour says gently.

'How are you feeling? Are the HIV tests still negative?'

'Yes, I'm fine. Don't worry about me. When do you see Andy next?'

'In a few hours, near dawn. Then, when he returns to work in the evening, I plan to stow away in the trunk of his car.'

'You'll need his cooperation. You can't go searching the compound for Joel.'

'Andy will cooperate, one way or the other.' I pause. 'Is there anything else you can tell me that might help?'

'Yeah. Practice that levitating trick. You never know when it'll come in handy.'

'I don't know what's causing it.'

'Obviously, Yaksha's blood. He must have developed the ability over the centuries. Could he fly when you knew him in India?'

'He never demonstrated that he could.'

'You vampires are full of surprises.'

I sigh. 'You're so anxious to become like me. You envy my powers. But what you don't know is that I envy you more.'

Seymour is surprised. 'What do I have that you could possibly want?'

I think of Lalita, my daughter.

But I cannot talk about children, on this of all nights.

'You're human' is all I say.

11 ~~~

When Andy gets to my suite, he acts stressed out but excited. He is in the door only a minute when I give him a hard kiss on the lips. He wants more, and reaches for it, but I push him away.

'Later,' I whisper. 'The night is still young.'

'It's almost morning,' he says, recalling my line from the night before.

I turn away. 'I want to gamble first.'

For a degenerate gambler, I know, dice are better than sex.

'Now you're talking, Lara,' he says.

We go down to the casino. It's only a few days before Christmas but the place is packed. The image of a nuclear bomb exploding on the Strip haunts me. Of course, that will never happen. Even if we set a nuclear warhead to go off at the compound, it would not affect Las Vegas, except for slight fallout – if the wind is blowing the wrong way. I wonder if Seymour's dream means I will succeed in my mission or fail.

A glowing angel, flying above the world?

We play craps, dice, and I am the designated roller. Without trying, I throw ten passes in a row and the table cheers me on. Andy bets heavily, wins plenty, and drinks even more. Before we leave the first table, he is drunk. I scold him.

'How can you be a scientist when you keep killing off your brain cells?' I ask.

He laughs, throwing an arm over my shoulder. 'I'd rather be a lover than a scientist.'

We walk down the Strip to another casino, the Excalibur. Here it is even more crowded. It is a fact that the town never sleeps. We play blackjack, twentyone. I count cards, only betting heavily when the deck favours the player. But the advantage from even perfect counting is limited, and we don't win any money. Andy drags me back to the dice table – his favourite. The dice come to me, and again I throw another six passes in a row. But I don't want Andy to win too much and be free of debt. Just as the sun begins to colour the sky, I drag him back to the Mirage, to my hotel suite. Once there, he falls on my bed, exhausted.

'I hate what I do,' he mutters to the ceiling.

I hate that I can't read his mind. It must be the

booze. I sit beside him. 'Another hard night at work?'

'I shouldn't talk about it.'

'You can. Don't worry – I'm good at keeping secrets.'

'My boss is crazy.'

'The general?'

'Yes. He's stark raving mad.'

'What do you mean? What is he doing?'

Andy sits up and glanoes at me with bloodshot eyes. 'Remember I told you we were working on an amazing discovery?'

'Yes. You said it was one of the greatest discoveries of modern time.' I smile. 'I thought you were trying to impress me.'

He shakes his head. 'I wasn't exaggerating. We're playing with explosive genetic material, and that's putting it mildly. This general has ordered us to artifically clone it. Do you know what that means?'

I nod. 'You're going to make more of it – in a test tube.'

'Yes. That's a layman's view, but it is essentially correct.' He stares out the window, at the glitter that is the Strip. When he speaks again, his voice reflects the horror he feels. 'We are going to try to duplicate something that, if it got out, could affect all of mankind.'

It's worse than I thought. The charade must end.

He has given me an opening. I must seize it.

'Andy?' I whisper.

He looks at me. I catch his eye.

'Yes, Lara?' he says.

I do not push him, not yet, but I do not let him turn away either. A narrow tunnel of whirling blue fog exists between us. He is at one end, chained to a hard wall, and I am steadily rushing toward him, shadows at my back. I hold his attention but slightly blur his focus. Since ingesting Yaksha's blood, my mind-altering abilities are more refined, more powerful. I have to be careful I don't destroy his brain.

'My name is not Lara.'

He tries to blink, fails. 'What is it?'

'It doesn't matter. I am not who I appear to be.' I pause. 'I know what you are working on.'

He hesitates. 'How?'

'I know your prisoner. He is a friend of mine.'

'No.'

'Yes. I lied to you last night, and I'm sorry. I won't lie to you anymore. I came to Las Vegas for the purpose of freeing my friend.' I touch his knee. 'But I didn't come to hurt you. I didn't know I would end up caring for you.'

He has to take a breath. 'I don't understand what you're saying?'

I have to relax my hold on him. The pressure inside his skull is building. Sweat stands out on his forehead. Standing, I turn my back to him and walk to the window to look out at the Strip. The Christmas decorations glitter even amid the neon in the faint light of the dawn.

'But you do understand,' I say. 'You are holding a prisoner, Joel Drake. He is an FBI agent, but since you have begun to examine him you have come to see that he's much more than that. His blood is different from that of most humans, and this difference makes him very strong, very quick. That's why you keep him locked up in a special cell. Your general tells you he is dangerous. Yet this same general makes you and your partners work night and day so that you can change more people's blood to match that of the supposedly dangerous prisoner.' I pause. 'Is this not accurate, Andy?'

He is a long time answering. His voice comes out hesitantly.

'How do you know these things?'

I turn to face him. 'I told you. I am his friend. I am here to rescue him. I need your help.'

Andy can't stop staring at me. It's as if I'm a ghost.

'They said there was another,' he mumbles.

'Yes.'

'Are you the one?'

'Yes.'

He winces. 'Are you like him?'

'Yes.'

He puts a hand to his head. 'Oh God.'

Once more, I sit beside him on the bed.

'We are not evil,' I say. 'I know what you must have been told, but it is not true. We only fight when threatened. The men and woman who died in L.A. trying to arrest us – we didn't want to harm them. But they came after us, they cornered us. We had no choice but to defend ourselves.'

His head is buried in his hands. He is close to weeping. 'But you killed many others before that night.'

'That is not true. The one who did the killing – he was an aberration. His name was Eddie Fender. He accidentally got ahold of our blood. I stopped him, but Eddie is a perfect example of what can happen if this blood gets out. You said it yourself a moment ago – it could affect all of humanity. Worse, it would destroy all of humanity. I am here to stop that. I am here to help you.'

He peers up at me, his fingers still covering much of his face. 'That's why you can throw the dice the way you do?'

'Yes.'

'What else can you do?'

I shake my head. 'It doesn't matter. All that matters is that more people are not allowed to become like me and my friend.'

'How many are there of you?' he asks.

'I thought there were just two of us left. But I suspect you have another at the compound.' I pause.

'Do you?'

He turns away. 'I can't tell you. I don't know who you are.'

'Yes, you know me better than anyone. You've seen what my DNA is like.'

He stands and walks to the far wall. He puts a hand on it for support, breathing rapidly. 'The man you speak of – Joel – he's ill. He has fever, severe cramps. We don't know what to do with him.' Andy struggles. My revelation is too much for him. 'Do you know?' he asks.

'Yes. Have you kept him out of the sunlight?'

'Yes. He's in a cell, in a basement. There is no sun.' He pauses. 'Is he allergic to the sun?'

'Yes.'

Andy frowns. 'But how does it make him ill? I told you, he doesn't see it.'

'The sun is not what makes him ill. I was only ruling out a possibility. He is sick because he is hungry.'

'But we have fed him. It doesn't help.'

'You are not feeding him what he needs.'

'What is that?'

'Blood.'

Andy almost crumbles. 'No,' he moans. 'You're like vampires.'

I stand and approach him cautiously, not wishing to scare him worse than I already have. 'We *are* vampires, Andy. Joel has been one only a few days. I changed him in order to prevent him from dying. Eddie had mortally wounded him. Believe me, I don't go around making vampires. It's against my – principles.'

Andy struggles to get a grip on himself. 'Who made you?'

'A vampire by the name of Yaksha. He was the first of our kind.'

'When was this?'

'A long time ago.'

'When?' he demands.

'Five thousand years ago.'

My revealing my age does not help the situation. The strength goes out of Andy; he slides to the floor. Rolling into a ball, he recoils as I come closer. I halt in midstride.

'What do you want from me?' he mumbles.

'Your help. I need to get into your compound and get my friend out before the world is destroyed. It is that simple. The danger is that great. And you know I'm not exaggerating. Our blood in the hands of your general is more dangerous than plutonium in the hands of terrorists.'

Andy nods weakly. 'Oh, I believe that.'

'Then you will help me?'

My question startles him. 'What? How can I help you? You're some kind of monster. You're the source of this danger.'

I speak firmly. 'I have walked this world since the dawn of history. In all that time, there have been only myths and rumours of my existence, and the existence of others like me. And those myths and rumors weren't based on fact. They were just stories. Because in all this time none of us has set out to destroy humanity. Yet your general will do this, whether he wants to or not. Listen to me, Andy! He has to be stopped and you have to help me stop him.'

'No.'

'Yes! Do you want him to clone Joel's blood? Do you want that material shipped to a weapons plant in the heart of the Pentagon?'

Anger shakes Andy. 'No! I want to destroy the blood! I don't need your lectures. I know what it can do. I have studied it inside out.'

I move closer, kneel on the floor beside him. 'Look at me, Andy.'

He lowers his head. 'You might cast a spell on me.'

'I don't need spells to convince you of the truth. I am not the enemy. Without my assistance, you won't be able to stop this thing from progressing to the next level. Try to imagine a society where everyone has our vampire strength and appetites.'

The visions I conjure make him sick. 'You really drink human blood?'

'Yes. I need it to live. But I do not need to kill or even harm the person I drink from. Usually, they don't even know what has happened. They just wake up the next day with a headache.'

My remark causes him to smile unexpectedly. 'I woke up with a headache this evening. Did you drink some of my blood without my knowing?'

I chuckle softly. 'No. Your headaches are your problem. Unless you cut down on the booze, your liver is going to give out. Listen to the advice of a five-thousand-year-old doctor.'

He finally looks at me. 'You're not really that old, are you?'

'I was alive when Krishna walked the earth. I met him in fact.'

'What was he like?'

'Cool.'

'Krishna was cool?'

'Yes. He didn't kill me. He mustn't have thought I was a monster.'

Andy is calming down. 'I'm sorry I called you that. It's just – well, I've never met a vampire before. I mean, I was never in a hotel room with one.'

'Aren't you glad you didn't sleep with me last night?'

He obviously forgot that small point. 'Would I have been changed into a vampire?'

'It takes more than sex with an immortal to make you immortal.' I speak delicately. 'But you may know that.'

He is grim. 'There has to be a blood transfer to bring about the change. I imagine a lot of blood is involved.'

'Yes, that is correct. Have your experiments established that?'

'We have established a few things. But the human immune system reacts violently to this kind of blood. It embraces it and at the same time tries to destroy it. We have postulated that a large infusion of this DNA code would transform the entire system. Actually, we think your DNA would just take over, and replicate itself throughout every cell in the body.' He pauses. 'Is that what happened when *Yaksha* changed you?'

I hesitate. I don't want to give him information that could be used later.

'When he changed me, I was young. I cried through most of it.'

'He is dead now?'

'Yes.'

'When did he die?'

'A few days ago.' I add, 'He wanted to die.'

'Why?'

I smile faintly, sadly. 'He wanted to be with Krishna. That was all that mattered to him. He was evil when he changed me. But when he died – he was a saint. He loved God very much.'

Andy stares at me, mystified. 'You're telling me the truth.'

I nod weakly. The thought of Krishna always shakes me.

'Yes. Maybe I should have told you from the beginning. You see, I was going to try to hypnotize you. I was going to seduce you and offer you money and set your head spinning – until you didn't know what you were doing.' I touch his leg gently. 'But none of that is necessary now. You are a true scientist. You seek the truth. You don't want to harm people. And you know that this blood can harm many people. Give it back to me. I know how to care for it, to keep it out of harm's way.'

'If I help you into the compound, they will lock me away for the rest of my life.'

'Vehicles go in and out of the compound all day. I've observed them from a distance. You can bring me inside in your trunk. When no one is looking, I will climb out, and no one will blame you.'

Andy's not convinced. 'Your friend is in a cell in the

basement of our main lab. The walls of the cell are made of a special metal alloy – even you couldn't break through. I know for a fact your partner can't. I've watched him try. Also, your friend is under constant surveillance. Cameras watch him twenty-four hours a day. Then, there is the security of the camp itself. It is surrounded by towers. The soldiers inside these towers are well armed. The place is a fortress. There are tanks and missiles behind every building.' He pauses. 'You won't be able to break him out.'

'This special cell where Joel is being held – how does the door to it open?'

'There is a button on a control panel just outside the cell. Push it and the door swings aside. But it is a long way from my car trunk to that button. It is a longer way back outside the compound. To escape with your friend, you'll have to become invisible.'

I nod. 'We can go over, point by point, the securtiy of the camp. But for now, answer my earlier question. Is there another vampire in the place?'

He hesitates, lowers his head. 'Yes.'

'How long has he been there? A month?'

'Yes.'

'Was he captured in Los Angeles?'

'Yes. He's a black youth. He lived in South Central L.A. before he was changed.' Andy looks up. 'But he never said anything about an Eddie. The person who changed him was someone else. I forget the name right now.'

My theory was correct. 'That other person was changed by Eddie. Trust me – I know the ultimate source of this other vampire. Where is he located in relation to Joel?'

'In the cell beside Joel's. But he's virtually comatose. He has the same disease as your friend – cramps and fever.' Andy shakes his head. 'We didn't know what to do for him. He never asked for blood.'

'Your people must have captured him right after he was changed. No one told him what he is now.' It isn't pleasant to contemplate the pain this poor soul is going through. 'I'll have to take him out as well.'

'You'll have to carry him then.'

'I can do that, if I have to.'

Andy studies me. 'You say you are so old. That must mean you're smarter than we short-lived mortals. If you are, you must know how the odds are stacked against you.'

'I have always managed to beat the odds. Look how well I do at the dice tables.'

'You will probably die if you do this.'

'I'm not afraid to die.'

He is impressed. 'You really aren't a monster. You're much braver than I am.'

I take his hand. 'I was wrong a minute ago when I said your helping me would not put you at risk. It will take a brave man to sneak me inside the compound in the trunk of his car.'

He squeezes my hand. 'What's your real name?'

'Sita.' I add, 'Few people have known me by that name.'

He touches my red hair. 'I was wrong only to say your blood scares me. It fascinates me as well.' He pauses and a sly grin crosses his face. 'Sex is not enough to make me immortal?'

'It hasn't worked in the past. But these days are filled with mysterious portents.' An unexpected warmth for him flows over me. His eyes – they have *me* hypnotized, with their uncanny depth, their gentle kindness. Smiling, I lean over and hug him and whisper in his ear, 'The dawn is at hand. In ancient times, it was considered a time of transformation, of alchemy. I'll stay with you, for now.' I pause. 'Who knows what may happen?'

12 ~

I dream a dream I've had before. A dream that seems to go on forever. It takes place in eternity, at least, my idea of such a place.

I stand on a vast grassy plain with a few gently sloping hills in the far distance. It is night, yet the sky is bright. There is no sun, but a hundred blue stars blaze overhead, shimmering in a long nebulous river. The place feels familiar to me. The air is warm, saturated with sweet aromas. Miles away a large number of people walk into a vessel – a violet-coloured spaceship of gigantic proportions. The vessel shines from the inside with divine radiance, almost blinding in its brilliance. I know it is about to depart and that I am supposed to be on it. Yet I cannot leave until I have finished speaking with Lord Krishna.

Hc stands beside me on the wide plain, his gold flute in his right hand, a red lotus flower in his left. We both have on long blue gowns. He wears an exquisite jewel around his neck – the Kaustubha gem, in which the destiny of every soul can be seen. He stares up at the sky, waiting for me to speak. But I can not remember what we were discussing.

'My Lord,' I whisper. 'I feel lost.'

His eyes remain fixed on the stars. 'You feel separate from me.'

'Yes. I don't want to leave you. I don't want to go to earth.'

'No. You misunderstand. You are not lost. The entire creation belongs to me – it is a part of me. How can you be lost? Your feeling of separation gives rise to your confusion.' He glances my way, finally, his long black hair blowing in the soft wind. The stars shimmer in the depths of his dark eyes. The entire creation *is* there. His smile is kind, the feeling of love that pours from him overwhelming. 'You have already been to earth. You are home now.'

'Is this possible?' I whisper, straining to remember. Faint recollections of being on earth come to me. I recall a husband, a daughter – I can see her smile. Yet a dark film covers them. I view them from a peculiar perspective, from a mind I can scarcely believe is connected to me. In front of them many centuries stretch out, choked with endless days and nights, suffering people, all awash in blood. Blood that I have spilled. I have to force the question from my lips. 'What did I do on earth, my Lord?'

'You wanted to be different – you were different. It doesn't matter. This creation is a stage, and we all play roles as heroes and villains alike. It is all *maya* – illusion.'

'But did I – sin?'

My question amuses him. 'It is not possible.'

I glance toward the waiting vessel. It is almost full. 'Then I don't have to leave you?'

He laughs. 'Sita. You have not heard me. You cannot leave me. I am always with you, even when you think you are on earth.' He changes his tone – he becomes more of a friend than a master. 'Would you like to hear a story?'

I have to smile, although I am more confused than ever.

'Yes, my Lord,' I say.

He considers. 'There was once a fisherman and his wife, who lived in a small town by the ocean. Every day the fisherman would go out to sea in his boat, and his wife would stay behind and care for the house. Their life was simple, but happy. They loved each other very much.

'The wife had only one complaint about her husband – he would eat only fish. For breakfast, lunch, and dinner, he would eat only what he caught. It didn't matter what she cooked and baked: bread or pastries, rice or potatoes – he would have none of it. Fish was his food, he said, and that was the way it had to be. From an early age, he had been this way, he had taken a vow his wife could not understand.

'It came to pass one day that his wife finally got fed up with his limited diet. She decided to trick him, to mix a piece of cooked lamb in with his fish. She did this cleverly, so that from the outside the fish looked as if it had come straight from the sea. But hidden beneath the scales of the fish was the red meat. When he returned home that evening and sat down at the table, the fish was waiting for him.

'At first he ate his meal with great relish, noticing nothing amiss. His wife sat beside him, eating the same food. But when he was halfway through, he began to cough and choke. He couldn't catch his breath. It was only then he smelled something odd on his plate. He turned to his wife, eyes blazing with anger.

' "What have you done?" he demanded. "What is in this fish?"

'The wife sat back, scared. "Only a little lamb. I thought you might enjoy the change."

'At these words the fisherman wiped the plate from the table and onto the floor. His anger knew no bounds. Still, he could not catch his breath. It was as if the lamb had caught in his windpipe and refused to shake loose.

' "You've poisoned me!" he cried. "My own wife has poisoned me!"

' "No! I only wanted to feed you something different." She stood and slapped him on the back, but it did not help. "Why are you choking like this?"

'The fisherman fell onto the floor, turning blue. "Don't you know?" he gasped. "Don't you know who I am?"

'"You are my husband," the wife cried, kneeling beside him.

'"I am . . ." the fisherman whispered. "I am what I am."

'Those were his last words. The fisherman died, and as he did, his body changed. His legs turned into a large flipper. His skin became covered with silver scales. His face bulged out and his eyes became blank and cold. Because, you see, he was not a person. He was a fish, which is what he had been all along. As a big fish, he could eat only smaller fish. Everything else was poison to him.' Krishna paused. 'Do you understand, Sita?'

'No, my Lord.'

'It doesn't matter. You are what you are. I am what I am. We are the same – when you take the time to remember me.' Krishna raises his flute to his lips. 'Would you like to hear a song?'

'Very much, my Lord.'

'Close your eyes, listen closely. The song is always the same, Sita. But it is always changing, too. That is the mystery, that is the paradox. The truth is always simpler than you can imagine.'

I close my eyes and Lord Krishna begins to play his magical flute. For a time, outside of time, that is all that matters. The music of his enchanted notes floats on a wind that blows from the heart of the galaxy. Overhead the stars shine down on us as the universe slowly revolves and the ages pass. I do not need to see my Lord to know that he is present everywhere. I do not need to touch him to feel his hand on my heart. I do not need anything, except his love. After a while, that is all there is – his divine love pouring through the centre of my divine being. Truly, we are one and the same.

13 ~~~

I lie flat on my back in the trunk of Andy's car. My hearing is acute – up ahead I hear the noises of the compound, the guards talking at the gate. The blackness in the trunk is not totally dark to me. I clearly see the white lab coat I have donned, the fake security badge pinned to my breast pocket. The badge is an old one of Andy's. I have cleverly put my picture over his, and changed the name. I am Lieutenant Lara Adams, Ph.D., a microbiologist on loan from the Pentagon. Andy says a large number of scientists have arrived from Back East. My makeup makes me look older. I should be able to blend in.

We stop at the security gate. I hear Andy speak to the guards.

'Another long night, Harry?' Andy asks.

'Looks like it,' the guard replies. 'Are you working till dawn?'

'Close. This night shift is a bear – I don't know whether I'm coming or going.' Andy hands something to the guard, a pass that must be electronically scanned. He has to have one to leave the compound as well. I have one in my back pocket. Andy continues in a natural voice, 'I just wish I could do a little better at the tables, and quit this stupid job.'

'I hear you,' the guard says. 'How's your luck been holding out?'

'I won a couple of grand last night.'

The guard laughs. 'Yeah, but how much did you lose?'

Andy laughs with him. 'Three grand!'

The guard hands the pass back. 'Have a good night. Don't piss off the man.'

I hear Andy nod. 'It's a little late for that.'

We drive into the compound. Andy has promised he'll park between two sheds, out of sight of the manned towers. From my earlier examination of the place, I am familiar with the spot. As the car moves, I feel confident we are heading straight for it. Especially when Andy turns to the left, stops, and turns off the engine. He climbs out of his car, shutting the door behind him, and walks away. I listen to his steps as he enters the main lab. So far so good.

I pop open the trunk and carefully peer out.

The car sits in shadow. No one is around. After

slipping out of the car, I silently close the trunk. I smooth my lab coat over my slim body, adjust my red hair. My thick glasses make me look almost nerdy but smart.

'Lara Adams from Back East,' I whisper. *Back East* means the Pentagon, Andy said. They never called the place by name.

'You have to get to the general. You have to control him.'

Seymour's advice remains with me. Resisting the temptation to follow Andy into the main lab – where I know Joel is being held captive – I turn instead in the direction of a small house located behind the lab. This is the general's private quarters. I move onto his front steps, then pause. I don't press the doorbell; I know without knocking that there is no one at home. Andy warned me of this. In fact, he said the general was seldom at home. Andy wants me to get Joel and get the hell out of the place, as quickly as I can. He doesn't, of course, know I need to control the general in order to blow the place up. But I have warned him that when the fireworks start, he should get out of the compound as quickly as possible.

For a moment, I stand undecided.

'The general knows you'll come for Joel.'

Seymour is wise, but I still think he overestimates the intelligence of the man. For example, I tell myself, look how easily I entered the compound. The general couldn't know that I was on my way. Certainly, I can't search the entire compound for him.

I decide to have a peek at Joel. After seeing exactly

where he is, I'll be in a better position to figure out what to do next. I head back to the front entrance of the lab, where Andy disappeared.

The interior of the lab is a complex maze of halls and offices. It seems clear the real work of dissecting and analyzing is done downstairs. Men and women in lab coats mill about. There is an occasional armed soldier. No one pays any attention to me. Listening for an elevator, I hear the sound of people going up and down steps. I prefer a stairway to an elevator. The latter can be a death trap for an invading vampire.

I find the stairs and go down a couple of flights. Andy told me Joel is being held two stories below the surface, and that his cell is at the east end of the building, farthest from the main gate. On this lower floor there are fewer people. They speak in soft tones. Moving like the sharp professional I'm supposed to be, I make my way down a narrow hall toward the rear of the building. Faintly, I smell Joel's scent. But I cannot hear his heart beating, his breathing. The walls of his cell must be thick. The scent is my compass and I follow it carefully, sensitive to the way it is spread by the ventilation ducts, the passage of people.

I come to a security center, equipped with monitors and two armed soldiers. I hear everything inside the closed room. Cracking the door, I peer inside and see Joel on one of the screens. He sits in the corner of a brightly lit cage, pinned to the corner by a metallic wrist chain.

I do not see another vampire on a separate monitor. Odd.

I close the door and knock. One of the guards answers.

'Yes? Can I help you?'

'Yes. My name is Dr Lara Adams.' I nod to Joel on the screen. 'I am here to talk to our patient.'

The guard glances at his buddy, back to me. 'You mean, over the speaker, right?'

'I would prefer to talk to him in person,' I say.

The guard shakes his head. 'I don't know what you've been told, but no one talks to the – to the patient directly. Only over the speaker.' He pauses, glances at my badge, my breasts. Boys will be boys. 'Who gave you clearance to interview this guy?'

'General Havor.'

The guy raises an eyebrow. 'He told you himself?'

'Yes. You can check with him if you like.' I nod to the interior of the room. 'May I come in?'

'Yes.' The guard stands aside. 'What did you say your name was?'

'Dr Lara Adams.' I gesture to the monitor. 'I see this guy but where is he really? Nearby?'

'He's just around the corner.' the other guard answers, while his buddy reaches for the phone. 'He's in a box so thick an atomic bomb couldn't blast through it.'

'Oh,' I say. That is useful information.

My hands lash out, my fingers cutting the air like knives.

Both guards crumple on the floor, unconscious, not dead.

I hang up the phone. Around the corner I go.

I push the large red button to open the cage.

There is a hiss of air. A door as thick as a man's body swings aside.

'Joel,' I cry softly, seeing him huddled in the corner, chained to the wall, burning like a dying coal as he shakes. I rush toward him. 'I'm going to get you out of here.'

'Sita,' he gasps. 'Don't!'

The door slams shut at my back. Locking me in.

Overhead, a TV monitor comes to life.

Andy stares down at me. Behind him stands the cruel-faced General Havor, wearing a barely disguised smirk. Yet there is no joy in Andy's expression as he slowly shakes his head and sighs. It is strange, but it is only then that I see my adversary clearly. The many years have reshapen his face, dulled his eyes, bruised his soft voice. Yet it is no excuse, not for a vampire as supposedly careful as I am. Right from the start I should have known who it was I was dealing with.

'Sita,' he says sadly with a faint Italian accent. *'E'passato tanto tempo dall' Inquisizione.'*

'Sita. It's been a long time since the Inquisition.'

In a single horrifying instant, I understand everything.

'Arturo,' I whisper.

14 ~

Several hours have elapsed since my capture. I have spent the majority of it sitting on the floor with my eyes closed, like a meditating yogi. But I enjoy no blissful nirvana. Inside, I seethe with rage: at General Havor, at Arturo, and most of all at myself. Arturo left signs for me everywhere, and I missed them all. Again and again my mind forces me to review the list.

1. When Joel was captured, he was brought before Andy. It was Andy who confirmed the special nature of Joel to General Havor. But rather than stay to examine Joel, Andy left the compound and went gambling. What an odd thing to do right after the catch of the century! Of course Andy was not out for

fun. He knew I would be watching. He knew I could be lured in.

2. I never saw Andy out in the sun, and it wasn't just because he worked the night shift. He was sensitive to the sun as a vampire should be. Yet he is not a pure vampire.

3. Andy talked about his highly classified work – to me, a total stranger. I hardly had to prod it out of him. He planted all the right clues for a person dissatisfied with his job – not enough pay, a totalitarian boss, a lousy work schedule. He tricked me in the most insidious way – by handing me all the ammunition I needed to think I could trick him.

4. He protested when I asked him to help me break into the compound. He put on a great show of defiance. But the fact that he helped me at all, without my having to manipulate his brain, was peculiar.

5. Andy had Arturo's model of vampire DNA. I passed it off, figuring he had already examined another vampire and broken the genetic code. The only problem was – there was no other vampire. I had destroyed all of Eddie's bastards. The only one the government had was Joel.

'Because, you see, he was not a person. He was a fish, which is what he had been all along. As a big fish, he could eat only smaller fish.'

In my dream, Krishna had been trying to tell me that

the hidden truth was the most obvious truth.

Andy was able to construct Arturo's model because he was Arturo!

Why did he leave it out for me to see? To taunt me, no doubt.

I open my eyes. 'Damn,' I whisper.

Joel looks over. I have broken his chains; he is no longer pinned to the wall, but is able to lie down properly and rest. The chains have accomplished their purpose, however. Had Joel been at the door, I would not have walked into the cage. I have tested the strength of the walls. The guard was right – a nuclear bomb couldn't blast through them.

The walls of the cell are a flat white colour, metallic. The space is square – twenty feet by twenty feet. A seatless toilet is attached to one wall, a single cot to the opposite one. Joel lies on the thin mattress.

'We all make mistakes,' he says.

'Some make more than others.'

'I appreciate your trying to rescue me. You should have left me to die after Eddie opened my veins.'

'You're probably right. But then I wouldn't have the pleasure of your company right now.' I pause. 'How are you feeling?'

The first thing I did after being captured, before sitting down to berate myself, was let Joel drink a pint of my blood. The transfusion alleviated his more severe symptoms but he still looked gaunt. Yet I am reluctant to give him more nourishment. We both know I need to be at full strength if we are to break out.

'I feel fine.' He adds, 'Better than I have in days.'

I reach out and squeeze his hand. 'It must have been hard for you. Have they been examining you inside out?'

'That's a literal way of putting the question.' He gestures to the screen. I have told him nothing of Arturo. 'I take it he is an old friend?'

I know our every word is being recorded. I don't know what can and will be used against me in a court of law. But I do know I don't have the right to remain silent. I wonder if they will try to torture information out of me. It will be a waste of their time. I doubt they're going to let me call a lawyer.

'We go way back' is all I say.

'How was Vegas?'

'Fine. Won a lot of money at craps.'

'That's great. Where did you stay?'

'At the Mirage.' I sigh. 'I'm sorry, Joel. Neither of us should be in here. I messed up.'

'Don't be so hard on yourself. After all, you stopped Eddie.'

'Yeah. Only to set up a situation where there might be a thousand Eddies.' I abruptly raise my voice and yell at the monitor. 'Did you hear that, Arturo? A thousand Ralphes running loose! Is that what you want?' My voice sinks to a whisper. 'That's what you're going to get.'

I don't expect to get a response to my outburst, but

a minute later the TV monitor comes back to life. Arturo is alone, sitting at a desk in the security room. Around the corner, as they say.

'Sita,' he says. *'None oho mai pensato che ti avrei rivista.'*

'I never thought I would see you again.'

'Same here,' I mutter.

'Are you comfortable?' he asks, switching languages effortlessly. When he wishes, he has no accent. He must have been living in America for a long time.

'No cage is ever comfortable.' I pause. 'Are you comfortable?'

He spreads his hands. I remember how large they were. Suddenly, I recall many details about him: the warm grey of his eyes, the strength of his jawline. Why didn't I recognize him? There are the obvious reasons. He has aged twenty-five years since we last met, and yet, his face has changed more than the two and a half decades warrant. Probably since it has, in reality, been over seven hundred years.

Yet none of that should have fooled me. I didn't recognize him for two sound reasons: I knew he couldn't possibly exist in our time, so I never even considered the idea; and the Andy I stalked did not possess the same soul as the Arturo I once loved. This man who stares down at me – I hardly know him, and I slept with him for months.

'What would you have me do?' he replies. 'You had to be stopped.'

My voice is filled with scorn. 'Stopped from what?'

152

'There were the violent murders in Los Angeles. I knew that was you.'

'You knew it was not me! You knew it was some other vampire! Don't start off our first conversation in seven centuries with a lie. You know I never killed for pleasure.'

My wrath makes him pull back a step. 'I apologize. I should say I knew you were indirectly involved.' He pauses. 'Who committed the killings?'

I forget my resolve to say as little as possible. The information cannot help them, anyway. My blood is all that matters.

'A psychotic vampire by the name of Eddie Fender started the murders. The LAPD and the FBI were doing everything they could to stop him. But it was I who put a halt to the killings. And what do I get for it? A medal? No, the entire police force comes after me.'

'You killed two dozen of those officers.'

'Because they were trying to kill me! I am not the villain here. You and the scum you are associated with are.' I pause, settle down. 'Why are you with these people?'

'I can help them. They can help me. We have vested interests. Isn't that the reason for most partnerships?'

'It is among people who have selfish goals. But I never remember you as selfish. Why are you working for the U.S. military machine?'

'Surely you must understand by now. I need to complete my experiments.'

I laugh. 'Are you still searching for the blood of Christ?'

'You say it as if it were a fool's errand.'

'It's a blasphemous errand. You saw what happened last time.'

'I made an error – that's all. I will not make the same error again.'

'That's all? Just some error? What about Ralphe? I loved that boy. You loved him. And you turned him into a monster. You forced me to kill him. Do you know what that did to me?'

Arturo's voice goes cold. 'It made you want to testify against me?'

'You had to be stopped. I didn't have the strength or the will to do it myself.' I pause. 'You had a chance to talk to me in the inquisitor's dungeon. You chose not to.'

'I had nothing to say.'

'Well, then, I have nothing to say to you now. Come, get your fresh supply of vampire blood. Send plenty of scientists and soldiers. Not all of them will be coming back to you.'

'You present no danger to us as long as you are in your cell. And you will remain in there for the remainder of your life.'

'We will see,' I whisper faintly.

'Sita, I'm surprised at you. Aren't you curious how I'm still alive?'

I draw in a weary breath. 'I have an idea as to how

you survived. Even when you swore to me you weren't experimenting on yourself, you were. That's why you began to have visions of DNA. You were seeing it through the eyes of your blessed hybrid state.'

'I did experiment on myself. That is true. But I never reached the full hybrid status. That must be obvious to you.'

I nod. 'Because you have aged. Does it hurt, Arturo, that you're not the dashing young priest anymore?'

'I may yet achieve immortality.'

'Hmm. And I always thought you wanted to die and go to heaven.' He is right, of course; I am curious about those days. 'What happened after the trial? How did you escape? I heard they burned you at the stake.'

'The inquisitor granted me a private audience. He couldn't let me go, he said, but in exchange for my confession of witchcraft, he agreed to hang instead of burn me.'

'And you recovered?'

'Yes.'

'Were you surprised?'

'Yes. It was a calculated risk. I didn't have many options.'

I hesitate. 'What did you do to Ralphe?'

For once, Arturo looks ashamed. 'I exposed him to the vial of your blood – with the midday sun pouring through it.'

I was aghast. 'But you said you'd never consider that. The vibration would destroy a man or woman.'

'You saw how the word was spreading about me. I had only a limited time to complete my experiments. Ralphe had been spying on us all along. Neither of us knew. He saw what we were up to. He wanted to try it.'

Fury possesses me. 'That's a ridiculous rationalization! He was a child! He didn't know what would happen to him! You did!'

'Sita.'

'You were a coward! If your experiment was so precious to you, why didn't you perform it on yourself, with the midday sun pouring through my bloody vial?'

My words wound him, but he is still full of surprises. 'But I did subject myself to the blood in the sunlight. That morning, when the mob approached the church, I heard them coming. I hurried down to the basement and let the full power of the vampire vibration wash over me. I believe that is why I have been able to live as long as I have. If the mob had not stopped me, maybe the transformation would have been complete, and I would have achieved the perfect state. I was never to know. The first thing the mob did was break the vial.'

His words sober me. 'Then what went wrong with Ralphe? Why did he turn into a monster?'

'There could be many factors that influenced his outcome. One was that I laid him on the copper sheets when the sun was high in the sky. Also – and I think this is the primary reason the experiment failed – Ralphe was ordinarily fearless by nature. But when the transformation started, he got scared. The power of the magnetic field magnified his fear, which in turn warped his DNA. When the process was complete, I couldn't control him. He had the strength of ten men. He was out the door before I could stop him.'

'You should have told me. I could have stopped him before he killed anyone. We might have been able to change him back.'

Arturo shook his head. 'I don't think there was any going back.' He adds, 'I was too ashamed to tell you.'

'Finally, the high priest confesses.' I continue to sneer at him. 'All your talk doesn't disguise the fact that you experimented on a child before yourself. And that you lied to me, after swearing on the name of your precious God that you would always tell me the truth.'

'Everyone lies,' he says.

'*Guarda cosa sei diventata, Arturo,*' I say, reverting to the language of his youth, out of frustration, hope. '*Look what's become of you, Arturo.*' 'When we first met, you wouldn't have hurt a fly. That's why I gave you my blood. I trusted you.'

Even on the monitor, I see his gaze is focused in the far distance. My words stir painful memories, for both of us. My hatred for him is matched only by my love. Yes, I still love him, and I hate that about myself. He seems to sense my thoughts for he suddenly glances back at me and smiles. It is a sad smile.

'I cannot defend my acts to you,' he replies. 'Except to say I thought the rewards of success outweighed the possibility of failure. Yes, I should never have used

Ralphe. Yes, I should never have lied to you. But if I had done these things – where would we be today? I'd be long dead in a forgotten grave and you'd be safe and secure in your own selfish universe. We wouldn't have your blood now so we could continue with our noble quest to finish what was started seven centuries ago.'

I snicker. 'I can't help but notice that you apply the word *selfish* to me. What sickness was magnified in your field when you lay beneath the vibration of my blood? You have become a megalomaniac. You were a priest, a good priest. You used to humble yourself before God. Now you want to be God. If Jesus were alive today, what would you say to him? Or would you give him a chance to explain himself before stealing his blood?'

'Do *you* want a chance to explain yourself?' Arturo asks gently.

'I answer to no man. My conscience is clear.'

He raises his voice. I have finally hit a button. 'I don't believe you, Sita. Why couldn't you look at me when you accused me of witchcraft?'

'You were a witch! And you haven't changed! Goddamn you, Arturo, can't you see how dangerous it is for me to be held captive by these people? I just have to look at General Havor to know he wants to rule the world.'

'He's not the monster *Andy* led you to believe.'

'You talk about beliefs. What do you believe in these days? I never met Jesus, it's true. But you must know as well as I that he would never condone your methods.

Your lying and ambushing and torture. The means do not justify the end. You did not watch Ralphe chew on human flesh. If you had seen him, you'd know that this path you want to take stinks of the devil.'

Arturo sits back from the screen. He is as tired as I am, perhaps shaken as well. In that moment, his face becomes much older than forty-five. He appears ready for the grave. Yet he is resolved, his destiny will be fulfilled. He shakes his head as he sighs.

'We can do this the hard way, Sita,' he says. 'Or we can do it the easy way. It is up to you. I need your blood and I am going to have it.'

I smile grimly. 'Then you'd better prepare yourself for a fight. Let me warn you, Arturo – I've shown you only a fraction of my powers. But if you come after me now, you will see all of them. There aren't enough soldiers and bullets in this compound to contain me for the remainder of my life. Tell your general that people will die if I'm not released. Their deaths will be on your conscience, Arturo. I swear in the name of my God, you will never get to heaven – in this world or the next.'

The screen goes dead.

But not before I see the fear in his eyes.

15 ⟋⟍

More hours pass. Joel lies sleeping. Once again I sit silently on the floor, my legs crossed, my eyes closed. Yet this time my attention is turned outward. Through the wall, I can just hear the guards at the security station talk. There are three of them now. They discuss a football game.

'Those Forty-Niners are amazing,' Guard One says. 'Their offence works like a machine gun – it just keeps firing. I felt sorry for the Cowboys.'

'You know, everybody looks at the quarterback,' Guard Two says. 'But I think when you got the receivers, you got all you need. Even a lousy pro quarterback can look good throwing to players who are wide open.'

'I think it's the other way around,' Guard Three says.

'You got a great quarterback, he can hit a player who's totally covered. Not many teams win the Super Bowl with an average quarterback.'

'Not many teams win the Super Bowl, period,' Guard one says.

'Only one a year,' Guard Two says.

'Wouldn't be a Super Bowl if everyone could win it,' Guard Three says.

Beyond their chattering, I sense their thoughts. The gift of Yaksha's blood grows stronger the more still I become. Guard One is contemplating his sour stomach. He has an ulcer, and when he pulls an all-night shift, it always hurts. He wonders if he should go to his car on the next break and get his bottle of Maalox. But he needs to drink it in private. The other guys always kid him about having a stomach ache like a little kid. Actually, Guard One has a lot of guts going into work in the pain he's in.

Guard Two's thoughts are dull. He is thinking about his wife, his current mistress, and a woman he just met in the cafeteria two hours earlier – all of them naked together in bed with him. He drank a large Coke before starting his last shift. He has to pee real bad.

Guard Three is interesting. Unknown to his buddies, he writes science-fiction in his spare time. His brother-in-law, who's a lawyer, just read his last book and told him to forget about becoming a writer. But Guard Three thinks that just because his brother-in-law has a law degree, it doesn't mean he can spot talent. And he's right – Guard Three's mind is rich in creative ideas.

I need to concentrate hard to sense their thoughts. I can only *read* one at a time. Since ancient times I have been able to influence people's thoughts by staring hard at them and whispering suggestions in their ears. But in here I am deprived of the power of my gaze, of the soothing allure of my velvety voice. Yet the longer I concentrate on these guys, the more certain I am that I can introduce thoughts into their minds. I focus in on Guard Three – he's the most sensitive. Creating a strong image in my mind, I send it through the wall.

'This girl is real dangerous. She can kill us all.'

Guard Three is saying something that he suddenly breaks off in midsentence. I hear him shift uneasily in his chair. 'Hey, guys,' he says.

'What?' the other two ask.

'That chick in there is dangerous. We have to be careful with her. You saw what she did to Sam and Charlie.'

'She knocked them out cold,' Guard Two agrees. 'But I'd like to see her try it on me. She wouldn't get far.'

'I don't think you want to mess with her,' Guard One says. 'She's supposed to be super strong.'

'Yeah, but they don't tell us why she's strong,' Guard Three says. 'They just tell us to watch her. But what if she gets out? She could kill us all.'

'Yes,' I whisper softly to myself.

'Relax,' Guard One says. 'There's no way she's getting out of that box.'

'Even if she does break out,' Guard Two says. 'We can stop her. I don't care about orders, I'm opening fire.'

'I hear bullets can't stop her,' Guard Three says, continuing to dwell on how dangerous I am.

I shift my focus to Guard One and send out another suggestion.

'We mustn't lose sight of her.'

'We'll keep an eye on her,' Guard One says.

I place the same thought in Guard Three's mind.

'Yeah,' Guard Three echoes. 'We have to be alert, keep watching her.'

I try to put the thought in Guard Two's mind.

'I've got to take a piss,' Guard Two says.

'Oh, well,' I whisper to myself. 'Two out of three ain't bad.'

Over the next thirty minutes – pausing only when Guard Two goes to the bathroom – I steadily build up their paranoia about how dangerous I am and how bad things will be if they don't keep me under constant surveillance. Pretty soon Guards One and Three are talking paranoid gibberish. Guard Two is not sure how to calm them down, or even *why* they need to be calmed down.

'If we don't watch her every second,' Guard One says. 'She'll escape.'

'And if she escapes,' Guard Three says. 'She'll rip our hearts out and eat them.'

'Stop!' Guard Two yells. 'She's not going to escape.'

'We know that,' Guard One says. 'If we don't blink, if

we keep the lights on her, she won't escape.'

'But if the lights go out, we're doomed,' Guard Three says.

'Why would the lights go out?' Guard Two wants to know.

Taking a few deep breaths, I slowly ease out of my deep state of concentration. I reach over and gently shake Joel. He opens his eyes and smiles at me. In all the confusion I have forgotten how handsome he is. His dark blue eyes are filled with affection.

'What a pleasant sight to wake up to,' he whispers.

'Thank you.'

'Did you sleep?'

I lean over and whisper directly into his ear. 'No. I've been planting the seeds of our escape. The guards outside are now terrified of losing sight of us.'

He's curious. 'You know this for a fact?'

'Yes. I'm going to break the lights in here, which will cause them to panic and call for help. I'm sure General Havor himself will come.'

'Then what?'

'I have a plan of sorts, but it's not set in stone. Just follow my lead. Get up – get ready to act when I say the word.'

Joel moves to the wall closest to the door. Standing in the centre of the cell, staring at the overhead cameras, I give the guards on the other side of the wall one last thing to think about.

'I'm coming for you now,' I say in a wicked voice.

'You'd better run, you'd better hide.' I lick my lips. 'Because I'm *very* hungry.'

Then, in a series of blindingly fast moves, I shatter every light on the ceiling and plunge the cell into darkness. I see perfectly, but Joel has to reach for the wall to get his bearings. At the security station, I hear Guard One and Guard Three screaming in terror. Guard Two fumbles for his weapon, yelling at his partners to stop. I suppress a giggle.

'Come to me, General,' I whisper. 'Come, Arturo.'

Five minutes later I hear Arturo and Havor pounding down the narrow hall, speaking heatedly. Although I have not heard the general's voice before, I recognize it by the authority it commands. Arturo has influence within the confines of the compound, but the man with the star on his shoulder is in charge. I wonder about the details of their relationship. All about them, clutching machine guns and trying not to panic, are dozens of soldiers.

'She's not a danger as long as we keep the lock in place,' Arturo says to the general. 'This is a stunt she's pulling to get us to open the door.'

'I don't like it that we can't see her,' General Havor snaps back. 'You heard what she told you. We don't know the full extent of her powers. For all we know she's cutting through a wall of the cell as we talk.'

'She's a master of manipulation,' Arturo counters. 'She talked about her unknown powers to plant a seed of doubt in our minds – for just this occasion. If you open the door to check on her, she'll be on you in a second. You'll have to kill her to stop her and you can't kill her.'

'We'll wait and see what she does next,' General Havor says.

'What's happening?' Joel hisses in the dark.

I whisper softly so that only he can hear. 'The general and Arturo are coming. They don't want to open the door, but I think I can do something to inspire them to relent. There will be a lot of noise in a few minutes. Besides creating the racket, I will be mentally projecting into the general's mind. Please don't speak to me during this time. I need to concentrate. Then, when they start to open the door, I need you to wedge yourself in the corner behind the door. But don't do it until I give the signal. There'll be gunfire, and the space behind the door will be the safest. Do you understand?'

'Yes. You really think they'll open the door?'

'Yes. I'll make them.'

Once more I sit cross-legged on the floor, this time in the centre of the room. Quieting my thoughts with several deep breaths, I project myself into the general's mind. It is easy to locate – the psychic energy that emanates from him is like molten lava from an erupting volcano. Yet his resolve will not be so easily manipulated with a few implanted thoughts. With a strong individual, even when I can look him in the eye and whisper in his ear, I have trouble getting him to do what I want. Now, I have neither of those options at my disposal. What I am attempting to do is set up several conditions that will work on the general and prompt him to give the order to open the door. Getting the guards nervous and knocking out the lights were the first of my conditional steps. The next ones will be more difficult.

I slip into General Havor's mind.

It is a black cavern, draped with the webs of poisonous spiders. When he does get my power, I see, General Havor fantasizes about raping me. He also plans to kill Arturo, as soon as the alchemist completes his experiments. There is no trust between the two. General Havor fears Arturo will alter his own DNA and then kill the general. But what Arturo thinks I cannot read. His mind is heavily cloaked – not unexpected in a partial hybrid. Anyway, I must concentrate on the man who gives the orders. General Havor must push the button that opens the door – this is all that matters.

I reach out with my mental claw.

'The witch will break down the door.'

I hear the general speak to Arturo.

'Are you positive she cannot break down the door?' he asks.

'Even she cannot destroy this alloy,' Arturo reassures him.

'The blood of a dead witch is as good as the blood of a living witch.'

General Havor does not speak this thought aloud to

Arturo. But I know he fantasizes about shooting me in the head, killing me, and immediately injecting my blood into his veins. It is an attractive idea to him. Arturo will not be able to stop him, or to come back at him later at an unexpected time, with an unseen dagger in his hand. It is this latter point that is the general's primary worry. My suggestion hits home, and I watch as my mental implant expands and warps. General Havor can almost feel what it will be like to have my blood flow through his veins in the next few minutes. I give the idea another nudge.

'Why wait for the witch's blood?'

Again, General Havor does not share this idea aloud with Arturo.

Still, he is not ready to open the door.

Stretching and breathing normally, I slowly come out of my trance. Enough for mental gymnastics. It is time for brutal force. Climbing to my feet, I study the supposedly impenetrable door, then launch my attack. I leap into the air and plant three extremely powerful kicks on the hard metal with my feet. In quick succession I leap again and again, alternately pounding the door with first my right then my left foot. The door doesn't give, but the noise I create is deafening. Outside I can hear them shouting to one another, and I know what the general is thinking. The witch is going to break out. I may as well open the door and kill her while I have her cornered. To hell with Arturo.

I keep up the pounding.

By this time, I am sure, Guard One and Guard Three have wet their pants.

After five minutes, I pause. Something is happening.

I strain to listen with my ears. General Havor and Arturo are arguing again.

'You are playing right into her hands!' Arturo yells. 'The only protection we have from her is this cell. Open it and you open the door to death – both for yourself and your men.'

'How long do you think that door can withstand that barrage?' General Havor asks. 'See, there are cracks in the walls.'

'The cracks are in the walls that hold the metal cage! The cage itself shows no sign of giving.'

'I don't believe it!' General Havor snaps. 'I say we face her now when we're armed and ready. Better she die than escape.'

'But what about her blood? We need it.'

'There'll be plenty of her blood lying around when I finish with her.'

Arturo hesitates. He lowers his voice. 'Plenty of blood for what?'

General Havor does not answer. He knows there will be only enough blood left in my body for him to inject into his own veins. The more I listen to the two, the clearer it becomes that General Havor is not interested in Arturo's hybrid. He wants to be a full-fledged vampire. That's where it's at in his mind.

I return to my pounding.

My feet ache. It doesn't matter.

The noise shakes the whole building.

I imagine even the men in the perimeter towers are trembling.

Outside the door, the guards shout to their general for orders.

General Havor and Arturo continue to argue. I hear them.

'We will die!' Arturo screams.

'She's only one!' General Havor yells. 'She can't get us all!' He pauses, makes a decision, and shouts to his men. 'Stand ready! We're going in!'

I relax for a moment and catch my breath. 'They're coming,' I whisper to Joel. 'Get behind the door.'

'Can't I help?' he asks, moving. 'I am a vampire, after all. Not just FBI.'

I chuckle softly. 'Later, Joel.'

Outside, I hear what sounds like a platoon of guards gathering around the red button. Each is more than a little reluctant to push it. The heavy metal door has become awfully comforting. But the general is shouting at them again to open it. Loaded magazines are popped onto M16s. Bullets are locked into firing chambers. Rifles are shouldered. I can smell the sweat of their fear.

Somebody gathers the courage to push the button.

The door begins to open.

I leap up and into a corner near the ceiling.

I don't need to use my newfound levitating abilities. I am able to wedge myself against the ceiling by pressing the back of my neck against one corner wall, and my feet against the other. Supernatural strength has its advantages. I leave my arms free – I am a black widow ready to swoop down and snatch her prey. They are going to rue the day they decided to lock me in a solid metal cage.

The door opens wider.

I hear them outside in the hall. Their frightened breathing.

You could hear a pin drop. Even without vampire ears.

'She's not there,' someone whispers.

They aren't even worried about Joel. Just me, that damn witch.

'She's behind the door,' General Havor snarls from farther down the hall.

It's good to know exactly where he is.

'What do we do?' someone croaks. Sounds like Guard Three.

'I'm not going in there,' Guard One moans. His ulcer must be killing him.

'I don't like this,' Guard Two agrees.

The door will not close again, no matter what happens. I will not let it. But now I am faced with a decision to make. There is only one hostage who will get me to where I want to go, and that is the kind-hearted General Havor. If I abduct Arturo, the general will tell his men to open fire on both of us. Certainly, any guard I would grab would be expendable in the general's mind. Friendly fire, they call it. Yet the general is maybe fifty feet up the hall. Between us are many soldiers. I am going to have to reduce the numbers. I need the men to panic and flee.

I know I will have to cause pain to make that happen.

In a move too swift for the soldiers to see, I slide onto the top of the door, reach outside the cage, grab one of the soldiers by the hair, and pull him back up into the corner with me. The man screams in my hands and I let him carry on for a bit. No doubt he feels like a victim in an *Alien* movie. Because he is crying so loudly, it takes me several seconds to recognize his voice.

It is Guard Three – the one who writes science-fiction in his spare time.

I am sure he has seen *all* the *Alien* movies.

I take his weapon and put my hand over his mouth.

'Shh,' I whisper. 'Things are not so bad as they seem. I am not going to kill you, not if you cooperate. I know about you and I like you. The problem is, I need to scare your friends out there. Now I know they are already pretty spooked, but I've got to get them to the point where they want to flee, no matter what your general orders. Do you understand?'

He nods, his eyes ready to burst out of his head.

I smile. 'That's good. They are probably imagining that I am ripping your heart out right now. And with a little help from you, I can make them think that is *exactly* what I am doing. I will hardly have to hurt you at all. Oh, I see you notice I use the word *hurt*. To be honest, I will have to cut you enough so that I can blow the stream of your warm blood out into the hall. Splashing blood always creates a wonderful effect, especially when vampires are involved. While I do that, I want you to scream bloody murder. Can you do that?'

He nods.

I pinch him. 'Are you sure?'

'Yes,' he croaks. 'I don't want to die. I have a wife and two kids.'

'I know, and your brother-in-law is a lawyer. By the way, don't listen to a thing he tells you. He is like all lawyers – envious of those who do honest work for a living. You just keep writing your stories. If you want, you can even write one about me. But make me a blond – this red hair is store-bought.'

'What's your name?' he asks, relaxing slightly.

I don't want him too relaxed. 'I am Mrs Satan.' I scratch him on the inside of his right arm, tearing his flesh and drawing plenty of blood. 'Start screaming, buddy.'

Guard Three does as he's told. His performance is admirable – he believes half of it. *'Oh God! Stop it! Save me! She's ripping my heart out!'* Actually, he didn't have to get so specific, but I let it pass. While he cries to his fellow soldiers, I purse my lips and blow on the blood that trickles from his arm. I have quite the set of lungs. The blood splatters over the exterior of the wall, and onto the floor outside. I hear the men moaning in horror. This is worse than 'Nam, many think.

They haven't seen anything yet.

'Now let out a real loud death scream,' I tell Guard Three. 'Trail off into silence. Then, I'll drop you behind the door where my friend is hiding. You might want to stay there when the shooting starts. I warn you ahead of time, I am going to have to kill many of your friends. When I am through, you may leave this building. Get out as fast as you can. Steal a truck if you have to. Things are going to get awfully hot here. Do you understand?'

'Yes. You're not going to kill me?'

'No. Not tonight. You can relax, after you do exactly what I say.'

The guard lets out the death scream. I spray an especially wide shower of blood through the doorway. Then I drop the guy down beside Joel, who pats him on the back and tells him to relax. I hand Joel the man's weapon and order him to keep it handy. Several guards outside the door are crying. They have backed away, but not far enough to be safe. I reach out and grab another. He carries a high-powered machine gun, which I wedge between the door and frame. He smells of hamburger and fries. His food is probably not digesting well. I don't know this soldier, which doesn't bode well for him.

'You're going to die now,' I tell his horrified face. 'I am sorry it has to be this way.'

I kill him slowly, painfully, so that his throat-tearing screams and red blood mingle to create an image so ghastly that many of the soldiers feel they are trapped in a nightmare from which they cannot awaken. When I am done, I throw what is left of his body into the hall. It is very messy – the terror in the air is as palpable as the hard metal door that can no longer be closed.

This last execution has disturbed me. If I am forced to kill, I prefer to do so efficiently and painlessly. I will not make another example – I don't have the stomach for it. It is time to leave the building, with Joel and General Havor in hand. To grab the machine gun the soldier brought in, I drop from my position on the ceiling and immediately retrieve it and open fire. The men outside the door stand frozen in place. They fall to their deaths like tenpins.

I kill eight of them before I step into the hall.

Arturo and General Havor are at the far end. They are a hundred feet away and backing up fast. Between us there are many soldiers. I cannot allow the big boss to leave the building without me. But the bloody examples I made of the first two men have had an effect. The soldiers are pushing and crowding behind General Havor and Arturo, slowing them down, preventing them from simply leaving. Also, General Havor has lost control of his men. I stand a clear and easy target in the hallway, but no order to fire comes. In their hearts, the men do not believe this witch can be killed with mere bullets.

They wish they hadn't opened the door.

'Drop your weapons and I will let you live!' I yell.

Most in front of me surrender right then. The few who don't, who take aim, I shoot in the head. The sheer number of deaths does not numb me. I look in the eyes of each one I destroy, and wonder about his life and who he leaves behind. If it was just my life – honestly, if there was no danger of my blood falling into the wrong hands, I would let them cut me down. But I have a responsibility to mankind. I know that is the rationale of every great man or woman, of every merciless monster. The smell of blood is too thick even for my taste.

Arturo and General Havor disappear around the corner.

I call to Joel to join me in the hallway.

He cautiously peeks out. He groans.

'Nothing can be worth this,' he whispers.

'You may be right,' I say. 'Still, we have to get out of here. To do that, we need General Havor.'

'Where is he?'

'On the second floor.' I grab Joel with my free arm and shield the top of his head with my palm. 'Let's join him.'

I leap straight up and smash through the ceiling. Again, Yaksha's blood comes to my aid. Without it, such a move would have given me a righteous headache. This time the ceiling barely slows me down. Pulling Joel through the hole I have created, we stand up on the floor of the basement, level one. I see soldiers down the hall jamming the stairs, frantic to exit. Arturo and

General Havor struggle in the midst of the human flood. Raising the machine gun to my shoulder, I take aim at General Havor's right thigh. For a split second it is clearly visible. I put a bullet in it. The general stumbles and lets out a cry. No one stops to help him, least of all Arturo. I grab Joel's arm.

'Come,' I say.

As I wade into the crowd, they scream and scatter. I guess my red hair does not suit me. Or perhaps it is the fact that I am soaked from head to toe in blood. I must look like a beast that has climbed from the depths of hell. Arturo is already out of sight, but General Havor lies helpless at the side of the stairway. He is lucky that he was not trampled to death. But he is not lucky that it is me who reaches out to help him to his feet.

'General Havor,' I say. 'Pleased to meet you face to face. Sorry I have to ask a favour so soon after saying hello. But I need you to take me and my friend into the cave behind this compound. I need one of those thermonuclear warheads you keep there. I have a thing about fire, you see, about explosions. For me, the bigger the better.'

16 ～～

The cave turns into another prison. We reach it without excessive bloodshed, but once inside I am forced to kill all the soldiers. The endless slaughter weighs heavily on me. Joel's broken expression begs me to stop. But I can't stop until it is over, one way or the other. It is my nature never to quit.

We are scarcely inside when the remaining soldiers close the door on us. The metal is as thick as the door on the cell – it cuts in half the miniature rail tracks that run between the compound and the depths of the hill. They also turn off our lights, but there are emergency lanterns. For Joel's sake, and the general's, I turn on several. The stark rays cast ghastly shadows over the carnage I have inflicted. There is blood everywhere. The red blurs in the silent gloom, in my racing mind; it is as if the walls of the cave bleed. I try not to count the dead.

'I didn't want this,' I say, pointing my weapon at the general, who sits on the edge of the small railroad car that carries supplies into this place of secrets. His leg continues to bleed but he doesn't complain. He is a horrible human being, but he is not without strength. A hard man with a blunt face, he wears his hair as if it were a disease growing on top of his head. I add, 'It's your fault.'

My accusation does not faze him. 'You can always surrender.'

I kneel beside him. To my left Joel sits on the ground, looking weary beyond belief. 'But you see that is not an option,' I tell the general. 'When history started, I was there. And the only reason mankind has been able to move steadily forward is because I have chosen to stand apart from history. I watch what happens. I have no desire to have important roles. Do you understand that I tell you the truth?'

General Havor shrugs. 'You've changed your style today.'

My voice hardens. 'You made me change.' I gesture to the dead men who lie around us. 'All this is because of you. Look at them. Don't you care about them?'

He is bored. 'What do you want? A nuclear bomb?'

I stand and look down at him. 'Yes. That's exactly what I want. And after you show it to me, I want you to arm it.'

He snorts. 'Do you think I'm crazy?'

'I know you're crazy. I have seen inside your mind. I know what you planned to do once you had my blood in your veins. You were going to murder Arturo and rape me.'

He's cocky. 'You flatter yourself.'

I slap him in the face, hard enough to break his nose. 'And you sicken me. I don't know how Arturo ever teamed up with you. He must have been desperate. He and I are not alike, by the way. I never beg for anything, but I know how to make you beg. Give me the warhead and arm it or I will subject you to such physical and mental torture you will think that soldier I ripped apart inside the cell died peacefully.' I raise my hand to strike again. 'Yes?'

He holds his nose; the blood leaks through his thick fingers. 'May I ask what you plan to do with the warhead?' he asks.

I catch his eye, push hard enough to make him cower. 'I am going to clean up your mess,' I reply.

General Havor agrees to furnish me with a bomb. He digs it out of the back, and wheels it into view on the railroad cart. A black squat affair with a pointed tip and an elaborate control box on the side, it looks like something from an old sci-fi movie. The general informs us that it is rated ten megatons – ten million tons of TNT.

I point to the colour-coded buttons on the side.

'Can it be rigged to go off at a specific time?' I ask.

'Yes. It can be set to detonate in ten minutes, or in ten years.'

'Ten years is a little long for my tastes. But your men may escape, if they listen to me. You will want to argue my position to them, once we get back outside. Which leads me to my next point.' I gesture to the metal wall that blocks the exit. 'How do we open this door?'

'It can't be opened from the inside. They've cut our power.'

'Is there a radio in here?' Joel asks. 'Can you talk to them?'

General Havor shrugs. 'I have nothing to say to them.'

I grab the general by the collar.

It doesn't take much for him to piss me off.

'You will tell them that we have an armed warhead in here set to detonate in fifteen minutes,' I say. 'That will be, by the way, the literal truth. You will also inform them that if they wish to prevent the bomb from exploding, they are to let us out. Finally, you will mention that I am willing to negotiate.'

He laughs at me. 'You can do what you want to me, I am not going to arm this warhead.'

I let him go, take a step back. 'You think you can play with me, General. You think the worst I can do is kill you. Arturo never told you of the power of my eyes. How my gaze can permanently fry your brain.' I pause. 'If in the next ten seconds you don't tell me the code to arm this warhead, I will stab such a needle into your forehead that you will have the IQ of a chimpanzee for the rest of your life – however long that may be.'

He lowers his head. 'I cannot allow you to set off this bomb.'

'Very well.' I step forward and grab him by the jaw, thrusting his head up, forcing him to stare at me. 'Look deep, General! Into the eyes of the witch you thought to control. See where I have prepared a place of fire for you to burn.'

17 ～

Ten minutes later the door is opened by the highest ranking commander on the outside and we wheel a fully armed warhead into the night time air. The detonator clicks off the seconds. Fifteen minutes to Armageddon. Driving at high speed should give us and the soldiers time to get clear of the blast. Overhead, the full moon shines down on our heads, bathing the entire desert with a milky white radiance. The setting is dreamlike, as if there has already been a nuclear explosion, thousands of years ago and the radioactive fallout remains.

A small army aims a line of high-tech weapons at us.

On all sides, from the guard towers to the rocks in the hill, we are surrounded.

A minute before, a mumbling General Havor had ordered them to let us go.

But they're not listening.

The highest ranking commander on the outside is now Arturo.

He steps forward as we move out of the cave.

'Sita,' he says. 'This is madness.'

'You tell me about madness, Arturo.' I hold a pistol to General Havor's head, shielding myself and Joel with his wobbly figure. He wept as I bored into his brain, but he resisted me as well. I had to destroy most of his mind to get what I wanted. Gesturing to the bomb, I add, 'This warhead is set to detonate in less than fifteen minutes. That gives you and your men barely enough time to get clear.'

Arturo shakes his head. 'We cannot let you escape. An order has come from the President of the United States. At all costs, you are to be stopped.' He gestures to the men around us. 'We are expendable.'

I force a chuckle. 'You will not sacrifice all these people.'

'It is not my decision to make.'

'That's nonsense! They look to you to command them now. Command them to drop their weapons and get the hell out of here.' I pause. 'You are bluffing.'

Arturo looks me in the eye. He is not intimidated by my gaze.

'I pray that you are the one who is bluffing,' he says softly.

The timer on the detonator goes to fourteen minutes.

I meet his gaze. 'When was the last time you prayed, Arturo? Was it before the inquisitor's court? The day they hanged you? I did what I did then because I know the danger my blood poses for the world. Tonight, I killed all these people for the same reason – to protect humanity.'

Arturo challenges me. 'To protect us from what? A chance to evolve into something greater? Into creatures that need never grow old, that need never hurt one another? Earlier you laughed at my mission. Seven hundred years ago you also laughed at me. But mine is still the noblest quest on earth – to perfect humanity, to allow it to become godlike.'

'You do not become godlike by merging with a monster!'

My words surprise him. 'You're not a monster, Sita.'

'I am not an angel, either. Or if I am, I am an angel of death – as far as humanity is concerned. True, I have the right to live. Krishna granted me that right. But only if I lived alone, and made no more of my kind. Now I have broken that sacred vow. Krishna will probably judge me harshly. Perhaps he has already judged me, and that is why I am being forced to suffer in this place, to hurt all these people. But what is done is done. I am what I am. Humanity is what it is. We can never join. Don't you see that?'

'Don't you see me, Sita? I am an example of what can

be accomplished with a merger of our DNAs. And I am only an incomplete example because I never got to complete the process. Think what mankind can change into if you'll just let me experiment with your blood for the next few weeks. Even a few days would be enough. That's all I'm asking. Then, when I'm finished, I promise to let you go. I will arrange it so that you can go free.'

I speak with sorrow. 'Arturo, I *can* see you. I see what's become of you. As a young man, you were the ideal person: devout, loving, brilliant. But your brilliance was perverted the day you received my blood. Your love was twisted. For the sake of your experiments, you even sacrificed a boy you loved. You sacrificed us – the love we had for each other. You lied to me, and I think you lie to me again. Your devotion is no longer to Christ – it is to yourself. And even though I have also lied to my God, I still love Krishna and pray he will forgive me for my sins. I still love you, and I pray you will order these people to let us go. But because of both of these loves, I cannot surrender. You cannot have my blood.' I pause. 'No man can have it.'

Arturo knows me.

He knows I'm not bluffing, not when it comes to matters of life and death.

The timer goes to thirteen minutes. Unlucky thirteen.

His face and voice show his resignation. 'I cannot let you go,' he says quietly.

I nod. 'Then we will stand here until the bomb goes off.'

Joel looks at me. I stare silently at Joel. There are no words left.

Arturo stands still as a statue. The moon shines down.

Twelve. Eleven. Ten.

Ten minutes might be long enough to get clear of the blast.

'Arturo, ti prego,' I say suddenly. *'Arturo, please.'* 'At least warn your men. Let them flee. I have enough blood on my conscience.'

'The blast will leave no blood,' he says, turning his eyes upward, toward the sky. 'We will be like dust, floating on the wind.'

'That is fine for you and me. We have lived long lives. But most of these men are young. They have families. Give the order – enough will remain to prevent Joel and me from escaping.'

Arturo sighs and turns. He raises his arms and shouts. 'Units G and H are free to go! Hurry! A nuclear bomb is about to detonate!'

There is a great commotion. I suspect more than units G and H want to leave. The men pour into their trucks. Engines roar to life. Tires burn rubber. The front gate is thrown open. The vehicles roar out of sight. Driving at a hundred miles an hour, they can put at least twelve miles between themselves and the blast in the time they have left. They should survive. Yet many remain behind who will not survive. Too many men still stand guard over us. If we try to escape, we will be cut down. It is better to go out like this, I think. Standing on our feet. Disintegrating in an all-consuming wave of fire.

Then I remember something.

'He's in a box so thick an atomic bomb couldn't blast through it.'

But if we move and try to flee toward the lab basement, they'll open fire.

For the first time in my long life, I can see no way out.

Time creeps by.

Eight. Seven. Six. Five.

'I don't even know if the warhead can be deactivated once it's armed,' I mutter.

'It can't be,' General Havor mumbles with what is left of his mind.

'Oh,' I say.

Then I begin to feel a peculiar sensation, a subtle but constant vibration inside my body. The moon is directly overhead, of course. It has been shining down on us since we left the cave. But what I didn't realize – with all that was going on around me – was that the moonlight has been filling my body all the time we have been out in the open. It has become more and more transparent. I feel as if I am made of glass. Interesting, I think – and I didn't even have to take my clothes off. It is Arturo who is the first one other than myself to notice the effect.

'Sita!' he cries. 'What's happening to you?'

Standing beside me, Joel gasps. 'I can see through you!'

I let go of the general. Staring down at my hands, I glimpse the ground through my open palms, through my fingers. Yet I can still see the blood pulsing in my veins, the tiny capillaries glowing like a complex web of fiber optics. A cool energy sweeps over me, yet my heart is strangely warmed.

It warms even as it starts to break.

The white glow spreads around me.

I realize I can just lift off and fly away.

Yaksha's blood, maybe Krishna's grace, gives me another chance.

Do I want it? I feel myself leave the earth.

I reach out to hug Joel, to carry him away with me.

My arms go right through him!

'Joel,' I cry. 'Can you hear me?'

He squints. 'Yes, but it's hard to focus on you. What's going on? Is this a special vampire power?'

My luminous body floats a foot off the ground now.

'It is a gift,' I say. Despite my unusual physical state, I feel tears on my face, white diamonds that sparkle with a red sheen as they roll over my transparent cheeks. Once more, I have to say goodbye to those whom I love. 'It is a curse, Joel.'

He smiles. 'Fly away, Sita, far away. Your time is not over.'

'I love you,' I say.

'I love you. The grace of God is still with you.'

The ground is two feet below me now. Arturo tries to grab me, but can't. He stands back and shakes his head, resigned.

'You are probably right,' he says. 'Mankind is not ready for this.' He adds, 'Everything you require is in my basement. It is your choice.'

I don't understand. But I smile at him as I float higher.

'*Ti amo,*' I whisper.

'*Ti amo anch'io,* Sita.'

A wind takes hold of me. Suddenly I am soaring. The stars shine around me. The moon beats down on the top of my head like an alien sun spawned in the centre of a distant galaxy. It is so bright! My now-invisible eyes can hardly bear the glare, and I am forced to close them. As I do an even greater light ignites beneath me. The fiery rays of it rise up and pierce through my etheric body. There is tremendous heat and noise. A shock wave as thick as a granite mountain strikes me. Yet I feel no pain – just swept away, on currents of destruction and tidal waves of death. The compound is gone, the stolen blood is vapour. The world is safe once again. But I, Sita, I am lost in the night.

Epilogue

There is, to my utter amazement, a basement in Arturo's Las Vegas home. The afternoon after the atomic blast, I peer through the carefully hidden trapdoor and discover sheets of copper, magnetic crosses arranged in odd angles, and, most important of all, an empty crystal vial, waiting to be filled with blood. A mirror rests above the vial. It can reflect either the sun or the moon, depending on how much you want to wager.

I call Seymour Dorsten, explain the possibilities to him.

Wait, he cautions. He is on his way.

I sit down and wait. Time passes slowly.

'Everything you require is in the basement.'

Do I still want a daughter? Do I still crave immortality?

Deep questions. I have no answers.

Seymour arrives and tries to talk me out of it.

Being human is not so great, he says.

Being a vampire gets old, I counter.

I know that I will attempt the transformation.

But I need some of his blood.

Make me a vampire first, he pleads.

That will not work, I remind him.

But, he protests.

The answer is no, I say firmly.

I take his blood, fill the vial to the brim, then tell him to get lost.

When the sun is at its peak, I lie down on the copper sheets.

The magnets draw out my aura. The magic begins.

When I awake, I feel weak and disoriented. Someone is knocking at the door. I have to struggle up the steps to answer it. There is a spongy texture to my skin I have never noticed before, and my vision is blurred. I am not even sure where I am – only that it is dark. Blood pounds in my head, and I feel I will be sick.

I reach the front door.

A shadow moves outside the glazed side window panel.

Just before I open the door, I remember everything.

'Am I human?' I whisper to myself.

Yet I am not given a chance to know.

The knocking continues.

'Who is it?' I call in a hoarse voice.

'It's your darling,' the person replies.

Odd. It doesn't sound like Seymour.

Yet the voice is familiar. From long ago.

But the tone is a little demanding. Sort of impatient.

'Open the door,' the person calls.

I wonder if I should.

Staring down at my trembling hands, I wonder many things.

book four

PHANTOM

For Scott, who loves female vampires

1 ～～

Someone knocks at the door of the Las Vegas home where I stand. It is late evening; the living room is dimly lit, four walls of blurred shadows. I don't know who this person is. For that matter, I'm not sure who I am. I have just awakened from a dead alchemist's experiment. My mind is foggy and my nerves are shot. But before I embarked on the experiment, only hours ago, I was a steel-willed vampire – the last vampire on earth. Now I fear – and hope – that I may once again be human. That I may be a young woman named Alisa, the humble offspring of a five-thousand-year-old monster called Sita.

The person continues to knock.

'Open the door,' he says impatiently. 'It's me.' Who

is me? I wonder. I do not recognize the voice, although it does sound familiar. Yet I hesitate to obey, even to respond. Of those few I call friends, only Seymour Dorsten is supposed to know I am in this Las Vegas home. My other friends – well, a couple recently perished in the Nevada desert, in a nuclear blast. A lot has been happening in the last few days, and most of it has been my doing.

'Sita,' the person outside the door says. 'I know you're in there.'

Curious, I think. He knows my ancient name. He even says it like he knows me. But why doesn't he tell me his name? I could ask him, but some emotion stops me. It is one I have seldom known in my five thousand years.

Fear. I stare down at my hands.

I tremble with fear. If I am human, I know, I am practically defenseless. That is why I do not want to open the door. I do not want to die before I have had a chance to taste mortality. Before I have had the opportunity to have a child. That is perhaps the primary reason I employed Arturo's alchemetic tools to reverse my vampirism – to become a mother. Yet I am still not a hundred percent sure the experiment has succeeded. I reach down with the nails of my right hand and pinch my left palm. The flesh breaks; there is a line of blood. I stare at it.

The wound does not immediately heal.

I must be human. Lord Krishna save me.

The knocking stops. The person outside takes a step back from the door. I hear his movements, even with my mediocre human ears. He seems to chuckle to himself.

'I understand, Sita,' he says. 'It's all right. I'll return soon.'

I hear him walk away. Only then do I realize I have been standing in the dark with my breath held. Almost collapsing from relief, I sag against the door and try to calm my thumping heart. I am both confused and exalted.

'I am human,' I whisper to myself.

Tears roll over my face. I touch them with my quivering tongue. They are clear and salty, not dark and bloody. Another sign that I am human. Moving slowly, striving to maintain my balance, I step to the living room couch and sit down. Looking around, I marvel at how blurred everything is, and wonder if the experiment has damaged my eyesight. But then I realize I must be seeing things as a human sees, which means to see so little. Why, I can't even distinguish the grain in the wood panel on the far wall. Nor can I hear the voices of the people in the cars that pass outside. I am virtually blind and deaf.

'I am human,' I repeat in wonder. Then I begin to laugh, to cry some more, and to wonder what the hell I'm going to do next. Always, as a vampire, I could do anything I wished. Now I doubt if I will ever leave the house.

I pick up the remote and turn on the TV. The news – they are talking about the hydrogen bomb that exploded in the desert the previous night. They say it destroyed a top-secret military base. The wind was blowing away from Las Vegas so the fallout should be almost nonexistent. They don't say anything about me, however, even though I was there and witnessed the whole thing. The experts wonder if it was an accident. They don't connect it to the mass police killings I committed in Los Angeles a few days earlier. They are not very imaginative, I think. They don't believe in vampires.

And now there are no more vampires to believe in.

'I beat you, Yaksha,' I say aloud to my dead creator, the vampire who sucked my blood five thousand years ago and replaced it with his own mysterious fluids. 'It took me a long time but now I can go back to an ordinary life.'

Yet my memories are not ordinary. My mind is not either, although I suddenly realize I am having trouble remembering many things that hours ago were clear. Has my identity changed with my body? What percentage of personal ego is constructed from memory? True, I still remember Krishna, but I can no longer see him in my mind's eye as I could before. I forget even the blue of his eyes – that unfathomable blue, as dear as the most polished star in the black heavens. The realization saddens me. My long life has been littered with pain, but also much joy. I do not want it to be forgotten, especially by me.

'Joel,' I whisper. 'Arturo.'

I will not forget them. Joel was an FBI agent, a friend I made into a vampire in order to save his life. An alteration that caused him to die from a nuclear bomb. And Arturo, another friend, a hybrid of humanity and vampires from the Middle Ages, my personal priest, my passionate lover, and the greatest alchemist in history. It was Arturo who forced me to detonate the bomb, and destroy him and Joel, but my love for him is still warm and near. I only wish he were with me now to see what miracle his esoteric knowledge has wrought. But would the vampire blood-obsessed Arturo have still loved my human body? Yes, dear Arturo, I believe so. I still believe in you.

Then there was Ray, my Rama reincarnated. My memories of him will never fade, I swear, even if my human brain eventually grows forgetful. My love for Ray is not a human or vampire creation. It is beyond understanding, eternal, even though he himself is dead. Killed trying to kill a demon, the malignant Eddie Fender. There are worse reasons to die, I suppose. I still remember more than a few of them.

Yet, at the moment, I do not want to dwell on the past.

I just want to be human again. And live.

There comes another knock at the front door.

I become very still. How quickly frightened a human can become.

'Sita,' this person calls. 'It's me, Seymour. Can I come in?'

This voice I definitely recognize. Standing with effort, I walk to the front door and undo the lock and chain. Seymour stands on the porch and stares at me. He wears the same thick glasses and hopelessly mismatched clothes of the high school nerd I met in a stupid PE class only a few months before. His face changes as he studies me; his expression turns to one of alarm. He has trouble speaking.

'It worked,' he gasps.

I smile and open the door all the way. 'It worked. Now I am like you. Now I am free of the curse.'

Seymour shakes his head as he steps in the house and I close the door. He liked me as a vampire, I know. He wanted me to make him a vampire, to poison him through the metamorphosis, an act that was strictly forbidden by Krishna five thousand years ago. Now Seymour is upset. Unable to sit, he paces in front of me. There are unshed tears in his eyes.

'Why did you do it?' he demands. 'I didn't think you would really do it.'

I force my smile wider and spread my arms. 'But you knew I would. And I want you to be happy for me.' I gesture for him to come to me. 'Give me a hug, and this time I won't be able to squeeze you to death.'

He hugs me, reluctantly, and as he does so he finally does shed his tears. He has to turn away; he is having trouble breathing. Naturally his reaction upsets me.

'It's gone,' he says to the far wall.

'What's gone?'

'The magic is gone.'

I speak firmly. 'It is only Yaksha's blood that has been destroyed. Maybe you don't like that. Maybe your fantasies of being a vampire are ruined. But think of the world – it is safe now from this curse. And only you and I know how close it came to being destroyed by it.'

But Seymour shakes his head as he glances at me. 'I am not worried about my own personal fantasies. Yeah, sure, I wanted to be a vampire. What eighteen-year-old wouldn't want to be one? But the magic is gone. You were that magic.'

My cheek twitches; his words wound me. 'I am still here. I am still Alisa.'

'But you are no longer Sita. The world needed her in order to be a place of mystery. Even before I met you, I *knew* you. You know I knew you. I wrote my stories late at night and your darkness filled them.' He hung his head. 'Now the world is empty. It's nothing.'

I approach and touch his arm. 'My feelings for you have not changed. Are they nothing? Good God, Seymour, you speak to me as if I were dead.'

He touches my hand but now it is hard for him to look at me. 'Now you will die.'

'All who are born die,' I say, quoting Krishna. 'All who are dead will be reborn. It is the nature of things.'

He bites his lower lip and stares at the floor. 'That's easy to say but it's not easy to live through. When you met me, I had AIDS. My death was certain – it was all I could see. It was like a slow-motion horror film that never ended. It was only your blood that saved me.' He pauses. 'How many others could it have saved?'

'Now you sound like Arturo.'

'He was a brilliant man.'

'He was a dangerous man.'

Seymour shrugs. 'You always have an answer for everything. I can't talk to you.'

'But you can. I'm a good listener. But you have to listen as well. You have to give me a chance to explain how I feel. I'm happy the experiment has succeeded. It means more to me than you can imagine. And I'm happy there's no going back.'

He catches my eye. 'Is that true?'

'You know it is true. There is no more vampire blood, anywhere. It's over.' I squeeze his arm and pull him closer. 'Let it be over. I need you now, you know, more than I needed you before.' I bury my face in his shoulder. 'You have to teach me how to be a nerd.'

My small joke makes him chuckle. 'Can we have sex now?' he asks.

I raise my head and plant a wet kiss on his cheek. 'Sure. When we're both a little older.' I shake him, but not so hard as I used to. 'How dare you ask me a question like that? We haven't been on a date yet.'

He tries hard to accept the loss of his world, the death of his magic. He forces a smile. 'There's a vampire movie in town. We could see it, and eat popcorn, and jeer, and then have sex afterward.' He waits for an answer. 'It's what most nerd couples do every Saturday evening.'

I suddenly remember. It has taken me this long. There must be something wrong with my mind. I turn away and swear under my breath. 'Damn.'

'What is it?' he asks. 'You don't like popcorn?'

'We have to get out of town. We have to leave now.'

'Why?'

'There was someone here a few minutes ago. A young man – he was knocking at the door.'

'Who was it?'

'I don't know. I didn't open the door. But this guy – he called me by name. He called me Sita. He kept insisting I open the door.'

'Why didn't you?'

'Because I didn't know who he was! Because I'm human now!' I pause and frown. 'His voice sounded familiar. I swear, I knew it, but I just can't place it.'

'What makes you think he's dangerous?'

'Do you have to ask that question? No one alive, except you, knows me by the name Sita.' I stop again. 'He said he would come back. He laughed as he said it. He sounded so sure of himself.'

'What else did he say?'

'He called himself my darling.'

Seymour was thoughtful. 'Could Arturo have survived the blast?'

'No.'

'But he was a hybrid. Half human, half vampire. It's possible. Don't dismiss the possibility.'

I shake my head. 'Even Yaksha could not have survived that blast.'

'But you did.'

'I floated away at the last minute. You know, I told you.' I turn toward the kitchen, my car keys. 'The sooner we leave the better.'

Seymour grabs my arm. 'I disagree. You have said there are no more vampires. What do we have to fear from this person? Better we stay and find out who he is.'

I consider. 'The government must have known Arturo was using this house. Such records were probably kept somewhere else besides the army base I destroyed. The government might be watching this house now.'

'But you said you knew this person.'

'I'm not sure about that. There was something in his voice, though . . .'

'What?' Seymour demands when I don't finish. I strain to remember through my newfound human fog. 'His tone – it gave me a chill.'

Seymour acts like a wise guy. 'In the real world not everybody who comes to the front door wants to kill you. Some guys just want to sell you a vacuum cleaner.'

I remain stubborn. 'We're getting out of here now.' Grabbing the keys off the kitchen table, I peer out the back window and see nothing significant. In the distance, the lights of the Strip come alive and shimmer, coloured beacons in a desert wasteland. A nuclear bomb just exploded but human vice will not be postponed. Of course the wind was blowing the other way, but I do not judge. I have always been a gambler. I understand better than most why the atomic dice did not betray the city of sin. Why the fallout fell the other way. Still, I swear again. 'Damn. I wish I had my old vision right now. Just for a minute.'

'And I bet your old hearing.' Seymour comes up at my side and pats me on the back. 'You're going to make that same wish a lot of times in the next few days.'

2

I own houses all over the world, some modest places to relax when I enter a foreign country in search of fresh blood, others so extravagant one would think I was an Arabian princess. My home in Beverly Hills, where we drive after leaving Las Vegas, is one of the most opulent ones. As we enter the front door, Seymour stares in wonder.

'If we stay here,' he says, 'I have to get new clothes.'

'You can have the clothes, but we're not staying. Ray's father knew about this house, so the government might as well. We're just here to get money, credit cards, clothes, and fresh identification.'

Seymour is doubtful. 'The government knew you were at the compound. They'll think you died in the blast.'

'They'll have to know for sure that I died. They were obsessed with my blood, so they'll research every possible lead concerning me.' I step to the window and peer outside. It is the middle of the night. 'They may be watching us now.'

Seymour shrugs. 'Are you going to get me fresh ID?'

I glance at him. 'You should go home.'

He shakes his head firmly. 'I'm not going to leave you. Forget it. I mean, you don't even know how to be human.'

I step past him. 'We can discuss this later. We don't want to be here a minute more than we have to be.'

In the basement of my Beverly Hills home, I pick up the things I mentioned to Seymour. I also take a 9mm Smith & Wesson equipped with a silencer and several rounds of ammunition. My reflexes and vision are not what they used to be, but I believe I am still an excellent shot. All my supplies I load into a large black leather suitcase. I am surprised how much it weighs as I carry it back upstairs. My physical weakness is disconcerting.

I don't let Seymour see the gun.

We leave Beverly Hills and drive toward Santa Monica. I let Seymour drive; the speed of the surrounding cars disturbs me. It is as if I am a young woman from 3000 B.C. who has been plucked from her slow-paced world and dumped into the dizzyingly fast twentieth century. I tell myself I just need time to get used to it. My euphoria over being human remains, but the anxiety is there as well.

Who was at the door?

I can't imagine. Not even a single possibility comes to mind. But there was something about that voice.

We check into a Sheraton hotel by the beach. My new name is Candice Hall. Seymour is just a friend helping me with my bags. I don't put his name down on the register. I will not stay Candice long. I have other ID that I can change my hair style and colour to match, as well as other small features. Yet I feel safe as I close the door of the hotel room behind me. Since Las Vegas, I have kept an eye on the rearview mirror. I don't believe we've been followed. Seymour sets my bag on the floor as I plop down on the bed and sigh.

'I haven't felt this exhausted in a long time,' I say.

Seymour sits beside me. 'We humans are always tired.'

'I am going to enjoy being human. I don't care what you say.'

He stares at me in the dimly lit room. 'Sita?'

I close my eyes and yawn. 'Yes?'

'I am sorry what I said. If this makes you happy, then it makes me happy.'

'Thank you.'

'I just worry, you know, that there's no going back.'

I sit up and touch his leg. 'The decision would have been meaningless if I could have gone back.'

He understands my subtle meaning. 'You didn't do this because of what Krishna said to you about vampires?' he asks.

I nod. 'I think partly. I don't think Krishna approved

210

of vampires. I think he just allowed me to live out of his deep compassion for all living things.'

'Maybe there was another reason.'

'Perhaps.' I touch his face. 'Did I ever tell you how dear you are to me?'

He smiles. 'No. You were always too busy threatening to kill me.'

I feel a stab of pain. It is in my chest, where a short time ago a stake pierced my heart. For a moment the area is raw with an agonizing burning, as if I am bleeding to death. But it is a brief spasm. I draw in a shuddering breath and speak in a sad voice.

'I always kill the ones I love.'

He takes my hand. 'That was before. It can be different now that you're not a monster.'

I have to laugh, although it is still not easy to take a deep breath. 'Is that a line you use to get a girl to go to bed with you?'

He leans closer. 'I already have you in bed.'

I roll onto my side. 'I need to take a shower. We both need to rest.'

He draws back, disappointed. 'You haven't changed that much.'

I stand and fluff up his hair, trying to cheer him up. 'But I have. I'm a nineteen-year-old girl again. You just forget what monsters teenage girls can be.'

He is suddenly moved. 'I never knew the exact age you were when Yaksha changed you.'

I pause and think of Rama, my long dead husband,

and Lalita, my daughter, cremated fifty centuries ago in a place I was never to know.

'Yes,' I say softly. 'I was almost twenty when Yaksha came for me.' And because I was suspended so long between the ages, I add again, 'Almost.'

An hour later Seymour is fast asleep beside me on the king-size bed. But despite my physical exhaustion, my mind refuses to shut down. I can't be free of the images of Joel's and Arturo's faces from two nights earlier when I suddenly began to turn to light, to dissolve, to leave them just before the bomb was detonated. At the time I knew I was dead. It was a certainty. Yet one last miracle occurred and I lived on. Perhaps there was a reason.

I climb out of bed and dress. Before leaving the hotel room, I load my pistol and tuck it in my belt, at the back, pulling my sweatshirt over it.

The hotel is located on Ocean Ave. I cross over it, and the Coast Highway that separates me from the ocean. Soon I am walking along the dark and foggy Santa Monica Beach, not the safest place to be in the early morning hours before the sun rises. Yet I walk briskly, heading south, paying little attention to my surroundings. What work it is to make my legs move over the sand! It is as if I walk with weights strapped around my ankles. Sweat drips in my eyes and I pant audibly. But I feel good as well. Finally, after thirty minutes of toil, my mind begins to relax, and I contemplate returning to the hotel and trying to sleep.

It is only then that I become aware that two men are following me.

They are fifty yards behind me. In the dark it is hard to distinguish their features, but it is clear they are both Caucasian and well built, maybe thirty years old. They move like two good ol' boys, one dark featured, ugly, the other bright as a bottle of beer foaming in the sunlight. I think these boys have been drinking beer – and stronger – and are feeling uncomfortably horny. I smile to myself as I anticipate the encounter, even imagine what their blood will taste like. Then I remember I am not who I used to be. A wave of fear sweeps through my body, but I stand and wait for them to come to me.

'Hey, girl,' the one with dark hair says with a Southern accent. 'What are you doing out at this time of night?'

I shrug. 'Just out for a walk. What are you guys up to?'

The blond guy snickers. 'How old are you, girl?'

'Why?' I ask.

The dark-haired one moves slightly to my left. He flexes his fists as he speaks. 'We just want to know if you're legal.'

'I'm old enough to vote,' I say. 'Not old enough to drink. You boys been drinking tonight?'

They both chuckle. The blond guy moves a step closer. He smells of beer, whiskey. 'You might say we've been looking at the wrong end of a few bottles tonight.

But don't let that worry you none. We're still fully capable of finishing what we start.'

I take a step back. Perhaps it's a mistake that I show fear. 'I don't want any trouble,' I say. And I mean it, although I feel as if I can still take them. After all, I am still a master of martial arts. A series of swift kicks to their groins, their jaws, should settle any unpleasantness. The dark-haired guy steps off to my left, and wipes at his slobbering mouth with the back of his arm.

'We don't want trouble either,' he says. 'We're just looking for a good time.'

I catch his eye, and really do wish that my stare was still capable of burning into his brain. Seymour was right – my wishes have already settled into a pattern of wanting what I have lost. Yet I do my best to make my voice hard.

'Sometimes a good time can cost you,' I say.

'I don't think so,' the blond guy says. 'You agree, John?'

'She looks like a freebie to me, Ed,' John responds.

They've used their names in front of me. That is a bad sign. It means they're either too drunk to know better, or else they plan to kill me. The latter seems a distinct possibility since they clearly intend to rape me. I take another step back, and am tempted to reach for my gun. Yet I don't really want to kill them, especially since there is no need for their blood. Knocking them unconscious is my preference.

Actually, it is my second preference. Surviving is my first.

'If you touch me I'll scream,' I warn them.

'No one's going to hear you down here,' John says as he reaches out to grab me. 'Take her, Ed!'

They go for me simultaneously, John close on my left, Ed three feet in front of me. But it is John who reaches me first. He has pretty good reflexes for a drunk. Before I can twist away, he catches me in a bear hug. Briefly I struggle, and then go limp. When Ed closes within two feet, however, I shove back against John and jump up, lifting both my feet off the ground. Lashing out with the right, I catch Ed in the groin. He shouts in pain and doubles up.

'The bitch got me!' he complains.

'Goddamn it!' John yells in my ear. 'You're going to pay for that.'

In response I slash backward and up with my left elbow. The blow catches John square on the jaw and his hold on me loosens as he staggers back. In an instant I am free. Since Ed is still bent over, I do him the favour of kicking him in the face, breaking his nose. He drops to his knees, his face dark with blood.

'Help me, John,' he moans.

'Help him, John,' I mock as John regains his balance and glares at me with death in his eyes. I gesture with my little finger. 'Come on, John. Come and get your good-time girl.'

John charges like a bull. I leap up and lash out with

my left foot in order to kiss his jaw with the heel of my boot. The only trouble is that my timing and balance are all off. I have not risen far enough off the ground. Instead of striking him in the face, I hit him just above the heart, and the blow has not nearly the power I anticipated. John is a big man, over two hundred pounds. He grunts in pain as I strike but he doesn't stop. The momentum of his charge brushes aside my leg and now it is me who is suddenly off balance.

Frantically, I try to bring my left leg back in beneath me before I land but I am too late. With a thud, I topple on my right foot and hit the sand with the right side of my face. John is on me in a second, grabbing me from behind and pinning my arms midway up my spine. He's strong. My upper vertebrae feel as if they will explode. With his free hand he smacks me on the back of the head.

'You are one nasty bitch,' he swears as he presses my face into the sand. Straining, I twist my head to the side so that I can breathe and see what is going to happen to me. 'Ed, give me a hand with this whore. She looked like a good sport to begin with but I'm afraid when we're done pleasing ourselves we're going to have to bury her in this spot.'

'We'll let the crabs eat her,' Ed agrees as he staggers over, still bleeding profusely from his smashed nose. Behind me, John reaches around for the button on my pants. That is something of a break because if he had just tried to pull my pants down from behind, he would have found the gun. Also, reaching around as he is, I realize, John is slightly off balance.

Digging in with my right knee and pushing off with the tip of my left foot, I shove up as hard as possible. The move catches John by surprise, and I momentarily break free and roll in the sand. But my freedom will be measured in fractions of a second if I don't take drastic action. Squirming onto my back, I see both John and Ed staring down at me with stupid grins. They look ten feet tall and as ugly as highway billboards. Together they reach for me.

'Wait!' I cry as I move my right hand slowly under my lower back. 'If I lie still and cooperate will you please not hurt me?'

They pause to think about that. 'You better lie still, bitch,' John says finally. 'But you've messed up my friend too much to just walk away from tonight.'

'But we might give you a chance to crawl away,' Ed says wiping at his bloody face and picking at his broken nose all in the same move.

'I won't leave here crawling,' I say in a different tone of voice as my hand finds the butt of the gun. Leaning slightly to the left I whip it out and point it at the good ol' boys. They stare at it, frankly, as if they have never seen a gun before. Then they both take a step back. Maintaining my aim, I take my time getting back to my feet. I speak gently. 'That's right boys,' I say. 'No sudden moves. No screams for help.'

John chuckles uneasily. 'Hey, you got us, girl. You got

us good. We give you that. But you know we didn't mean you no harm. We just drank a little too much and didn't know what we were doing.'

'We weren't going to hurt you none,' Ed adds, sounding scared, as well he should. Still taking my time, I step within a foot of Ed and place the barrel of the gun between his eyebrows. His eyes get real big, and he wants to turn and run but I stop him with a faint shake of my head. To my left, John stands frozen in wonder and horror.

'You are both liars,' I say in a cold voice. 'You were not only going to rape me, you were going to kill me. Now I am going to kill you because you deserve to die. But you should be grateful I'm using a gun. A few nights ago I would have used my teeth and nails, and you would have died much slower.' I pause. 'Say goodbye to John, Ed.'

Ed is consumed with murderer's remorse. 'Please!' he says, his voice cracking. 'I have a wife and kid back home. If I die, who will take care of them?'

'I've got two kids back home,' John says passionately.

But I am unmoved. Being human has not made me more gullible.

Yet, I usually do not kill when I have the upper hand. I do not kill for pleasure. But I know these two will harm others in the future, and therefore it is better that they die now.

'It is better for your children not to grow up having to imitate trash like you,' I say.

Ed's face is awash with tears. 'No!' he cries.

'Yes,' I say, and shoot him in the head. He falls hard.

I turn the gun on John, who slowly backs away, shaking his head.

'Have mercy,' he pleads. 'I don't want to die.'

'Then you should never have been born,'I reply.

I shoot him twice in the face. In the eyes.

Yet that is all I do. The ancient thirst is gone.

I leave their bodies for the crabs.

3 〜〜

It is only on the way back that the shock of what has just happened overwhelms me. Ordinarily, killing a couple of jerks would occupy my mind for less than ten seconds. But now it is as if I feel the trauma in every cell. My reaction is entirely human. As I stumble off the beach and back onto Ocean Ave., I shake visibly. I scarcely notice that I'm still carrying the gun in my right hand. Chiding myself, I hide it under my sweatshirt. If I was in my right mind I would throw it in the ocean in case I'm stopped and searched. But I'm reluctant to part with the gun. I feel so vulnerable; it is like a safety blanket to me.

There is a coffee shop open three blocks from the sea. Staggering inside, I take a booth in the corner and order a cup of black coffee. It is only when the steaming beverage arrives, and I wrap my trembling hands around the mug, that I notice the faint mist of blood splattered on the front of my gray sweatshirt. It must be on my face as well, and I reach up and brush at my skin, coming away with red-stained palms. What a fool I am, I think, to be out like this in public. I am on the verge of leaving when someone walks in the coffee shop, heads straight to my table, and sits down across from me.

It is Ray Riley. The love of my life.

He is supposed to be dead.

He nods slightly as he settles across from me, and I am struck by the fact that he is dressed exactly as when he ignited the gasoline truck outside the warehouse filled with Eddie Fender's evil vampires and blew himself to pieces. When he sacrificed his life to save mine. He wears a pair of black pants, a short-sleeved white silk shirt, Nike running shoes. His brown eyes are warm as always, his handsome face serious even though he wears a gentle smile. Yes, it is Ray. It is a miracle, and the sight of him stirs so much emotion inside me that I feel almost nothing. I am in shock, pure and simple. I can only stare with damp eyes and wonder if I am losing my mind.

'I know this is a surprise for you,' he says softly. I nod. Yes. A surprise.

'I know you thought I was dead,' he continues. 'And I think I was dead, for a time. When the truck exploded,

I saw a bright flash of light. Then everything went black and I felt as if I were floating in the sky. But I couldn't see anything, know anything, even though I was not in pain. I don't know how long this continued. Eventually I became aware of my body again, but it was as if I was at a great distance from it. The strange thing was, I could feel only parts of it: a portion of my head, one throbbing hand, a burning sensation in my stomach. That was all at first. But slowly, more parts woke up, and I finally began to realize someone was trying to revive me by feeding me blood.' He pauses. 'Do you understand?'

I nod again. I am a statue. 'Eddie,' I whisper.

A spasm of pain crosses Ray's face. 'Yes. Eddie collected what was left of me, and took me away to some dark cold place. There he fed me his blood, Yaksha's blood. And I began to come back to life. But Eddie vanished before the process was complete, and I was left only half alive.' He pauses again. 'I assume you destroyed him?'

I nod again. 'Yes.'

He reaches across the table and takes my hands. His skin is warm, and it quiets the trembles that continue deep inside me. He continues his impossible tale, and I listen because I can do nothing more.

'Still, I continued to gain strength without Eddie's help. In a day – maybe it was two – I was able to move about. I was in a deserted warehouse, tied with rope. I had no trouble breaking out; and when I did I read about all the strange goings on in Las Vegas, and I knew you must be there.' He stops. 'It was me who was at the door.'

I nod for a fourth time. No wonder the voice sounded familiar. 'Why didn't you identify yourself?' I ask.

'I knew you wouldn't believe me until you saw me.'

'That's true.'

He squeezes my hands. 'It's me, Sita. I've come back for you. It's Ray. Why can't you at least smile?'

I try to smile but I just end up shaking my head. 'I don't know. You were gone. I knew you were gone. I had no hope.' My eyes burn with tears. 'And I don't know if I'm not just imagining this.'

'You were never one to imagine things.'

'But I'm no longer the one you knew.' I withdraw my hands from his and clasp them together, trying to hold myself together. 'I'm human now. The vampire is dead.'

He is not surprised. 'You let go of my hands too quickly, Sita. If you examine them, you will notice a change in me as well.'

'What do you mean?' I gasp.

'I watched you at that house. I watched you enter it, and I watched you leave it. I knew you were not the same, and I wondered what had happened in there. I explored the house, and found the basement: the copper sheets, the crystals, the magnets, the vial of human blood.' He pauses. 'I performed the same experiment on myself. I am no longer a vampire either.'

The shocks keep piling one on top of the other. I cannot cope. 'How did you know what to do?' I whisper.

He shrugs. 'what was there to know? The equipment was all set up. I just had to lie down and allow the vibration of the human blood to wash over my aura as the reflected sun shone through the vial of blood.' He glances out the window. There is a kind of light in the east. 'I did it this afternoon. Now the sunrise will no longer hurt me.'

The tears in my eyes travel over my cheeks. My mind travels with them as my disbelief washes away. Swallowing thickly, I finally feel as if my body returns to my control. In a burst I realize I am not imagining anything. Ray is not dead! My love is alive! Now I can live my life! Leaning across the table, I kiss his lips. Then I brush his hair and kiss that as well. And I am happy, more happy than I can remember being in thousands of years.

'It is you,' I whisper. 'God, how can it be you?'

He laughs. 'You have Eddie to thank.'

I sit back down in my seat and feel my warm human heart pounding in my chest. My anxiety, my fear, my confusion – all these things have now transformed into a solitary glow of wonder. For a while now I have cursed Krishna for what he has done to me, and now I can only bow inside in gratitude. For I have no doubt Krishna has brought Ray back to me, not that monster Eddie Fender.

'Let's not even speak his name,' I say. 'I cut off his

head and burned his remains. He is gone – he will never return.' I pause. 'I'm sorry.'

He frowns. 'What have you to be sorry for?'

'Assuming you were dead.' I shrug. 'Joel told me you were blown to pieces.'

Ray sighs and looks down at his own hands. 'He wasn't far wrong.' He glances up. 'I didn't see Joel at the house?'

My lower lips trembles. 'He's dead.'

'I'm sorry.'

'We both have to stop saying that.' I smile a sad smile. 'I made him a vampire as well, trying to save him. But it just killed him in the end.'

'Who created the equipment that transformed us back into human beings?'

'Arturo – old friend, from the Middle Ages. I was in love with him. He was an alchemist, the greatest who ever lived. He experimented with my blood and changed himself into a hybrid of a vampire and a human. That's how he was able to survive all these years.' I lower my voice. 'He died with Joel. He had to die.'

Ray nods. One didn't have to explain every detail to him in order for him to understand. He knew Arturo must have still been after my blood; that he was dangerous. Ray understood that I could kill those I loved, as I had almost killed him. Ray reaches for my hand again.

'You have blood on you,' he says. 'Surely you're not still thirsty?'

'No, it's not like you think.' I speak in a whisper. 'Two men attacked me at the beach. I had to kill them.'

'How?'

'I shot them in the head.'

Now it is Ray's turn to be shocked. 'We have to get out of here, away from here. Besides the government, you'll have the police after you too.' He glances toward the door of the coffee shop. 'I know you have Seymour with you.'

I understand what he wants to say. 'I have told him he has to go home.'

'He won't want to leave you. You'll have to leave him.'

'I have been thinking about that. I just don't know how to explain it to him.'

Ray is sympathetic, but a curious note enters his voice. For a moment he sounds like I used to as the pragmatist.

'Don't explain it to him,' he says. 'Just leave him, and don't tell him where you're going.'

'That seems harsh.'

'No. You of all people know that to keep him with you will be harsh. You'll expose him to danger for no reason.' He softens his tone. 'You know I speak from experience.'

'You're right. He's asleep at the hotel right now. I suppose I can sneak in, grab my things, and be away before he wakes up.' But inside I know I will at least leave him a note. 'Where are we going?'

It is Ray's turn to lean over and kiss me. 'Sita, we can

go anywhere we want. We can do anything we want.' He whispers in my ear. 'We can even get married and start a family if you want.'

I have to laugh, and cry as well. My happiness lingers like the warmth of the sun after a perfect summer day. It is the winter outside, the darkness, that seems the illusion.

'I would like a daughter,' I whisper, holding him close.

4

Two months later we are in Whittier, a suburb of Los Angeles, where the late President Nixon attended college. The city is largely middle class, completely nondescript, a perfect place, in Ray's opinion, to disappear. Certainly I have never been to Whittier before, nor harbored any secret desires to go there. We rent a plain three-bedroom house not far from a boring mall. Ray picked it out. There is a large backyard and an olive tree in the front yard. We buy a second-hand car and purchase our groceries at a Vons down the street. I have lived five thousand years to do all these things.

Yet my happiness has not faded with the passage of the eight weeks. Sleeping beside Ray, walking with him in the morning, sitting beside him in a movie – these simple acts mean more to me than all the earth-shattering deeds I have accomplished since I was conceived beneath Yaksha's bloody bite. It is all because I am human, I know, and in love. How young love makes me feel. How lovely are all humans. Shopping at the mall, in the grocery store, I often find myself stopping to stare at people. For too long I admired them, despised them, and envied them, and now I am one of them. The hard walls of my universe have collapsed. Now I see the sun rise and feel the space beyond it, not just the emptiness. The pain in my heart, caused by the burning stake, has finally healed. The void in my chest has been filled.

Especially when I discover that I am pregnant.

It happens the early morning of the full moon, two months after the nuclear bomb detonated in the desert beneath a previous full moon. A fifteen-dollar early pregnancy kit tells me the good news. I shake the blue test tube in the bathroom and Ray comes running when I let out a loud cry. What is the matter, he wants to know? I am shaking – there must be something wrong. I don't even get a chance to show him my blue urine because I accidentally spill it all over him. He gets the picture and laughs with me, and at me.

I am at the bookstore later the same day, browsing through the baby books, when I meet Paula Ramirez. A pretty young woman of twenty-five, she has long black hair as shiny as her smooth complexion and a belly larger than her enchanting brown eyes. Obviously she is expecting, much sooner than I am. I smile at her as she juggles six different baby books in one arm, while reaching for another with her free hand.

'You know,' I say. 'Women were having kids long before there were books. It's a natural process.' I put my own book back on the shelf. 'Anyway, I don't think any of these authors know what the hell they're talking about.'

She nods at my remark. 'Are you pregnant?'

'Yes. And so are you, unless I'm blind.' I offer my hand, and because I like her, without even knowing her, I tell her one of my more real names. Even as a human, I often trust my intuition. 'I'm Alisa.'

She shakes my hand. 'Paula. How far along are you?'

'I don't know. I haven't even been to the doctor. It can't be more than two months, though, unless God is the father.'

For some reason, Paula loses her smile. 'Do you live around here?'

'Yes. Close enough to walk to the mall. How about you?'

'I'm on Grove,' Paula says. 'You know where that is?'

'Just around the block from us.'

Paula hesitates. 'Forgive me for asking, but are you married?'

It is a curious question, but I'm not offended. 'No. But I live with my boyfriend. Are you married?'

Sorrow touches her face. 'No.' She pats her big

belly. 'I have to take care of this one alone.' She adds, 'I work at St Andrews. It's just down the block from where you live.'

'I have seen the crucifix. What do you do at St Andrews?'

'I am supposed to be an assistant to the Mother Superior but I end up doing whatever's necessary. That includes scrubbing the bathroom floors, if no one's gotten to them. The church and the high school operate on a tight budget.' She adds, almost by way of apology, 'But I take frequent breaks. I pray a lot.'

For some reason this girl interests me. She has special qualities – a gentleness of manner, a kindness in her voice. She is not a big girl but she seems to take up a lot of space. What I mean is there is a presence about her. Yet she acts anything but powerful, and that I also like.

'What do you pray for?' I ask.

Paula smiles shyly and lowers her head. 'I shouldn't say.'

I pat her on the back. 'That's all right, you don't have to tell me. Who knows? Prayers could be like wishes. Maybe they lose their magic if you talk about them.'

Paula studies me. 'Where are you from, Alisa?'

'Up north. Why'

'I could swear I've seen you before.'

Her remark touches me deeply. Because in that exact moment, I feel the same way. There is something familiar in her eyes, in the soft light of their dark depths. They remind me of, well, the past, and I still have much of that, even if I grow older with each day.

Yet I intend to brush her comment aside, as I brush aside thoughts of my own mortality that come in the middle of night, when Ray is asleep beside me, and sleep is hard to find. My insomnia is the only obvious curse of my transformation. I must still be used to hunting in the middle of the night. Prowling the streets in a black leather miniskirt. Death with a sexy smile and an endless thirst. Now, instead, I get up from bed and have a glass of warm milk and say my prayers – to Krishna, of course, whom I believe was God. I still remember him best during the darkest hours.

Krishna was once asked what was the most miraculous thing in all of creation, and he replied, 'That a man should wake each morning and believe deep in his heart that he will live forever, even though he knows that he is doomed to die.' Despite my many human weaknesses, a part of me still feels as if I will never die. And that part has never felt so alive as when I stare at Paula, a simple pregnant young woman that I have met by chance in a mall bookstore.

'I just have one of those faces,' I reply.

We have lunch, and I get to know Paula better, and I let her know a few censored facts about myself. By the time our food is finished, we are fast friends, and this I see as a positive step on my road to becoming truly human. We exchange numbers and promise to stay in touch, and I know we will. I like Paula – really; it is almost as if I have a crush on her, though I have had few female lovers during my fifty centuries, and certainly Ray now takes care of my sexual needs. It is just that as I say goodbye to her, I am already thinking of the next time we will meet, and how nice it will be.

Paula is the rarest of human beings. Someone with intelligence and humility. It has been my observation that the more intelligent a man or woman is, the more dishonest he or she is. Modern psychologists, I know, would not agree with me, but they are often dishonest themselves. Psychology has never impressed me as a science. Who has ever really defined the mind, much less the heart? Paula has a quick mind that has not destroyed her innocence. As we part for the first time, she insists on paying for our meal even when it is clear she has little money. But I let her pay since it seems to mean a lot to her.

5 ~

And so, for a week, life went on, sweetly, smoothly, with a new friend, a reborn lover, and a baby growing inside me. A daughter, I am sure, even though I pray to God to make it an absolute certainty. Yet fifty centuries cannot be forgotten. History cannot be rewritten. I live in the suburbs and abide by my country's laws. I have a new library card and am thinking of buying a little dog. Yet I have murdered thousands, tens of thousands, brutally and without mercy. That is a bloody fact, and perhaps there is such a thing as karma, of sin and judgment. I wonder if I am being judged when I begin to have trouble with the baby.

It is not normal trouble.

It is the worst kind. The supernatural kind.

The baby is growing much faster than she should. As I said to Paula, I can only be two months pregnant, and yet, one week after I meet Paula, I wake with something kicking in my abdomen. After hurrying to the bathroom and turning on the light – for I cannot see very well in the dark anymore – I am astounded to see that my stomach bulges through my nightgown. In the space of hours, even, the baby has developed through an entire trimester. This does not please me.

'Ray,' I say. 'Ray!'

He comes running, and takes forever to see what the problem is. Finally he puts his hand on my belly. 'This is not normal?'

'Are you nuts?' I brush his hand aside. 'She can't be human.'

'We're human,' he says.

'Are we?' I ask the empty bathtub.

He puts a hand on my shoulder. 'This accelerated growth doesn't have to be a bad thing.'

I am having trouble breathing. I had put so much hope in the past being past. But there is no future, not really. It is only a phantom of what we want to deny, a dream in a time that will never actually be.

'Anything abnormal is bad,' I say. 'Especially when you have to answer yes to the question on the medical form: Have you ever been a vampire?'

'The child cannot be a vampire,' Ray says simply. 'Vampires cannot reproduce this way.'

'You mean they haven't done so in the past,' I say.

'When has a vampire ever turned human again? This is new terrain.' I lean over and spit in the sink. My spit is bloody – I bit my lower lip the instant the light went on. 'It's an omen,' I say.

Ray rubs my back. 'Maybe you should see a doctor. You were going to start looking for one anyway.'

I chuckle bitterly. 'I cannot see a doctor. We're in hiding, remember? Doctors report local monsters to the authorities. Young women who have babies in three months.' The baby kicks again. I stare in the mirror at my bulge. 'If it even takes that long.'

My words prove prophetic. Over the next four days the baby grows at an insane pace, a month of development for each twenty-four-hour period. During this time I am forced to eat and drink constantly, but seldom do I have to use the rest room. Red meat, in particular, I crave. I have three hamburgers for breakfast and in the evening four New York steaks, washed down with quarts of Evian. Still, I burn with hunger, with thirst, and with fear. What would an ultrasound show? A horned harlot grinning back at the sound waves?

During this time, I avoid Paula and the world. Ray is my only companion. He holds my hand and says little. What is there to say? Time will tell all.

Five days after waking in the middle of the night to see my swollen belly, I awake again in the early morning hours in horrible pain with cramps in my abdomen. Just before Ray wakes, I remember when I had my first child, five thousand years earlier. My dear Lalita – she who plays. That birth had been painless, ecstatic even. I had intended to name this child by the same name. But as another spasm grips me, seemingly threatening to rip me in two, I don't know if such a gentle title will be appropriate. I sit up gasping for air.

'Oh God,' I whisper.

Ray stirs beside me. His voice is calm. 'Is it time?'

'It's time.'

'Do you want to go to the hospital?'

We have discussed this, but never come to a decision. I can withstand tremendous physical pain, and of course I have delivered babies many times and know human anatomy inside out. Yet this pain is a thing of demons. It transcends any form of torment I have ever experienced. Literally, I feel as if I am being ripped apart, consumed from the inside. What is my child doing to me? I bury my face in my hands.

'It feels like it's eating my womb,' I moan.

Ray is on his feet. 'We have to get help. We have to risk the hospital.'

'No.' I grab his hand as he reaches for the car keys. 'I won't make it. It's coming too fast.'

He kneels at my side. 'But I don't know what to do.'

I fight for air. 'It doesn't matter. It's all being done.'

'Should I call for Paula?' Ray approves of my relationship with Paula, although, for some strange reason, he has avoided meeting her. How I long for her company right then, her soothing smile. Yet I know she is the last person who should see me like this. I shake my head and feel the sweat pour off my face.

'No,' I say. 'This would terrify her. We have to face this alone.'

'Should I boil some water?'

For some reason his remark amuses me. 'Yes, yes. Boil some water. We can put the baby in it when she comes out.' I snort when I see his stunned expression. 'That's a joke, Ray.'

Yet he stares at me strangely. He speaks to me as if he is speaking to a third person in the room. 'Sometimes I feel I came back just for this baby. I don't want anything to happen to her.'

Another spasm grips me, and I double up and ignore his serious tone. The agony angers me. 'If anything is going to happen to anyone,' I whisper, 'it will happen to me.'

'Sita?'

'Get the goddamn water.'

My daughter is born fifteen minutes later, and she puts a nice rip in me as she comes into the world. My blood is everywhere, even in my hair, and I know I am in danger of hemorrhaging to death. It is only now I let Ray call for an ambulance. But before he gets on the phone, he puts my bloody child on my chest. He has already cut the umbilical cord with a sterilized knife from the kitchen drawer. Cuddling my daughter as I lie on the verge of blacking out, I stare into her dark blue eyes and she stares back at me. She does not cry nor make any other sound. For the moment I am just relieved she is breathing.

Yet there is an alertness in her eyes that disturbs me. She looks at me as if she can see me, and all the books say a child of five minutes cannot even focus. Not only that, she stares at me as if she knows me, and the funny thing is, I do likewise. I do know her, and she is not the soul of my gentle and joyful Lalita returned to me from the ancient past. She is someone else, someone, I feel, they may have constructed temples to long ago, when mankind was closer to the gods in heaven and the forgotten creatures beneath the earth. I shiver as I look at her, yet I hold her tight. Her name just springs from my cracked and bleeding lips – I do not bring it forth consciously. The name is a mantra, a prayer, and also a name for that which cannot be named.

'Kalika,' I call her. Kali Ma.

Not she who plays. She who destroys.

Still, I love her more than can be said.

6 ⮆

Kalika is two weeks old, really a year in size and ability, when she refuses to take my milk. For the last fourteen days I have enjoyed feeding her, although I have not relished the speed at which she grows. Each morning when I wake to her sounds, I find a different and older daughter. This morning she pushes me away as I try to hold her to my breast. She is strong and actually bruises my skin as she refuses what I have to offer. Ray sits across from me and tries to comfort me in my despair.

'Maybe she's not feeling well,' he says.

I stare out the window as Kalika squirms on my lap. 'Maybe she wants something else to drink,' I say.

'She's not a vampire.'

'You don't know.'

'But sunlight doesn't bother her.'

It is true, I have tested my daughter under the bright sun. She just stares at it as she stares at everything else. Indeed, the glare does not seem to annoy her young eyes, a fact that does nothing to comfort me.

'No one knows what she is,' I say.

'Well, what are we going to do? We have to feed her.'

Maybe Kalika understands the question. Already she has begun to speak, simple words as many twelve-month-old children do. But it is probable she understands more than she says, certainly more about herself than either of her parents is willing to admit. While I am gazing out the window at the sky, she leans over and bites my left nipple. She has teeth now and she bites so hard that she draws blood. The pain, for me, is sharp, but the flow, for her, is steady. And the blood seems to satisfy her.

I look at Ray and want to cry.

Another day has gone by and Kalika is in her bedroom screaming. She is hungry but my breasts are too sore – too drained actually – to give her another feeding. Ray paces in front of me as I lie on the living room couch and stare out the big window. My thoughts are often of the sky, and of Krishna. I wonder where God is at times like this, if he is not browsing in the horror section of the cosmic library searching for another chapter to slip in my life story.

I am exhausted – I have yet to regain my strength

from the delivery. I'm a smashed doll who's been sewn together by an emotionless doctor, an aching mother whose daughter disembowels Barbies in search of something to eat. Kalika lets out another loud cry and Ray shakes his head in disgust.

'What are we going to do?' he asks.

'You asked me that five minutes ago.'

'Well, we've got to do something. A child's got to eat.'

'I offered her a steak, a raw steak even, and she didn't want it. I offered her the blood from the steak and she didn't want it. She just wants my blood and if I give her any more I will die.' I cough weakly. 'But considering the circumstance that might not be bad.'

Ray stops pacing and stares down at me. 'Maybe she doesn't just crave *your* blood.'

I speak in a flat voice. 'I have thought of that. I would have to be stupid not to have thought of that.' I pause. 'Do you want to give her some of your blood?'

Ray kneels on the floor beside me. He takes my hand and gives it an affectionate squeeze. But there is a look in his eyes, one I have never seen before. Of course having a child like Kalika in the house would give the Pope a new look. Ray speaks in a low conspiratorial voice and there is no affection in his words.

'Let us say she is not a human being,' he admits. 'I suppose that is obvious by now. Let's even go so far as to say she's some sort of vampire, although not a vampire in the traditional sense. Her indifference to the sun makes that seem certain. Now, all of this is not necessarily a bad thing if we can teach her right from wrong as she matures. She doesn't have to be a monster.'

'What's your point?'

'Isn't it obvious? She's still our daughter. We still love her, and we have to give her what she needs to survive, at least until she can fend for herself.' He pauses. 'We have to get her fresh blood.'

I smile without pleasure. 'You mean we have to get her fresh victims.'

'We just need blood, for now. We don't have to kill anyone to get it.'

'Fine. Go down to the hospital and buy some. Take one of my credit cards. They're in my purse on the kitchen table.'

Ray drew back. 'I'm serious, Sita.'

I chuckle bitterly. 'So am I. I have experience in these matters, in case you've forgotten. The only blood she will take will be warm blood from a human being.'

'I thought you sometimes survived on animal blood.'

'I offered her the blood of a cat I caught and killed in the backyard and she didn't want it.'

'You didn't tell me.'

'Killing a cat wasn't something I felt like bragging about.'

A peculiar note enters his voice, to match the strange look in his eyes. 'You used to kill people all the time.'

I brush off his hand and sit up. 'Is that what you want me to do? Murder people for her?'

'No. No one has to die. You told me that the day you made me a vampire.'

My temper flares. 'The day I made you a vampire I had an arsenal of supernatural powers at my command. I could lure dozens of people into my lair, and let them go with little more than a headache. To get Kalika fresh blood, I will have to kill, and that I refuse to do now.'

'Now that you're human?'

'Yes. Now that I'm human. And don't remind me of those two I wasted the night you returned. That was an act of self-defense.'

'This is an act of self-preservation,' Rays says.

I speak impatiently. 'How am I supposed to get someone to donate blood for Kalika's breakfast? Where do you find people like that? Not in Whittier.'

'Where did you go to find victims before? To bars? You went to them to lure men back to your place.'

'I never took them back to my place.'

Ray hesitates. 'But we need someone, maybe a couple of someones we can take blood from regularly.'

I snicker. 'Yeah, right. And when we let them go we just tell them to please not mention what has been going on here. Just chalk the bloodletting off to a unique experience.' I fume. 'Whoever we bring here, we'll have to kill in the end. I won't do that.'

'Then you'll let your daughter die?'

I glare at Ray, searching for the loving young man I

once knew. 'What's happened to you? You should be on the other side of this argument. Before the blast, you would have been. Where did you go when you died? Huh? You never told me. Was it hell? Did the devil teach you a few new tricks?'

He is offended. 'I'm just trying to save our daughter. I wish you'd drop your self-righteous, pompous attitude and face the facts – Kalika needs blood or she will die. We have to get her blood.'

'Fine, go out and get a young woman victim. You're handsome and you've got style. It shouldn't take you long.'

He stops. 'I don't know how to pick up people. I've never done it before.'

I have to laugh. 'You sure picked me up easily enough.'

Kalika screams again.

Ray loses his dark expression and looks pained. 'Please,' he says. 'She's all we've got. You're the only one who can save her.'

Fed up with arguing, I stand and grab my black leather coat, the one I used to wear for hunting. Heading for the door, I say over my shoulder, 'We used to have a lot, Ray. Remember that next time you order me to go out and kill.'

7 ~~~

I drive around for an hour before ending up at a local park. There are a couple of basketball courts, a baseball diamond, a circular pond with white ducks in it, and a wide field where children fly long-tailed kites. Sitting between the pond and the basketball courts, I try to think how I can fix my miserable life in one brilliant stroke.

For the last twenty-four hours I have considered taking Kalika to Arturo's secret laboratory, where the paraphernalia that completed my transformation is located: the crucifix-shaped magnets, the long copper sheets, the coloured crystals. Yet the attempt, I know, to make Kalika into a human, would be a desperate act at best. One of the few times Arturo experimented on a boy – dear Ralphe – the results were disastrous. Ralphe

246

was transformed into a flesh-eating ghoul, and I had to break his neck with my own hands to stop him from killing. No, I realize, I cannot experiment on Kalika, not until every other alternative has been explored.

Which means I need human blood. Now.

A young man on the basketball court glances over at me. I may not be a vampire anymore, but I know I'm cute. This guy is maybe nineteen, with blond hair and a strong build, an easy six-two. His size is important to me. The more pounds he has, the more blood he can stand to lose. Yet the more difficult he will be to contain. But my daughter is screaming at home. I heard her screams as I drove away in the car, echoing in my ears like the cries of a thousand past victims.

I catch this young man's eye and smile.

He flashes me a grin. He is interested, doomed.

When his game finishes, he strolls over to say hi.

'Hi,' I say in response, nodding to the court, to his companions. I sit with my profile to them – I don't want them to get a good look at me. 'You know, you're pretty good. You have a great jump shot.'

'Thanks. I still enjoy these pick-up games.'

'You used to play in high school?'

'Yeah. Just got out last year. How about you?'

I laugh softly. 'I was too short to play basketball.'

He blushes. 'I mean, did you just graduate?'

'Not long ago.' I pause, let my eyes slide over him. 'What's your name?'

'Eric Hawkins. What's yours?'

I stand and offer him my hand. 'Cynthia Rhodes. Do you come here often?'

'I usually play at Centinela. This park – I haven't been here in ages.'

That's good, I think. 'What brings you here today?'

He shrugs. 'Nothing in particular. I was just out driving around.'

That's also good. The other guys he's playing with – they're not close friends.

'I was just doing the same,' I say.

He glances at the ground, fidgets shyly. 'Hey, would you like to go have a Coke or something?'

'Sure. I'm not doing anything.'

We go to a coffee shop, and I order coffee. I have become a big coffee drinker since becoming human. It does wonders for my insomnia. Eric has a hamburger and french fries. I am happy he eats heartily. He will need his strength. Yet as he talks about himself, I begin to feel sad. He seems like such a nice boy.

'I'm taking a year off from college, but I'll be in school next year,' he says. 'I just got accepted to SC. I'm going to major in pre-med. My old man's a doctor and he's encouraged me to follow in his footsteps since the day I learned to talk.'

'Why didn't you go straight to college?'

'I wanted to travel a little, work a little. I spent the summer in Europe. Spent a month in the Greek islands alone. You ever been there?'

I nod as I sip my coffee. 'Yes. Did you visit Delos?'

'The island with all the ruins?'

'Yes. It's supposed to be the most sacred island in the Aegean Sea. Apollo was born there.' I lower my voice. 'At least, that's what the stories say.'

'Yeah, I was there. When were you there?'

'A few years back.' I pause and catch his eye, and hate myself for the blatant manipulation. 'I'm glad I went to the park today.'

He smiles shyly and stares down at his hamburger. 'Yeah. When I saw you sitting there all by yourself – I don't know – I just felt like I had to talk to you.' He adds, 'I don't usually go around hitting on girls.'

'I know, Eric.'

We chat a while longer and he finishes his food, and then glances at his watch. 'Boy, I better get going. My dad's expecting me at his office. I help out there Tuesday and Thursday afternoons.'

I feel a moment of panic. I cannot imagine returning to Kalika's screams empty-handed. Reaching across the table, I touch his hand. 'Could you do me a quick favour?'

'Sure. What is it?'

'It's kind of embarrassing to explain. You see, I have this ex-boyfriend who is sort of stalking me. He's not violent or anything like that, but if he sees me return home he immediately jumps out of his car and runs over and starts hassling me.' I pause. 'Could you follow me home in your car? Just to make sure I get in OK.' I add, 'I don't live far from here.'

'You don't live with your parents?'

'No. Both my parents are dead. I live alone.'

Eric is troubled. 'Sure, I can come. But I won't be able to stay.'

'I understand. If you can just walk me to my door.'

Eric is agreeable, although his reluctance remains. As a human, I'm not the actress I used to be. He likes me, but he is slightly suspicious of me. I have to wonder exactly what I'm going to do with him once he's in my house.

To my immense bad luck, Paula is standing on my front porch as I drive up and park. Waving to her, I quickly run back to Eric's car, which is in the middle of the block. I ask if he can wait a minute, but he's anxious to get to his father's office.

'He loses his temper if I'm even ten minutes late,' he explains.

'I'm grateful you followed me this far,' I say. 'But I'm still worried my ex is around. He could even be in the house.'

Eric nods to Paula, who waits patiently for me. 'Who is she?'

I snort, and feel another layer of guilt. 'She's just this pregnant girl who stops by from time to time looking for money. I have to get rid of her, or she'll stay all afternoon.' I touch his arm. 'Please stay. Give me two minutes.'

Eric hesitates. 'OK.'

Paula flashes me a warm smile as I hurry toward her. 'What are you doing here?' I ask.

'I was worried about you. I haven't heard from you in so long.' Paula studies me, and I know how perceptive she is. 'Have you been sick? You look pale.'

'I've had a bad flu. Look, I can't talk right now. That guy in the car – he's my boyfriend's brother, and he's in deep trouble that I can't go into right now. He needs my help.'

Paula is hesitant. 'Fine, I can go. I was just out for a walk.' She glances at Eric. 'Are you sure you're all right?'

'Yeah, no problem.' I gesture to her swollen belly. 'It won't be long now.'

Paula is radiant. 'No. Another three weeks is all.'

'That's great.' I nod to my door. 'Did you knock? Did you talk to Ray?'

'I knocked but no one answered.'

'Oh.' That's strange. Ray is almost always at home. He would have to be at home, with Kalika and all. I can't imagine him taking her out. But perhaps our daughter is the reason he didn't answer. I cannot hear either of them inside. I add, 'I'll talk to you soon, Paula. I promise, we'll have lunch.'

Paula is gracious as she carefully moves down the steps. 'You take care. I'll be thinking of you.'

'Thanks. Say a prayer for me.'

'I always do, Alisa.'

Paula leaves, and I gesture for Eric to join me on the front porch. He parks in my driveway and approaches reluctantly. He has antennae of his own. I am definitely giving off bad vibes. His car will have to be moved

251

quickly, I think, before it makes an impression on my neighbours. I fumble for my keys, like I'm nervous. And I am nervous – I can't imagine hurting him. For that matter, he might end up hurting me.

'Sometimes my ex comes in a back window,' I say as I put the key in the lock.

'You should lock your windows,' Eric mutters.

'Can I get you something to drink?' I ask as we step inside. A quick look around shows neither Ray nor Kalika. Maybe he did go out with her. Eric stays near the door.

'I really should be going,' he says.

'At least have a lemonade. I made some fresh this morning.' I move toward the kitchen. 'I really appreciate you doing this for me.'

Eric feels trapped. 'I'll have a small glass,' he says without enthusiasm.

In fact, I did make lemonade that morning, from concentrate. Pouring a couple of glasses, I hurry back to the living room. My resentment toward Ray continues to grow. For seducing Eric to come into the house, it is good Ray is out of sight. Yet I could use Ray to knock Eric unconscious. I mean, I am a hundred-and-ten pound blond chick who just had a baby. Eric accepts his drink and I toast him with our glasses. Eric drinks without relish.

'It's good,' he mumbles.

'Thanks. We have lemon trees in our backyard.'

'They give fruit this time of year?'

I smile. 'No, but they do in the summer.'

Eric finishes half his drink and sets the glass down on the coffee table. 'Well, my dad's waiting. Let's talk another time. It was nice to meet you.'

I jump slightly, and speak in a hushed tone. 'Did you hear that?'

Eric is puzzled. 'What?'

I point down the hall. 'I think he's here.'

Eric frowns. 'I don't hear anything.'

I am a picture of fear. 'Would you check? Just to be sure.'

'Cynthia, really. I don't think anyone's there.'

I swallow heavily. 'Please? It's terrible when he sneaks up on me like this. I can't get rid of him by myself.'

Eric eyes the hallway. 'You're sure he's not violent? Why does he break into your house?'

'He's never violent. He's just a pest. I hope I'm imagining the whole thing.'

Eric starts up the hallway. I follow close behind him, silently. Even as a human, I can move like a cat. As he reaches for the last bedroom door on the left, I lash out with my right foot, striking behind his right knee. There is a mushy tearing sound – the spot is especially vulnerable. Letting out a painful cry, Eric topples to his knees. Before he can recover, I slash out with my left hand and catch him in the left temple, which is the thinnest part of the skull. The blow stuns him but does not knock him out. Disgusted, I strike again, at the opposite temple, hitting as hard as I can, the side of my hand throbbing from the effort. Still on his knees, he sways precariously. Yet he refuses to go down. Quite the contrary, he grasps at the near wall, trying to pull himself up. He is a fighter and it breaks my heart not to let him go. But I'm committed now. Backing up a step, I jump in the air and kick him in the back of the head with the heel of my left boot. That does the trick. Eric falls forward like a sack of flour. Blood drips off the back of his head, staining the carpet. Just what we need.

'I'm sorry,' I whisper as I kneel by his side, checking the pulse at the side of his neck to make sure I haven't killed him. His face against the floor, Eric breathes heavily but his pulse is strong.

Suddenly I am aware of someone at my back.

'Good job,' Ray says.

I turn on him angrily. 'Yeah, it's good I was able to handle him all by myself. Where have you been?'

He shrugs. 'I was in the other room.'

'Where's Kalika?'

He nods to the door Eric was about to open. 'In there. I told her to remain silent.'

'And she listened to you?'

Ray speaks seriously. 'She always listens to me.'

'Lucky you.' I nod to Eric. 'Where are we going to put him?'

'In the spare room. We'll tie him up and gag him, and take only as much blood as our daughter needs.'

'That might be more than he can give,' I say, stroking Eric's hair.

'We'll have to worry about that later.' Ray pauses. 'How should we withdraw the blood?'

'We need needles, syringes, tourniquets, tubing, flasks. I have them at my house in Beverly Hills.' I stand, wiping Eric's blood from my hands. 'I'll go now.'

Ray stops me. 'That house might be watched, you said.'

I don't like being stopped. 'I'll have to risk it. I'm not breaking into a drugstore to get this stuff.'

'I want you to help me tie him up before you leave.'

'Can't you tie him up? The sooner I leave, the sooner I can get back.' I glance at the bedroom door. My daughter hasn't made a peep. 'Kalika must be starving by now.'

'It won't take us long if we work together. Then I can go with you to the other house.'

'No,' I say. 'I'm going alone.'

Ray hesitates. 'Fine. But I think it's better this guy sees only one of us.'

'Why?'

'Isn't it obvious? If he can identify me, it doubles our chances of being caught.'

I stare at Ray. 'You really have changed.'

He shrugs. 'Maybe it was Eddie's blood.'

'Maybe.' I hold his eye. 'All right, I'll deal with him, like I deal with everything else. As long as we both understand that we're not pushing Eric beyond his limit. This boy is not going to die.'

Ray nods his head, but his eyes do not seem to agree.

8 ~

Before entering my Beverly Hills house, I search the street and the surrounding houses for signs of anyone watching. The FBI's methods are not unfamiliar to me. The house appears unwatched. Once inside, I gather the supplies I need to turn Eric into a serious anaemic. But before leaving I stop to call Seymour. I haven't spoken to him since I said good night in the hotel by the beach. Even the note I left said little.

Sorry, Seymour. Got to go. You know this is for the best. Love, Sita.

'Hello?' he says.

'It's me.'

He takes a long time to answer. His voice comes out harsh. 'What do you want?'

I speak with sincerity. 'Just to hear your voice, Seymour. I miss you.'

'Yeah, right.'

'I do. I really do.'

'Where are you?'

'I can't tell you.'

'I have to go.'

'No! Wait! You know why I can't tell you.'

'No, I don't know why. I thought you were my friend. Friends don't leave each other in the middle of the night.' He lowers his voice and there is pain in it.

'Why did you leave?'

I hesitate. I didn't plan to tell him.

'Ray's come back.'

Seymour is astounded. 'That's impossible.'

'It's true. We're living together.' I add, 'We've got a daughter.'

'Sita, what kind of fool do you think I am? You haven't had time to have a daughter.'

My voice cracks. 'I know that. But this one came rather fast.'

He hears that I'm serious. 'Tell me everything that's happened since I last saw you.'

So I tell him because I need someone to talk to. As always he listens patiently, closely, and I have to wonder what insights he will provide when I'm finished. He's so smart – he always has something interesting to say about my numerous predicaments. Yet the next words out of his mouth shock me.

'Why do you assume this guy is Ray?' he asks when I finish.

I have to laugh, although I almost choke on it. 'What kind of question is that? Of course it's Ray. I know it's Ray. Who else could it be?'

'I don't know who else it could be. But how do you know it's Ray? Remember, he died.'

'Because he looks like Ray. He acts like Ray. He knows everything Ray knew. He can't be an impostor.'

Seymour speaks calmly. 'Let's take each of your statements. He looks like Ray you say. OK, I grant you that because you've seen him and I haven't. But you say he acts like Ray? I don't think so. The Ray you describe isn't the Ray I remember.'

'He's been through a lot. In a sense, he died during the blast. It was only Eddie's blood that brought him back to life.'

'That worries me right there. Eddie was the incarnation of evil. What would his blood do to someone's psyche? Even the psyche of another vampire?'

I close my eyes and sigh. 'I've worried about that myself. But please believe me, he can't be an impostor. Dozens of times we've discussed things only Ray and I knew.'

'But you do accept you're dealing with a guy that has his priorities twisted?'

'Am I? I've asked myself that question many times. When you get right down to it, I would do anything to save Kalika. Ray's her father. Is he so different from me?'

'I don't know. There's something in your story – something I can't put my finger on. I think Ray's dangerous, and I'd keep an eye on him. But let's leave that for a moment. Let's talk about Kalika. How can she be a vampire and not be sensitive to the sun?'

'I wasn't that sensitive,' I say.

'Because you'd been a vampire for over five thousand years. And still the sun did bother you; it sapped your strength. You say it doesn't affect her at all?'

'Not as far as I can tell. She plays out in it.'

'Does she make any effort to move into the shade?'

'No. She likes the sun as much as the moon.'

'Yet she wants human blood,' Seymour muttered, thinking aloud. 'Hmm. Is she exceptionally strong?'

'Yes. Pretty strong. She must be a vampire.'

Seymour considers. 'What does she look like?'

'A lot like me, except her features are darker.'

'You mean she has brown hair, brown eyes?'

'Her hair is brown, but her eyes are a dark blue.' I add painfully, 'She's very pretty. You'd like her.'

'Not if she wants to drink my blood. Sita, let's be frank with each other. You're not superhuman anymore. You're not going to be able to go around abducting people without getting caught. As far as I can tell, you were lucky with this Eric guy. And how are you going to let him go when you're through with him? He'll go straight to the police.'

I bite my lower lip and taste the blood. The flavor gives me no strength.

'I know,' I say.

'If you know then you've got to stop now.'

There are tears pooled in my eyes but I won't shed them. Not tonight. 'I can't, Seymour. Ray's right about one thing. I can't let her die.'

Seymour speaks gently. 'You know what I'm going to ask next.'

I nod weakly. 'Yes. Does the world need a monster like her? All I can say is, I'm hoping she turns out all right. For godsakes, she was just born. She hasn't had a chance to show what she's like.'

'But by the time she does, it might be too late. You might not be able to stop her.' He adds carefully,

'But you can stop her now.'

I'm aghast. 'I can't murder my own daughter!'

'You can stop feeding her. Think what those feedings will cost you and your victims. You'll need a dozen Erics to keep her satisfied if she's growing at the rate you say. In fact, she'll be getting her own Erics soon enough. I know this is painful for you to face, but you should probably end it now.'

I shake my head vigorously. 'I can't do that.'

Seymour is sympathetic. 'But then I can't help you.' He adds, 'Unless you tell me where you are.'

'It won't help for you to see her. You'll just fall in love with her. When she's not hungry, she's really very lovely.'

'I was thinking I'd like to speak to this new and improved Ray.'

'I don't think that's a good idea. Not now.'

Seymour speaks with feeling. 'You've trusted me in the past, Sita. Trust me now. You're too close to this. You can't see what's real. You need me.'

'It's too dangerous, Seymour. If something happened to you, I'd never forgive myself. Stay where you are, I'll call you again. And I'll think about what you've said.'

'Thinking won't stop her from growing into what she really is.'

'I suppose we'll see what that is soon enough.'

We exchange goodbyes. As I leave the house, I think of Eddie Fender's blood circulating in my lover's body. And I wonder what blood pumps through Kalika's veins. What it is capable of doing.

9 ~~~~

At home, Eric has regained consciousness. His feet and hands are firmly bound, and there is duct tape over his mouth, but he has somehow managed to squirm his way so that he is sitting upright in the far corner of the spare bedroom. His eyes are wide with fear as I approach him with a syringe. It is hard to blame him. As I kneel by his side, I start to stroke his head but he trembles under my fingers so I stop.

'I'm sorry,' I say. 'This isn't easy for me either. I wish I could explain the whole situation to you but I can't. But I can promise you that you're not going to die. I swear this to you, Eric, and I keep my word. At the same time, I'm going to have to keep you here for a few days. I'm not exactly sure how long. And while you're here –

please don't freak out over this – I'm going to have to occasionally take some of your blood.'

The last sentence does not go over well. Eric's eyes get so round I'm afraid they're going to burst from his skull. He shakes his head violently from side to side and tries to wiggle away. But I pull him back.

'Shh,' I say. 'It's not going to be as bad as it sounds. I have clean needles, and am better trained than most doctors. You can lose a little blood and it won't damage you in the slightest.'

He works his mouth vigorously. His meaning is clear.

'If I remove your gag,' I say, 'will you promise not to scream? If you do scream, I'll have to shut you up quickly, and I don't want to have to hurt you any more than I have to.'

Eric nods rapidly.

'OK. But you mustn't raise your voice.' I tear off the tape. Ouch.

Eric gasps for air. 'Who are you?' he moans pitifully.

'Well, that's an interesting question. I am not Cynthia Rhodes if that's what you're asking, but I suppose you know that already.' I pause. 'I'm just a stranger in the park.'

'What do you want with me?'

'I told you. Your blood. A little of your blood.'

'But what do you want my blood for?' he cries.

'That's a long story.' I pat him on the shoulder. 'Just trust me that I really need it, and that in the end you're going to be OK.'

He is breathing heavily. He stares down at his leg and looks so pitiful it breaks my heart. 'You broke my knee. It hurts. I need a doctor.'

'I'm sorry. You can see a doctor later, in a few days. But until then you'll have to stay here. You'll have to eat here, and sleep here, and go to the bathroom here. Now you see that bathroom over there? I will let you use it from time to time if you just cooperate with me. In fact, if you're real good, I won't have to keep you tied up at all. You'll be able to walk around this room, even read and listen to music. But I warn you, I'm going to board up all the windows as soon as I take care of other business. And if you do try to escape, well, let's just say that wouldn't be a good idea.'

He is a little slow. 'Would you kill me?'

I nod gravely. 'I would kill you slowly, Eric, by draining away all your blood. It's not a pleasant way to die. So don't mess with me.' I fluff up his hair. 'Now stick out your arm and don't move.'

He tries to back up. 'No!'

'Don't raise your voice.'

'No!'

I ram the heel of my palm into his nose, which stuns him. While he tries to refocus his eyes, I replace the duct tape and grab his arm. I have the tourniquet on in seconds. His veins are big and bulging. Before he can pull away, I have a needle in his vein and blood flowing into a sterile tube. I lean over and whisper in his ear.

'Don't fight me,' I say. 'If you force me to hit you

again, it won't be in the face, but in a much more sensitive spot.' I tug on his earlobe. 'Understand?'

He stares at the tube as his blood drips into it. He nods.

'Good boy.' I kiss his cheek. 'Just think of all this as a nightmare that will soon be over.'

Kalika is waiting in the living room with Ray when I bring out the blood in a flask. She has a book on her lap. I assume it is one of the picture books that I have recently bought for her, but I am mistaken. Sitting beside her on the floor, I see she has been paging through an anatomy textbook that was in the house when we rented it. I don't ask if she knows what it is. I'm afraid that she might. Her dark blue eyes brighten when she sees the blood. Her little hands shoot out.

'Hungry,' she says.

'Is that all you took?' Rays asks. 'She's been waiting all day.'

'The less I take the more often I can take it,' I say, handing Kalika the flask. I am curious if she will notice the difference between my blood and Eric's. Actually, I wonder if she will drink it all. But that doubt is soon dispelled. She wolves it down in a few gulps. The flask is thrust back into my hands.

'Hungry,' Kalika says.

'I told you,' Ray says. 'You have to give her at least a pint.'

I stare at Kalika, who stares back at me, and a curious sensation sweeps over me. There is a coldness in my daughter's eyes, but also a great expansive feeling. Few people in the West, who know anything of Vedic deities, understand the meaning of Kali or Kalika. To most she is simply a dark, bloodthirsty goddess. Yet that meaning is superficial, and I certainly would not have named my daughter after a monster with no redeeming virtues.

Actually, Kali *is* black, but this is because she represents space, the abyss, that which is before the creation, and that which will exist after. Her necklace of skulls symbolizes how she cares for souls after life, not just through one incarnation. Even the funeral pyre she sits on is representative of the many sins she burns to ash, when she is pleased. Kali is a destroyer, true, but she also destroys evil. Many of India's greatest saints worshipped her as the supreme being.

And they say she is easy to please – if one is careful.

Staring at my daughter, I am reminded of Krishna.

Yet Krishna had love as well as infinity.

Kalika has never been an affectionate child.

There is a bloodstain on her right cheek.

'Hungry, Mommy,' she says softly.

Sighing, I take the flask and trudge back into the spare bedroom. Eric is upset to see me again so soon. Now this won't hurt a bit. I have to hit him again to get him to sit still, and I hate myself for the cruelty. I hate Krishna as well, for forcing me into this situation. But I know it is useless to hate God. It is like screaming at the night sky. The stars have no ears, and besides, they are too far away to hear. They just keep on shining, I must keep on living until death reaches my front door, or my own daughter comes for my blood in the dead of night. I have no doubt that, in a few days, she will be capable of killing me.

10 ~~~

After boarding up Eric's room and ditching his car a safe distance away, I go for another drive, this one entirely aimless. It is dark now and the time of day suits my mood. Kalika thrust back her second empty eight-ounce glass of blood with the same numbing words: *Hungry, Mommy.* I shudder to think what her appetite will demand tomorrow. Will I have to collect a whole team of basketball players? Maybe I should drive down to the Forum and wait for the Lakers to start practice. They have some big boys who know how to shoot a ball.

But should they bleed for my daughter?

Should Eric?

Seymour has scored with many of his points, as always.

Midnight finds me at the beach where I buried Yaksha's body, or rather, where I sunk it. There was little of Yaksha left when I sent him to a watery grave, with his full blessings. Eddie Fender had done his usual number on my creator: stabbed him, torn him, dissected him, drained him. Good old Eddie, never one to take a joke well. But Yaksha hadn't minded the horrific treatment. Indeed, in the end, the most feared of all earth's ancient demons had found peace of mind through faith in Krishna. Staring at the dark waves, I think of how the passage of the many years does not necessarily bring devotion, how my own suffering has more often than not brought cynicism.

I have to wonder if that is why I keep suffering.

'What am I missing?' I ask the ocean. 'Why do I have to go on like this?'

Yet now it is more important than ever that I continue. I am a mother; I have a responsibility to feed my daughter; but it is very possible my daughter is capable of destroying all mankind. No one knows, except perhaps Krishna, what weird alchemy of blood she possesses. Bowing my head in the direction of Yaksha's grave, I turn and leave the beach.

Another hour finds me at Paula's school, inside St Andrews church. It's peculiar how many churches don't have posted hours, how their doors are always open. The light of the candles, as I step inside, fill me with warm feelings. Despite my obsession with Krishna, my respect for Jesus has never faded, even during the

Middle Ages when the Catholic Church tried to burn me at the stake for witchcraft. Me, a witch? I'm a goddamn vampire. I almost told them that, but then, the Church was never one to enjoy a joke.

St. Andrews is comfortably stuffy. The smoke from the candles and incense fills my nostrils as I take a seat in the third pew and stare at the stained-glass windows, dark and sinister without the sun to give them colour. A statue of Mother Mary stands nearby, dozens of glowing red dishes flickering at her feet. I have not lit a candle for the Madonna in the last two thousand years, but I have a strong urge to do so now. But I won't pray to her, I won't ask for her help. Her own son was crucified, so I don't think she is the best person to run to with my problems. Yet I feel close to her, and that is reason enough to show her respect. Plus I like candles. I like fire of all kinds.

I have just lit my candles when I hear steps off to my right.

'Alisa?'

I smile as I turn. 'Paula. What are you doing here at this hour? Praying?'

She is happy to see me. As best as she can with her swollen belly, she gives me a hug. 'No, I was working on the school's books. I couldn't sleep tonight. I only stopped in here because I saw a car parked out front. I thought it might be yours. Why are you here?'

I gesture to Mother Mary. 'I'm making my confession.'

'You need a priest for that.'

I shake my head. 'I don't think there's a priest anywhere who would be able to sit through a list of my sins.'

'Nonsense. They hear all kinds of stuff. None of us is that unique. I think it all sounds the same to them after a while.'

'For once I have to disagree with you. My confession would set a record for the most difficult penance assigned.' I pause as a wave of nostalgia sweeps over me. 'Actually, I knew a Catholic priest once. He used to listen to my confessions. I think that's what drove him mad.'

Paula wonders if I am kidding. 'What was his name?'

'Arturo. He was Italian. I met him in Florence, a long time ago. But that is another story. I'm happy to see you. How are you feeling?'

Paula beams. 'Wonderful. If I didn't have such trouble sleeping, I wouldn't even know I was pregnant.'

'Not to mention the basketball in your belly. Well, that's great, I'm happy for you.' I glance at the main crucifix and lower my voice. 'Very happy.'

Paula touches my arm. 'Something's the matter?'

I nod grimly, still staring at Jesus, wondering how it felt to hang on the cross with so much power available to him, but unable to show it. In that instant I feel a great kinship with Jesus. Seldom in five thousand years was I allowed to demonstrate my full power, and then, when I did, people died.

Also, I think of how Krishna was killed, cut down in the forest by a hunter's arrow, mistaken for a beast and shot in the heel, the only portion of his divine body that was vulnerable to physical attack. So the legend of Achilles was born, not in Greece, but in the deep forests of central India. It is impossible for me to look at Jesus and not think of Krishna. Honestly, all the religious dogma aside, I believe they were one and the same. So universal that they were everybody, and nobody at the same time. Like Kali, Mother Kalika.

Who is my daughter? What is she?

'Something is the matter,' I say to Paula.

'What is it? Maybe I can help.'

'No. Thanks, but no. No one can help me.' I gesture to the empty pews. 'Could I remain here a while? I have to think, to meditate. I think that will clear my mind, and then I will know what to do.'

Paula kisses me on the cheek. 'Stay as long as you want. I will lock the doors as I leave, but they will still open from the inside. You'll be safe in here.'

I smile feebly. 'Thank you. You are a true friend. Sometime, when things are less hectic, we must talk.'

Paula stares deep into my eyes. 'I look forward to that talk.'

When she is gone, I curl up in one of the pews and close my eyes. I meditate best when I am unconscious, when I allow God to do most of the talking. Even though I am in a Catholic church, I pray Krishna will visit me in my dreams.

11 ~~~

The scene is the same as it has always been. It can be
no other way for it is constructed in eternity. It is only
here that dialogue with the Almighty can take place.

I stand on a vast grassy plain with many gently
sloping hills surrounding me. It is night, yet the sky is
bright. A hundred blue stars blaze overhead. The air is
warm and fragrant. In the distance a stream of people
move slowly toward a large spaceship. The ship is violet;
bright rays of light stab into the sky from it. I know that
I am supposed to be on this ship. Yet, before I go to it,
I have something to discuss with Lord Krishna.

He stands beside me on the plain, his gold flute in
his right hand, a red lotus flower in his left. His dress,
like mine, is simple – a long blue gown that reaches to

the ground. But he wears a jewel around his neck – the brilliant Kaustubha gem, in which the destiny of every soul can be seen. He does not look at me but at the vast ship, and the stars beyond. He waits for me to speak, to answer him, but for some reason I can't remember what he last said. I only know that I am a special case. Because I do now know how to respond, I say what is most on my mind.

'When will I see you again, my Lord?'

He gestures to the wide plain, the stars overhead. 'All this creation is an ocean, turbulent on the surface, silent in the depths. But like an ocean, the creatures in it are always searching for meaning in the creation, the ultimate element.' He smiles to himself at the irony. 'The fish searches for water in the ocean. He has heard so much about it. But he never finds it, and that is because he searches too hard.' He pauses. 'I am everywhere in the creation. There is nowhere that I am not. Why do you speak to me of separation?'

'Because, my Lord, I fear I will forget you when I enter into the creation.'

He shrugs, he has no worries. 'That is to be expected. You learn by forgetting what you once knew. Then, when you remember, it is that much sweeter.'

'When will you come to earth?'

'When I am least expected.'

'Will I see you, my Lord?'

'Yes, twice. At the beginning of Kali Yuga and then at the end of the age.'

'Will I recognize you?'

'Not at first, not with the mind. But inside you will know me.'

'How will I know you?'

He looks at me then, and his eyes are a wonder, windows into the cosmos. Time loses all meaning. It is as if the whole universe turns while I stare at him. I see thousands of people, millions of stars, so much life striving for small joys, so many illusions ending in shattering bitterness. Yet in the end it all turns to red, then to black, as the blood of the people runs cold and the fires of Kali burn the galaxies to ash. Still, none of this disturbs the eternal Lord for he never blinks, even though the sheer magnitude of the vision forces me to turn away trembling. He has stolen my very breath.

'Sri Krishna,' I pray, overwhelmed, 'take my soul now. Don't send me out. I surrender everything to you. I can't bear to forget you even for a moment.'

He smiles. 'I will tell you a story. This same story will be told by a simple man named Jesus, in the middle of Kali Yuga. Few people will recognize this Jesus with their minds, but some will know him inside.' Krishna pauses before he begins.

'There is a man named Homa, who is a good person but not a perfect soul. He is a friend of Jesus and one day Jesus asks him to go to the village to buy some food for a large meal Jesus wants to give for some elders of the nearby village. Jesus says to the man, "Take these ten coins and buy twelve loafs of bread, five jugs of wine, four fish, and one bag of a grain. Load it all on my donkey, and when you are done bring it here. I will be waiting for you."

'At this Homa is confused, as well as excited with greed. He can see Jesus does not understand the value of the coins because he knows he can get all the things Jesus has requested for only five coins. Yet Homa also knows Jesus will need twice as much as he has asked for in order to feed all the people who are expected. Still, Homa does not plan on spending all ten coins. He says to himself, "I will buy what I have been told to buy, and I will pocket the rest of the coins."

'So Homa takes the donkey to town, and sets about purchasing the food. At the bakery he buys twelve loafs of bread, but as he places them on the donkey, when he is not looking, they change to twenty-four loafs. Next, Homa gets the five jugs of wine and the four fish. But like before, when he is not looking, the five jugs turns to ten, and the four fish turn to eight. Finally, Homa obtains the bag of grain, but then, on the way back, he sees that he actually has two bags, and that everything else has doubled as well. He is astounded and feels to see if the five coins are still in his pocket.

'Jesus is waiting for him when he arrives and greets him with a kind smile. The smile of Jesus is a wonderful thing. Mankind's history will portray Jesus as filled with sorrow, but the love and joy that flow toward Homa when Jesus looks at him is all consuming. Still, Homa is worried about seeing Jesus, even though Jesus has only kind words for him.

'Jesus says, "Welcome back, Homa, you have brought everything we need for a great feast. Thank you."

'But in shame Homa lowers his head and takes the five coins and places them at Jesus' feet. "Don't thank me, Master, for I thought to cheat you. I knew you needed more than you asked for, but I was going to keep these extra coins for myself. It is only by some strange magic that all this food is here. I bought only half this." At that he kisses Jesus' feet. "I am unworthy to be called your friend, or even your servant."

'But Jesus lifts him up, and says, "No, Homa, you have done well because you have done my bidding. That is all you have to do. I ask nothing more of anyone."'

Krishna pauses and stares up at the sky. 'Did you enjoy this story?'

'Yes, my Lord. But I do not know if I understand it, or how it relates to me.'

'This man, Homa, he is like every man. He is goodhearted but he has his flaws. Yet he is perfect in the eyes of Jesus because he has done what Jesus asks. You see, Sita, God does not expect you to give him all that you have. He understands the ways of the world, that it requires effort to deal with them. God only asks that you grant him half of what you possess, and then God will make up the other half. That is why the food multiplied. That is the miracle of this tale.' Krishna pauses. 'This story will be a part of the Gospel of Jesus, but too soon it will be removed from the holy book by those who want the peasant class to give everything to the Church, who do not understand the compassion of Jesus for those who struggle in the world.' Krishna pauses again and smiles at me, that bewitching smile that steals even the hearts of the gods. 'You don't need to surrender *everything* to me. Keep your head and I will take your heart. You will need your head to deal with Kali Yuga, particularly the end of the age.'

'What will happen at the end, my Lord?'

Krishna laughs and raises his flute to his lips. 'You will not enjoy the tale if you know the end of the tale. Enough questions, Sita, now listen to my song. It dispels all illusions, all suffering. When you feel lost, remember it, remember me, and you see the things you desire most are the very things that bring you the greatest sorrow. My song is eternal, it can be heard at all times in all places.'

'But –'

'Listen, Sita. Listen in silence.'

Krishna starts to play. But as he does, a sudden wind comes up on the plain and the notes of his melody are drowned out. The dust rises and I am blinded, and I can't see Krishna anymore. The light of the stars fades and everything turns black.

Yet in this blackness an even darker shadow fills the sky, and I know I see Kali, who is without colour and who destroys all at the end of time. Sinners as well as saints, devils as well as angels, humans as well as vampires. And I know it is Kali who will eventually destroy me.

12 ~~~

Over the next three days Kalika grows to the approximate age of five, while Eric ages ten years. During this time she reads greedily and masters English, as well as many subtleties of conversation and social convention. I have tested her – her IQ appears off the charts. Her beauty flourishes as well. Her long dark hair is like a shawl of black silk, her face a fine sculpture of hidden mysteries. Even her voice is magic, filled with haunting rhythms. When she speaks, it is hard not to listen, to agree with her, to forget everything else. But it is seldom Kalika does speak, and what runs through her mind – besides her hunger for blood – I have no idea.

It is in the middle of night when my daughter wakes

me in my bed. She does this by gently stroking my hair. I am forced to wake to confusion.

'I can't wait,' she says. 'I need more.'

I shake my head. 'He can't take it. You're going to have to wait till later in the day. I have to get you another.'

Kalika is gently persistent. 'I can do it if you don't want to. I know how.'

I frown. 'Have you been watching me?' Naturally, I have not let Eric see where his blood is going. Somehow I doubt it would lift his spirits.

'Yes,' Kalika says. 'I watch you.'

I sit up. 'Has he seen you?'

'No.' She pauses and glances at Ray, who continues to sleep. 'He hasn't seen either of us.'

'You are not listening to me. This boy can give no more blood. Already his heartbeat is erratic. In a few hours, when it is light, I will go out and find another supply. Until then you will have to be patient.'

Kalika stares at me with her dark blue eyes. Perhaps it is my imagination, but I catch a glimmer of red in their depths. She smiles slightly, showing her front teeth.

'I have been patient, Mother.' That is her new name for me. 'I will just take a little of his blood, and then we can go for another supply. We can go in a few minutes.'

I snort. 'You're not going with me. You're a little girl.'

Kalika is unmoved. 'I will come with you. You will need me.'

I pause. 'Do you know that for sure?'

'Yes.'

'I don't believe you.'

Kalika loses her smile. 'I won't lie to you, Mother, if you don't lie to me.'

'Don't give me orders. You are to do what I say at all times. Is that clear?'

She nods. 'As long as you don't lie to me.' She adds, as if it were related, 'How is Paula doing?'

Her question confuses me. Kalika has never met Paula. How would I explain that I have given birth to a child and that she has grown to five years of age, all in a month? Of course, I have talked about Paula with Ray. Perhaps Kalika was listening.

'Why do you ask?' I say.

Kalika glances at Ray. 'I am curious about her. She means a lot to you.'

'She's my friend. She's doing fine. One day you will meet her.'

'Do you promise?'

I hesitate. 'We'll see.' I throw off the covers and put my feet on the floor. 'We can go out now, if you insist. But we're not disturbing Eric anymore.'

Kalika puts a hand on my leg. It is still a small hand but I have to wonder if I would be able to stand if she didn't want me to. I doubt it, and do not try to brush her fingers away.

It is a terrible thing to be afraid of one's own daughter.

'I will take only a little of his blood,' she repeats.

'How much?'

'Eight ounces.'

'That is not a little, not for him. He is weak, don't you care?'

Kalika is thoughtful. When she gets that way, she stares at the ground. I have no idea what she looks for. Her eyes close halfway, and her breathing seems to halt. The overall effect is disturbing. Finally she looks up.

'I care,' she says. 'But not in the way you mean.'

I am curious. She is still an enigma to me. 'What do you mean?'

She shakes her head. 'I cannot explain, Mother.'

Kalika leaves me to get dressed. Knocking lightly on Eric's door, I step in his room. I have not been able to untie him as I had hoped. As his strength has failed, his behaviour has become more desperate. He thinks only of escape, or of his own impending death. I wish I could release him. An unhappy bundle of nerves stuffed in a stale corner, he twitches as I step into the room.

'No,' he moans. 'I can't.'

I kneel by his side. 'I need just a little. Less than last time.'

He weeps. 'Why?'

'You know I can't tell you why. But it will be over soon, Eric, I promise. I'm going out right now to – to get someone else.'

He shakes his head sadly as he stares up at the ceiling. 'I'm not stupid. You're never going to let me go. You're going to keep me here till I die.'

'No.'

He speaks with passion. 'Yes. You're evil. You're a

vampire. You have to kill me to keep your evil ways secret.'

His words hurt. 'I'm not a vampire. I don't take this blood for myself.'

He is not listening. He continues to sob but grows more animated. 'You're some monster from another planet. You're going to rip me open and eat my guts. You're going to have a glass of wine and have my guts all over your face, dripping on your clothes, on the floor . . .' He raises his voice. 'You're going to eat me alive!'

'Shh.'

'You're an alien monster!'

'Eric!'

'Help! The monster's got me! The aliens are coming!'

I am forced to strike him hard in the face to shut him up. My reflexes are still excellent, my martial art skills sharp. I believe I break his nose. Yet he continues to moan softly as I tighten the tourniquet. After I have drained away eight ounces – I know Kalika will count them – he dozes, probably out of sheer loss of blood. I kiss the top of his head before I leave the room.

'You will go home, Eric,' I whisper. 'I am not a monster.'

While Kalika has her breakfast, I dress in my bedroom, in black leather pants, a tight leather coat. Ray sits up in bed. I do not need to turn to feel his eyes on me.

'Are you going out?' he asks.

'Yes. You know why.'

'Yes. You've waited too long anyway.'

'It's not an enjoyable task, you know, finding people to kill.'

'Eric's still alive.'

'Barely.'

'Find someone you don't like. A criminal, a rapist – you used to specialize in them if I remember correctly.'

I turn on him. 'I may not be able to handle a criminal or rapist nowadays, or does that concern you, my love?'

He shrugs. 'Take your pistol. It has a silencer on it. Just get someone you're not going to go to pieces over every time you have to take blood.'

I speak with thinly disguised bitterness. 'You didn't answer my question, my love. But I suppose that is answer enough. You know I enjoy this little family we have here. A gorgeous daughter who is a medical and historical first, and a supposedly loving boyfriend who has forgotten what the words *friend* and *love* mean. I mean, you've got to admit, five thousand years of intense experience has really helped me create the perfect domestic environment. Wouldn't you agree?'

He is unimpressed by my outburst. 'You create what you want. You always have. If you don't like it, you can always leave.'

I snort. 'Leave you with Kalika! She would starve in a day.'

'I doubt that Kalika will need either of us soon. She's not a normal child, you know.' He adds, 'Not like Paula's child will be.'

I stop. 'Why did you say that?'

He ignores me. 'When is her baby due exactly? Soon?'

I frown. Why were they both dropping remarks about Paula? 'She's not having a baby anymore,' I say carefully. 'She lost it.'

He waves his hand. 'Yeah, right, she got kicked by a donkey.'

A donkey, I think. 'Yeah, that is right.' I turn away. 'Seymour was right about you.'

Ray is instantly alert. 'You spoke to him. When did you speak to him?'

I reach for my black boots. 'None of your business.'

'What did he say about me?'

I glare at him. 'He said that Eddie Fender's blood has warped your mind. He told me not to trust you, which was probably good advice.'

Ray relaxes. 'Good old Seymour. Did you invite him down for a pleasant evening of food and conversation?'

I have my boots on and stalk out the door. 'He is not interested in our problems,' I lie. 'He has better things to do with his time.'

But Ray's final remark makes me pause outside the door.

'I hope you didn't tell him about Kalika. I really hope you didn't.'

I glance over my shoulder. 'Of course not. He would never have believed me if I had.'

Ray just nods and smiles.

13 ~

Kalika drives with me to a club in Hollywood. It is one in the morning but the place is still hopping. What I'm supposed to do with my daughter, I'm not sure. It is she who suggests she hide under a blanket in the backseat until I bring out whoever it is who is to be our next barrel of blood. As she crawls under the blanket, she peers up at me with her serious dark blue eyes.

'You'll be warm enough?' I ask.

'I am never cold,' she says.

'If you want, you can sleep. Just don't make any noise when I return to the car. I'll take care of everything.' I glance at the crowded parking lot. 'But I won't be able to knock him out here.'

'Take him to a secluded place,' Kalika says. 'I will help you.'

'I told you, I don't want your help.'

Kalika does the unexpected then. She reaches up and kisses me on the lips. 'Be careful, Mother. You are not who you used to be.'

Her kiss warms me, her words give me a chill. 'You know what I used to be?'

'Yes. He told me.'

'Ray?'

'Yes.'

'How come you never call him Father?'

'You call him Ray. I call him Ray.'

'But he calls me Sita.'

'Do you want me to call you Sita?'

'No, it doesn't matter.' I pause. 'Do you like Ray?'

She shrugs. 'How I feel – I can't explain to you at this time.'

'Why not?'

'You are not ready to hear.'

'When will I be ready to hear?'

'Soon.'

'You know this?'

She pulls the blanket over her head. 'I know many things, Mother.'

The music is loud as I enter the club, the strobe lights flashing, unnatural thunder and psychedelic solar flares to match the scrambled brains of the alcohol-saturated clientele. I am, of course, a superb dancer, even without my vampire strength. Without looking around, I leap onto the dance floor and wait for my daughter's next meal to come to me. Guilt makes me less discriminating. Let destiny decide who is to suffer, I will not.

A man about thirty, with an expensive sports coat and a thin black mustache joins me within a few minutes. His speech is educated; he could be an Ivy League graduate, a young lawyer with something profitable on the side. His watch is a Rolex, his single gold earring studded with a carat diamond. He is not handsome but his face is likeable. He speaks smoothly.

'Mind if I butt in?' he asks.

I smile, whirling, my hair in my eyes. 'There's no one to butt out.'

He chuckles. 'Hey, you're a real dancer.'

'You're not bad yourself. What's your name?'

'Billy. You?'

'Cynthia. But you can call me Cindy.'

He grins, he's having a good time. 'I'll call you whatever you want.'

After twenty minutes on the floor, he buys me a couple of drinks. We catch our breath over them at the bar. I was right, he's a lawyer but he insists he's an honest one.

'I don't represent shmucks and I don't fudge my billing hours,' he says proudly, sipping his Bloody Mary, my drink of choice when I am on the prowl. I am already on my second. The alcohol soothes my nerves, although I don't suppose it sharpens my reflexes. At my waist, above my butt and beneath my leather jacket, I carry my pistol and silencer. But I know I won't need it on Billy. He will go the way of Eric, to endless misery. Guilt hangs over my head but I keep it away with a stiff umbrella of denial.

'What firm are you with?' I ask.

'Gibson and Pratch. They're in Century City. I live in the valley. The traffic's hell coming over the San Diego Freeway in the morning. What do you do?'

'I'm a music teacher,' I say.

'Cool. What instrument do you play?'

'Piano, some violin.'

'Wow, that's incredible. I have an expensive piano that was left to me by my rich uncle. I've always meant to take lessons, but never got around to it.' He pauses and then has a brilliant idea. God inspires it. I know what it is; he hasn't been able to take his eyes off my body. 'Hey, will you play me something on my piano?'

I laugh and look around. 'Did you bring it with you?'

'No, at my place. It doesn't take long to get there at this time of night.'

I hesitate. 'Like you say, Billy, it's late. I have to get up in the morning.'

'Nah! You're a teacher. You call your students and tell them when you want to see them. Really, we can go in my car. I've got a brand-new Jag.'

I'm impressed. 'I love Jags.' I glance uneasily at my watch, playing the role to the hilt. 'OK, but I'm going to have to follow you there. That way I can head straight back to my place after your song.'

Billy is pleased as he sets down his drink. 'I'll drive slowly. I won't lose you.'

Kalika is asleep when I return to the car. Her soft rhythmic breathing follows me as I steam onto the freeway and chase Billy's Jag into the valley. He has lied to me – he drives like a maniac.

My plan is simple. I will knock him out the second we get inside, then load him into my trunk. He looks like he's been drinking all night, an easy mark. He won't even know what hit him.

Kalika is still asleep when we reach Billy's place.

I leave my gun in the glove compartment.

Billy's house is modest, considering his new car. The driveway is cracked, the landscaping neglected. He lives in a cul-de-sac. His car disappears into the automatic garage as I park in the street. A moment later he is on the front porch, waving to me. Making sure Kalika is resting comfortably, I get out and walk toward Billy, my boots clicking on the asphalt and concrete. Billy thinks he's in for a night of sex and more sex. His grin as he greets me belongs to a sixteen-year-old. I'm not surprised when he kisses me the moment we're inside with the door closed. His mouth is sweet with the taste of alcohol, his groping hands moist with the thrill of seduction. He presses me against the wall and I have to turn my head to catch my breath.

'Hold on a second, Billy,' I protest. 'You haven't even

shown me the house. And where's your piano?'

He stares at me with a gleam in his eye. 'I don't have a piano.'

'What do you mean. You said your uncle . . .'

'I don't have an uncle,' he interrupts.

Right then I smell it. The odor is faint, probably something most young women would miss, but I have had extensive experience with this smell. I don't need supernatural nostrils to identify it. Somewhere in Billy's house, perhaps buried beneath his bed, perhaps cemented into his bathroom floor, is one or more dead bodies. My best estimate as I look deeper into his manic eyes is that it is more than one. I curse myself for being such a fool, for being caught off guard. Certainly as a vampire I would have heard his lies a mile away.

Careful, I let none of my insights show on my face.

'That's all right, Billy,' I say. 'I don't know how to play piano anyway.'

He is dizzy with pleasure. 'You lied to me?'

'We lied to each other.'

There is a single metal click. The sound is very specific, the snap of a switchblade. His right arm begins to slash upward. He is close to me, though, perhaps too close. Giving him a nudge in the chest, I yank my right knee up as hard as I can, catching him clean in the groin. But Billy must have balls of steel. My blow stuns him but he doesn't double up in agony. His switchblade continues its terrifying course toward my throat. Only by twisting to the side at the last second do I manage to avoid having my jugular severed. But even though I momentarily break free, the blade catches the tip of my left shoulder and slices through my leather jacket. The knife is incredibly sharp; it opens a four-inch gash in my tender flesh. Blood spurts from my body as I stagger into the centre of the living room.

How I long for my pistol right then.

Billy limps toward me, holding his bloody knife in his right hand, his bruised crotch in his left. He grins again but he is no longer a happy-go-lucky serial killer.

'You are a spunky little bitch,' he says.

I grab a vase of flowers and cock it back in my right hand. 'Stop! I'll scream if you don't.'

He laughs. 'My nearest neighbours are all old and hard of hearing. This house is completely soundproof. Scream all you want, Cindy.'

'My name's not Cindy. Your's isn't Billy.'

He is surprised. 'Who are you then?'

'Why should I tell you?'

'Because I want to know before you die.'

I harden my voice. 'I am Sita, of the ancient past. I am older than I look and I have dealt with scum like you before. It is you who will die this night, and I don't care what your name is.'

He charges, and he moves fast for a human. The vase, of course, I throw at him merely to upset his balance. But he seems to know that ahead of time; he ducks and prepares for my real blow. I am already in the air, however, lashing out with my right foot, the heel of my boot, aiming for the sensitive spot on his jaw that professional boxers covet. One hard punch will put him out cold.

Unfortunately my human muscles fail me once again. I am short on the reach. As a result my devastating kick barely contacts his jaw. The blow backs him up, cuts him even, but it by no means puts him down. Wiping at his face, he has hatred in his eyes.

'Where did you learn this stuff?' he demands.

'Through a correspondence course,' I snap as I begin to circle. Now I have lost the element of surprise. He watches my feet as he stalks me with his knife. Someone has trained him as well, I see. He does not lunge carelessly, but plots his strikes. One such swipe of his knife slashes open the back of my right hand. The pain is electric, burning, my blood is everywhere. Still, I maintain my balanced stance, circling, searching for an opening. He is skilled at defense; however, he never stops moving his arms. I know I can't let him catch my leg. He would probably saw off my foot, and make me watch.

Then he makes a mistake. Going for my eyes, he subtly telegraphs his intention. My initial reaction is simple – I duck. Then I leap up just after the knife swishes over my head and sweep his lower legs with my left foot. The move is kung fu, very old and effective. Billy, or whoever the hell he is, topples to the floor. I am on him in an instant. When he tries to rise, I kick him in the face, then again in the chest. He smashes into his coffee table and his knife bounces on the blood-stained carpet and I kick it away. Lying on his back, breathing hard, he stares at me in amazement. Standing over him, I feel the old satisfaction of triumph. I step on his left wrist and pin his arm to the floor.

'I actually can play the piano,' I say. 'If you had an instrument here, I would play Mozart's *Requiem* for the dead after I stuff you in a closet.'

He still has a weird gleam in his eye. 'Is your name really Sita?'

'Yes.'

'How old are you? You're older than you look, huh?'

'Yes. How old are you and how do you want to die?'

He grins. 'I'm not going to die.'

'No?'

'No.' And with that, before I can react, he pulls out a snub-nose silver revolver and points it at my head. 'Not tonight, Sita.'

Once again I am furious at myself, for not taking him out immediately when he was helpless. I know what my problem is. I am used to playing with my victims, a luxury I can no longer afford now that I am mortal. There is no way I can dodge the bullet he can send hurtling into my brain. It is his game now. Taking my foot off his wrist, I back up a couple of steps. He gets up slowly and guards me carefully. He is not one to repeat a mistake, as the odor in his house testifies.

'How many girls have you killed here?' I ask.

'Twelve.' He grins. 'You're going to be lucky number thirteen.'

'Thirteen is traditionally an unlucky number,' I remind him.

He gestures with his gun. 'On your knees. Keep your hands on top of your head. No sudden moves.'

I do as he says. Like I have a lot of choice. The blood from my hand wound drips into my hair and over my face. Like those of a full-fledged vampire, my tears are once again dark red. My situation is clearly desperate, and I cannot think of a clear course of action. He ties my wrists behind my back with nylon cord. Although I can work my way out of any knot, even with my current strength, he complicates my dilemma by redoing the knots several times over. When he is finished he crouches in front of me and takes out his switchblade. He plays with my hair with the tip of the blade, with my eyes even, letting the silver razor brush the surface of the whites. I won't be surprised if he gouges one of my eyes out and eats it.

'You're so beautiful,' he says.

'Thank you.'

'All my girls have been beautiful.' He leans close, his breath on my face, his knife now inside my right nostril. 'You know, I never met a girl like you. Not only can you fight, you are totally fearless.'

I smile sweetly. 'Yeah, I could be your partner. Why don't you untie me and we can talk about it?'

He laughs. 'See! That's exactly what I mean. You

make jokes in the face of death.' He slides the knife a little farther up my nose and loses his smile. A typical serial killer, moody as hell. 'But some of your jokes aren't that funny. Some of them annoy me. I don't like to be annoyed.'

I swallow thickly. 'I can understand that.'

He pokes the inside of my nose and a narrow line of blood pours over my mouth and down my throat. His eyes are inches from mine, his mouth almost close enough to lick my blood. I am afraid he will do that next, and not like the taste. It hurts to have a switchblade up my right nostril. Still, I cannot think of a way out of my situation. Yet I find I am more concerned about Kalika, asleep in the car, than I am about myself. Truly I am a good mother. It was only my love for my daughter that brought me into this evil place. Krishna will understand.

I feel I will be seeing him soon.

'You know what I don't like about you?' Billy asks. 'It's your cockiness. I had a cocky girlfriend in high school once. Her name was Sally and she was so sure of herself.' He pauses. 'Until she lost her nose and her lips. A girl with only half a face is never a smart mouth.'

I wisely keep my mouth shut.

There is a knock at the front door.

Billy pulls the knife higher, still inside my nose, forcing my head back. 'Don't make a sound,' he whispers. 'There is dying all at once and there is dying piece by piece. Believe me, I can take a week to kill you if you try to get their attention.'

My eyelashes flash up and down. Yes, I understand and agree.

I know who is at the door. The person knocks again.

Billy is sweating. Clearly he fears some noise has escaped his soundproof spider's lair and that a neighbour has called the police. All he can do is wait and worry. But he is not kept in suspense long. The door slowly opens and a beautiful little girl with stunning dark hair and large black-blue eyes pokes her head inside.

'Mother,' Kalika says. 'Are you OK?'

Billy is astounded and immensely relieved. He lowers his switchblade. 'Is that your daughter?' he asks.

'Yes.'

'What is she doing here?'

'She came with me. She was sleeping in the car.'

'Well, I'll be goddamned. I didn't know you had a daughter.'

'There are a few things about me you don't know.' I glance at Kalika, wondering what I should do: be a good mother, warn her to get away, or remain silent and try to get out of this hell hole alive. Honestly, I don't know how quick Kalika is, exactly how strong she is. But a vampire her size and her age could take Billy. I speak carefully, 'I am not OK, darling.'

'I told you,' she replies.

Billy withdraws his knife and stands in front of me. He is bleeding as well, and he has plenty of my blood on him. He holds his messy knife in his right hand and he has his shiny revolver tucked in his belt. Plus the light in his eyes is radioactive. He looks as trustworthy as Jack the Ripper on PCP high. Yet he gestures to Kalika to come closer, as if he were Santa Claus anxious to hear her wish list.

'Come here, darling,' he says in a sweet voice.

And she comes, slowly, observing every blessed detail: the composition of the floor, how Billy stands, the height of the ceiling, the arrangement of the furniture – moving precisely the way an experienced vampire would move while closing in for the kill. Her arms hang loose by her sides, her legs slightly apart, well-balanced, and she is up on her toes so that she can move either way fast. Billy senses there is something odd about her. When she is ten feet from him, he drops his smile. For my part, I watch in wonder and terror. Only then do I realize the full extent of my love for my daughter. I would rather die a dozen times over than have anything happen to her.

'What's your name, sweetie?' Billy asks when she stops directly in front of him. His voice is uneasy, perhaps as a result of the power of her stare, which is now locked on his face. Kalika tilts her head slightly to one side, ignoring me for the moment.

'Kalika,' she says.

He frowns. 'What kind of name is that, child?'

'It's a Vedic name. It's who I am.'

'What does it mean?' he asks.

'It has many meanings. Most of them are secret.' She finally gestures to me. 'You've hurt my mother. She's bleeding.'

Billy gives an exaggerated sigh. 'I know that Kalika, and I'm sorry. But it was your mother who hurt me first. I only hurt her back to defend myself.'

Kalika doesn't blink. 'You are lying. You are not a good man. But your blood is good. I will drink it in a moment.' She pauses. 'You can put your knife and your gun down now. You will not need them.'

Billy is having a night of amazement. His face breaks into a wolfish grin and he looks down at me. 'What kind of nonsense have you been teaching this child, Sita?'

I shrug. 'She watches too much TV.'

Billy snorts. 'God, I can't believe this family.' He takes a step toward my daughter, his knife still in his right hand. 'Come here, girl. I'm putting you in the other room. I have business with your mother that can't wait. But I'll let you out in a little while, if you behave yourself.' Billy holds out his free hand. 'Come, give me your hand.'

Kalika innocently reaches up and takes his hand. She even allows his fingers to close around her tiny digits. But then, in a move too swift for human eyes to properly follow, she grabs his other hand, twists his wrist at an impossible angle, and rams the knife into his stomach. Literally the blade is sunk up to the hilt. An expression of surprise and grief swallows Billy's face as he stares down at what she has done to him. Slowly, as if in a dream, he lets go of the knife. It is obvious his right wrist is broken. Blood gushes over his pants and Kalika stares at it with her first sign of pleasure.

'I am hungry,' she says.

Billy gasps for air but finally he is getting the idea that he is in mortal danger, that he might be, in fact, already screwed. Summoning his failing strength, he makes a swipe for Kalika's head. But she is not standing where she was an instant before, and he misses. She is her mother's daughter. Twice she kicks with her right foot, with her shiny black shoes that I bought for her at the mall, and the cartilage in both his joints explodes. Falling to his shattered knees, he lets out a pitiful scream.

'How can you do this to me?' he cries.

Kalika steps over and grabs him by his hair and pulls his head back, exposing his throat. The calm on her face is eerie even for me to see.

'If you understood the full meaning of my name,' she says, 'you would have no need to ask.'

Billy dies piece by piece, drop by drop.

Kalika satisfies herself before she releases me.

Even I, Sita the Damned, cannot bear to watch.

14 ⁓

The following week Kalika attains full maturity, approximately twenty years of age, about the same age I was when I was changed into a vampire. At this point her growth seems to halt. I am not surprised. It is a fact that a human being is at his or her greatest strength, mentally and physically, just out of his or her teens. Certainly Kalika is very powerful, but how powerful I'm not sure. Except for the incident with Billy, she never demonstrates her abilities in front of me. One thing is sure, though – she no longer needs me to bring her lunch. Now she leaves the house for long stretches of time – on foot and at night. When she returns, I don't ask where she's been or who she's been with. I don't want to know.

Of course that's a lie. I scrutinize the papers each day for reports of unexplained murders. Yet I find none, and it makes me wonder.

The police have yet to find Billy – what is left of him. I know it is only a matter of time. I hope they will uncover his victims as well.

My hand and shoulder are still bandaged. I did not allow myself the luxury of a doctor and hospital, but I did manage to sew myself up fairly well. Still, I know I will be scarred for life.

The change in my daughter's eating habits means that I no longer need to keep Eric locked in the spare bedroom. Unfortunately, I can't figure out a way to let him go and keep him from running straight to the police. Simply moving to another city, or even another state, is not a solution. Well, it would probably help, but I don't want to move, not until Paula has her baby. Kalika and Ray don't want to move either. They have stated their opinion many times.

So I keep Eric locked up, but have stopped taking his blood. It had been my hope that this would cheer him up, and he'd be able to gain back his strength. But Eric is now deep in the throes of depression and won't eat a bite.

'Come on, Eric,' I say as I offer him a hamburger and fries. 'This is a McDonald's Big Mac and their golden delicious french fries, large size. I've even brought you a vanilla shake.' I touch his head as he refuses to even look at me. He has lost over thirty pounds since meeting me, and his skin is a pasty yellow. There are black circles under his eyes, from his grief, and from the times I hit him. His nose is still broken; he has trouble breathing, especially tied up as he is. I add gently, 'You've got to eat something. You're just wasting away in here.'

'Then why don't you let me go like you promised?' he asks quietly. 'I'm sick – you know I'm really sick.'

'I am going to let you go. Just as soon as I figure out the logistics of the release. You understand I have to worry about you talking to the police. I have to be long gone from this place before you are freed.'

'I won't talk to the police. I just want to go home.'

'I know you do. It won't be long now.' I push the hamburger his way. 'Have a bite, just for me, and I'll have some of your fries. We can pretend we're in that coffee shop you took me to on our first date.'

That is probably not the best thing to say. He begins to sob again. 'I thought you were a nice girl. I just wanted to talk to you. I didn't know you would hurt me and take all my blood.'

'But I stopped taking your blood. Things are looking up. Soon you'll see your mom and dad. And they'll be so excited to see you. Just think of that, Eric, and try to keep a positive attitude. Imagine what an incredible homecoming you're going to have. You'll be interviewed by every TV station in the country. You can even make your story more exciting than it really was. You can say how a whole horde of vampires tortured you night and day and used your blood for satanic rituals. The media will love that – they're really into the devil. You'll be a celebrity, a hero, and after that you'll probably get lots of dates. The girls will come to you. Heroes are sexy. You won't have to go looking for girls in the park.'

My pep talk is wasted on him. He stares at me with bloodshot eyes and sniffles. 'Even if you wanted to let me go, she'd never let you.'

I pause. 'Who's she?'

'The one you've been giving my blood to.'

'I don't know what you're talking about.'

'I've seen her. You serve her and you don't know it, but I know she's not human. I've seen her *eyes*, the red fire deep inside. She drinks human blood and she's evil.' He nods like a man who's been granted a vision by God and won't be convinced otherwise. 'After she kills me and eats my guts, she's going to kill you and eat your brains.'

Well, I don't know what to say to that.

Placing the hamburger in his lap, I leave the room.

Ray is sitting in the living room. Kalika is in the backyard, sitting in the full lotus and meditating with her eyes closed in the bright sun, wearing a one-piece black bathing suit. She sits on a white towel in the centre of the lawn and doesn't move a fraction of an inch, or even seem to breathe. This is a new habit of hers, but I am afraid to ask what she mediates on. Perhaps her own name, or the secret forms of it. They are reputed to be powerful mantras.

Ray looks up at me. 'Is he eating?'

'No.'

'What are we going to do with him?'

I sit on the couch across from Ray. 'I don't know. Let him go.'

'We can't let him go. Not now.'

'Then we'll let him go later,' I say.

Ray shakes his head. 'I think that's a bad idea. It will require us to cover our tracks. He'll just give the authorities information we don't want them to have. Think about it a minute before you dismiss it. You said yourself that the government might still be searching for you. What are they going to think when they hear the story of a young man who was held captive by a beautiful blond woman who systematically drained his blood? They'll put two and two together, and they'll start a manhunt for you unlike anything that's been seen in this country. Remember, they still want that vampire blood.'

I speak in a flat voice. 'What is it you want me to think about?'

Ray hesitates. 'Just getting rid of the problem.'

'You mean kill Eric and bury him in the backyard?'

'I don't think we should bury him there. But, yes, I don't see how we can let him go and expect to remain free ourselves.'

I smile as I stare at him. It is one of those smiles a salesperson gives to a customer. 'You know, something just occured to me.'

'What?'

'I don't know who you are. Oh, you look like Ray. You talk like him and you even have his memories. But I honestly don't know who you are.'

'Sita, be serious. You have to face reality.'

'That's exactly what I'm doing. The Ray I met and loved would never talk about killing an innocent young man. No matter what the consequences to himself. The idea would never even enter his mind. And one more thing, I've been watching our daughter the last few days and I swear she doesn't look a bit like you. You don't share a single feature. How can that be?'

Ray snorts. 'You're the one who should be able to answer that question. You're the one who got pregnant.'

'I wish I could answer it. I believe if I could, many other questions would be answered as well.'

'Such as?'

I lose my smile. 'I don't know how much I should tell you. I don't trust you, and I'm not going to kill Eric. We'll leave here before it comes to that. I don't care if he does set the government on my tail.'

'You will not leave here until Paula has her baby.'

'Paula's baby is not the topic of this conversation. Also, I notice you're not responding to my accusations. You're not even trying to defend yourself.'

'They're so ridiculous. What can I say?' He glances down the hall. 'Eric has to die, and the sooner the better.'

'Have you shared this with Kalika?'

'Yes.'

'Does she agree with you?'

Ray is evasive. 'She didn't say one way or the other.'

'She never says much.' I straighten up and point a finger at Ray. 'But let's make one thing perfectly clear. If you so much as harm a single hair on Eric's head, you'll regret it.'

Ray is amused. 'You're not a vampire anymore. You have nothing to back up your threats.'

I'm not given a chance to respond. By chance, if anything is chance, a police car pulls into our driveway at that moment. The two officers are almost to the door when I remember that I have not replaced Eric's gag. I've been letting him be without it for the last few days. He knows the penalty for crying out.

Yet if he hears the police in the house, what will he do?

Ray runs into the back room, not into Eric's. I answer the door. A blond-haired cop and a dark-haired one. The handsome black one holds a picture of Eric in his hand. Wonderful.

'Hello,' he says. 'I'm Officer Williams and this is my partner, Officer Kent. We're canvassing the neighbourhood for information concerning the whereabouts of this young man. His name is Eric Hawkins. He vanished close to three weeks ago.' He pauses. 'May we come in?'

'Sure.' I open the door wider. As they step inside, I

ask, 'Was this guy from around here? Excuse me, please, have a seat.'

Kent and Williams settle themselves on my couch. Williams does the talking. He is the leader of the two – his eyes are everywhere, searching for clues. Well-muscled Kent sits content like a comfortable jock after a hard game. I plop down across from them.

'Actually, Eric lives some distance from here,' Williams says. 'But we have a report from one of your neighbours that a guy who fit his description was seen entering your house. Also, this same neighbour believes she saw Eric's car parked out in front of your house on the day he disappeared.'

'So you're not just canvassing the neighbourhood. You've come here specifically to see me?' I gesture to Eric's picture. 'I've never seen this guy in my life.'

Williams is grave. 'We also have a description from two guys that Eric was playing basketball with on the day he disappeared. They say he left Scott Park in the company of a young woman who matches your description.'

I raise my hand, palm out. 'Hold on! You do not have *my* description. I don't even know where Scott Park is. What exactly did these guys say?'

Williams consults notes jotted on a piece of folded paper. 'That he left the park in the company of a beautiful blond girl approximately eighteen to twenty-one. Her hair was long, like yours.'

I'm not impressed. 'There are literally tens of

thousands of cute blond girls with long hair in Southern California.'

'That is true ma'am,' Williams says. 'You're just a lead we're checking out.' He pauses. 'Did you have a guest with a blue Honda Civic park in your driveway three weeks ago?'

'I can't remember. Lots of friends drop by. They have all kinds of cars.'

'Do you have a friend who looks like Eric?' Williams asks. 'Someone your neighbour might have mistakenly identified as Eric.'

I shrug. 'I have a couple of friends who resemble him superficially.'

Williams glances in the backyard. Kalika was no longer there. 'Would you mind if we looked around?' he asks.

'Do you have a search warrant?'

Williams is cagey. 'We just stopped by to ask a few questions.'

'Then I certainly do mind. Look, I live here with my boyfriend and a girlfriend. We're not kidnappers, and I resent your implying that we are.'

Kent speaks for the first time. 'Then why won't you let us look around?'

'That's my choice.'

'What happened to your hand?' Kent asks, pointing to the bandage that covers Billy's second good swing at me.

'I cut it on a broken glass,' I say.

'Hello?' Kalika says softly as she enters the living room from the direction of the hall, a towel tied around her waist over her bathing suit. 'Is there a problem?'

'No,' I say quickly. 'These men were just leaving.'

Williams stands and holds out the picture of Eric for Kalika to see. 'Have you ever seen this young man?'

Kalika studies the photograph. Then looks my way with a cool smile. 'Yes.'

That's my daughter. She would talk about Billy next.

'Where did you see him?' Williams demands, casting me a hard look.

Kalika is thoughtful. 'I can show you the place. It's not far from here. Would you like to take me there?'

I clear my throat. 'That's not necessary.'

'I don't mind,' Kalika says. 'It's not a problem.'

I lower my head. Arguing with her in front of these men will not help.

'Don't be gone long,' I say.

Kalika leaves with the officers. She doesn't even bother to change out of her suit. The men don't seem to mind. Kalika is more stunning than her mother, and they can't take their eyes off her. I pray they don't take their eyes off her, and that they don't have families. It is them I am worried about now.

Paula calls ten minutes after Kalika leaves.

She's in labour. I'll be there in two minutes, I promise.

Running out the door, Ray stops me. 'Call us when the baby's been born.'

I step past him. I haven't told him who was on the phone but I suppose it shows on my face. 'I'll think about it.'

He speaks to my back as I go down the steps. 'Remember, you promised Kalika you would let her see the baby. Don't forget.'

I ignore him, or wish I could.

15

Paula is having contractions in my car when I decide we are not going to the local hospital where her doctor is waiting. I turn left and head for the freeway. Paula is in pain, and in shock when I floor it.

'What are you doing ?' she cries.

'I don't like your hospital,' I say. 'It's ill equipped. I'm taking you to a much nicer one. Don't worry, I have money, I'll pay.'

'But they're expecting me! I called before I left!'

'It doesn't matter. This hospital is only thirty minutes away.' It is actually over forty minutes away. 'You'll like it, we can get you a room with a view of the mountains.'

'But I'm not going on vacation! I'm going to have a baby! I don't need a room with a view!'

'It's always nice to have a view,' I reply, patting her leg. 'Don't worry, Paula, I know what I'm doing.'

This baby – I don't know what's special about it. I don't know why Ray and Kalika are obsessed with it. But I do know they are the last people on earth who are going to see it.

The hospital I take her to, the famous Cedar Sinai, is surprised to see us. But the staff jumps to attention when I wave cash and gold credit cards in their faces. What a terrible thing it is that the quality of emergency care is often determined by money. Holding Paula's hand, I help her fill out the paperwork and then we are both ushered into a delivery room. The baby appears to be coming fast. A nurse asks me to put on a gown and a mask. She is nice, and lets me stay with Paula without asking questions.

Paula is now drenched in sweat and in the throes of *real* pain, which I have often been intimate with. An anesthesiologist appears and wants to give her Demerol to take the edge off the contractions, maybe an epidural to partially numb her lower body. But Paula shakes her head.

'I don't need anything,' she says. 'I have my friend with me.'

The anesthesiologist doesn't approve, but I am touched by the remark. I have become so human. Even sentimental nonsense has meaning to me. Paula's hand is sweaty in mine but I have seldom felt a softer touch.

'I am with you,' I say. 'I will stay with you.'

The baby fakes us all out. It is eight hours later, at night, when the child finally makes an appearance – a handsome male of seven pounds five ounces, with more hair than most babies, and large blue eyes that I assume will fade to brown over the next few months. I am the first to hold the baby – other than the delivering physician – and I whisper in his ear the ancient mystical symbol that is supposed to remind the child of its true essence or soul.

'Vak,' I say over and over again. It is practically the first sound the infant hears because he did not come out screaming, and the doctor and the others fell strangely silent at the moment of his birth. Indeed, it was almost as if time stood still for a moment.

Vak is a name for Saraswati, the Goddess of speech, the Mother above the head who brings the white light to saints and prophets. The baby smiles at me as I say Vak. Already, I think, I am in love with him. Wiping him gently off and handing him to Paula, I wonder who his father is.

'Is he all right?' she asks, exhausted from the effort but nevertheless blissful.

'Yes, he's perfect,' I say, and laugh softly, feeling something peculiar in my words, an intuition, perhaps, of things to come and a life to be lived. 'What are you going to call him?' I ask.

Paula cuddles her child near her face and the baby reaches out and touches her eyes. 'I don't know,' she says. 'I have to think about it.'

'Didn't you think about a name before?' a nurse asks.

Paula appears puzzled. 'No. Never.'

Death is a part of life. Calling home to see how Kalika has faired with the two police, I know the grave and the nursery sit on opposite sides of the same wall. That they are connected by a dark closet, where skeletons are hidden, and where the past is sometimes able to haunt the present. All who are born die, Krishna said. All who die will be reborn. Neither is supposed to be a cause for grief. Yet even I, with all my vast experience extending over fifty centuries, am not prepared for what is to happen next.

Kalika answers the phone. It is ten at night.

'Hello, Mother,' she says.

'You knew it was me?'

'Yes.'

'How are you? Did you just get home?'

'No. I have been home awhile. Where are you?'

I hesitate. 'Ray must have told you.'

'Yes. You're at the hospital?'

'Yes. How did you get on with the police?'

'Fine.'

I have trouble asking the next question. 'Are they all right?'

'You don't have to worry about them, Mother.'

I momentarily close my eyes. 'Did you kill them?'

Kalika is cool. 'It is not your concern. The baby has been born. I want to see it.'

How does she know the baby has been born? 'No,' I

say. 'Paula's still in labor. You can't see the baby now.'

Kalika is a long time in responding. 'What hospital are you at?'

'The local one. Let me speak to Ray a moment.'

'Ray is not here. What is the name of this hospital?'

'But he seldom goes out. Are you sure he's not there?'

'He's not here. I'm telling you the truth, Mother. You will tell me the truth. What is the name of the hospital where you're at?'

Even as a human, I do not like to be pushed around. 'All right, I will tell you. If you tell me why it is so important to you to see this baby?'

'You wouldn't understand.'

'I gave birth to you. I am older than you know. I understand more than you think. Try me.'

'It is not your concern.'

'Fine. Then it is also not my concern to tell you where the child is. Let me speak to Ray.'

Kalika speaks softly, but there is tension in her words. 'He's not here, I told you. I don't lie, Mother.' She pauses. 'But Eric is here.'

I hear my heart pound. 'What do you mean?'

'He's sitting on the couch beside me. He's still tied up but he's not gagged. Would you like to speak to him?'

I feel as if I stand on melting ice in a freezing river that flows into a black sea. A mist rises before me and the next moments are played out in shadow. There is no way I can second-guess Kalika because all of her actions – when judged by humans or vampires alike – are inexplicable. Perhaps it was a mistake to snap at her.

'Put him on,' I say.

There is a moment of fumbling. It sounds as if my daughter has momentarily covered the phone with her hand. Then the line is clear. Eric does not sound well.

'Hello?'

'Eric, it's me. Are you all right?'

He is breathing heavily, scared. 'I don't know. She . . . This person says you have to tell her something or something bad will happen to me.'

'Put her back on the line. Do it now!'

Another confused moment passes. But Eric remains on the line. 'She doesn't want to talk to you. She says you have to tell me which hospital you're in. She says if you lie she will know it, and then something *really* bad will happen to me.' Eric chokes with fear. 'Could you tell her the name of the hospital? Please? This girl – She's so strong. She picked me up with one hand and carried me out here.'

'Eric,' I say, 'try to convince her that I need to talk to her directly.'

I hear Eric speaking to Kalika. But Eric is forced to stay on the line. I imagine his arms and legs still bound, Kalika holding the phone up to his ear. The tears in his eyes – I can see them in my mind, and I hear the many vows I swore to him.

'But I can promise you you're not going to die. I swear this to you, Eric, and I keep my word.'

'You have to help me!' he cries. 'She has long nails, and she says she's going to open the veins in my neck unless you tell her what hospital it is. Ouch! She's touching me!'

'Tell her the hospital is called St Judes!'

'It's St Judes!' he screams. Another soul-shattering pause. 'She says you're lying! Oh God! Her nails!'

Sweat pours off my head. My heart is a jackhammer vibrating.

'Kalika!' I yell into the phone. 'Talk to me!'

'She keeps shaking her head!' Eric weeps. 'She's scratching my neck! Jesus help me!'

I fight to stay calm, and lose the fight. 'Eric, shove the phone in her face!'

'Oh God, I'm bleeding! She's cut my neck! The blood is gushing out! Help me!'

'Eric, tell her I'll tell her the name of the hospital! Tell her!'

He begins to choke. 'This can't be happening to me! I can't die! I don't want to die!'

Those are the last intelligible words he speaks. The rest – it goes on another two minutes – is slobbering sounds and pitiful weeping. It trails off into strangled gasps, then I must assume his heart has stopped beating. I sag against the wall of the hospital next to the place where the phone is attached. People stare at me from down the hall but I ignore them. Kalika lets me enjoy the silence. Another minute goes by before she returns to the phone.

'Then he should never have been born,' she says calmly. 'Is that what you wanted to tell him, Mother? Your famous quote.'

I am in shock. 'You,' I whisper.

'I want to see the baby, Mother,' she repeats.

'No.'

'What is the name of the hospital? Where is it located?'

'I would never tell you!' I cry. 'You're a monster!'

It is as if she smiles. I hear her unspoken mirth, somehow. Yet her voice remains flat. 'And what are you? What did Krishna say to you about vampires in Kali Yuga?'

I can only assume Ray explained my dialogue with Krishna to Kalika. It doesn't matter – I am not in the mood for philosophical discussions. There is an aching void inside me that I had always believed a daughter would fill. Well, the irony is bitter, for the real Kali has always been described as the abyss, and now the void inside me feels as if it stretches forever. Eric's death screams continue to reverberate inside my skull.

'I am human now,' I whisper. 'I don't kill unless I have to.'

'The same with me. This baby – you don't understand how I feel about it.'

'How *you* feel about it? You have no feelings, Daughter.'

'I will not argue. I will not repeat my questions. Answer now or you will regret it.'

'I will never answer to you again.'

Kalika doesn't hesitate. 'There is someone else here I want you to speak with. He also sits on the couch beside me. But I have gagged him. Just a moment and I will remove his gag.'

Oh no, I cringe. My demon child.

Seymour comes on the line. He strains to sound upbeat.

'Sita. What's happening?'

My voice is filled with agony. 'What are you doing there?'

'Your daughter called me six hours ago. She said she needed to speak to me. I think Ray gave her my number. You remember Ray and I used to be friends when we were both normal high school kids? I caught the first plane down. Your daughter met me at the airport.' He hesitates and probably glances at Eric's body. 'She seemed really friendly at first.'

'I told you not to come. I told you it was dangerous.'

'Yeah, but I was worried about you.'

'I understand. Is Ray there?'

'I haven't seen him.' Seymour coughs and I hear his fear. There is talking in the background. 'Your daughter says you're to tell me the name of the hospital where you are.'

'Or something bad will happen to you?'

'She didn't say that exactly, but I think it would be safe to bet that will be the case.' He pauses. 'She seems to know when you're lying.'

'She knows an awful lot.' Yet Kalika is unable to 'tune into' where I am. I find that curious, what with her incredible psychic abilities. 'Tell her I want to talk to her.'

I catch snatches of more mumbled conversation. Seymour remains on the line. 'She says you are to tell me the name and location of the hospital.' Seymour stops, and a note of desperation enters his voice. 'What she did to Eric – you'd have to have been here. She made the old you look like a Girl Scout.'

'I can imagine.' I think frantically. 'Tell her I'll make her a counter proposal. I'll bring the child to her in exactly twenty-four hours. At the end of the Santa Monica Pier at ten tomorrow night. Tell her if she so much as scratches you, she'll never see this baby, if she searches the entire globe.'

Seymour relays my offer. Kalika appears to listen patiently. Then the phone is covered and I imagine my daughter is talking to Seymour. A minute goes by. Finally Seymour returns.

'She wants to know why you need twenty-four hours?'

'Because the baby has to remain in an incubator for a day. Tell her that's normal hospital procedure.'

Seymour repeats what I say. He doesn't cover the phone this time but I still can't hear Kalika speak – her voice is too soft. I tire of this game. But there is a reason why my daughter doesn't let me talk to her directly at critical times. It heightens my helplessness, and her strategy says a lot about how her mind works. She is a master manipulator. I have as much hope for the two missing police officers as I do for Eric. Seymour finally relays her latest message.

'She says you are lying about the incubator but she doesn't care,' he says. 'As long as you bring the baby, she will wait to meet you.'

'She has to bring you as well,' I say. 'Alive.'

Seymour acts cheerful. 'I made that a condition of the bargain.'

'Does she know where the Santa Monica Pier is?'

'We both know where it is, in Santa Monica.'

I try to sound optimistic. 'Hang loose, Seymour. I'll get you out of this mess somehow.'

He pauses. 'Do what you have to, Sita.'

Kalika must have taken the phone from him. It goes dead.

16 ~

Midnight has arrived, the witching hour. I stand in a clean hallway and stare through the glass at the newborn babies in their incubators. There are six – they all look so innocent, especially Paula's. A paediatric nurse busies herself with the infants, checking their temperatures and heartbeats, drawing blood. She sees me peering through the glass, and I must look like a sight because she comes to the door and asks if I'm all right. I shuffle over to her.

'Yeah, I was just wanting to hold my friend's baby again. Before I leave the hospital.' I add, 'I'm not sure when I'll be able to come back.'

The nurse is sweet. 'I saw you earlier with the mother. Put on a gown and mask and you can hold him.

I'll get you the stuff. Which one is he?'

'Number seven.'

'He doesn't have a name?'

'Not yet.'

Soon I am dressed appropriately and I am led into the newborns. I watch as the nurse draws blood from Paula's baby and places the vial in a plastic rack, with the other vials. *Ramirez* is all she writes on the label. The nurse hands me number seven to hold.

'He's so beautiful,' she says.

'Yeah. He takes after his mother.'

It is good to hold the baby after the shock I have been through. Somehow the nearness of the child soothes me. I stare into his lovely blue eyes and laugh when he seems to smile at me. He is full of life; he kicks the whole time, tries to reach up and touch me with his tiny hands. It is almost as if I am his mother, I treasure him so.

'Why couldn't this have been my child?' I whisper.

Of course I had prayed for a daughter.

Ten minutes later, when the nurse is prepared to leave, she says I can take the baby to Paula's room if I want. The nurse has her back to me as she speaks.

'I'll do that,' I say.

'I'll come check the child again in an hour,' she says, working with the last baby on her rotation. I turn toward the door.

'I'll tell Paula,' I say.

Then I stop and stare at the vials of blood. Warm red blood – it has been the centre of my life for five thousand years. Perhaps that is why I halt. I want to be near it, to smell it, to enjoy its dark colour. Yet a part of me has doubts. There is *something* about this blood in particular – number seven's – that draws me. It is almost as if the red liquid hypnotizes me. Hardly thinking, I remove the vial from its plastic rack and slip it into my pocket. The nurse doesn't look over.

I take the baby to Paula.

She is sitting up and praying when I enter, a rosary in her hands. Standing silently at the door, I watch her for a full minute. There is something about how she focuses as she prays. She projects an intensity and at the same time an ease that baffles me. She hardly speaks above a whisper but it is as if her words fill the room. 'Our Father, who art in heaven . . .'

'Hello,' I say finally. 'I brought you a present.'

Paula is pleased. But she only smiles as I hand her the child. The boy is wise – he immediately searches for and finds her right nipple. I sit by Paula's bed in the dim room. The window is open, we are high up. The city lights spread out beneath us like a haze of jewels and dust. Seymour never leaves my thoughts, nor does Eric. I have twenty-two hours left to do the impossible.

'How do you feel?' I ask.

'Wonderful. I'm hardly sore at all. Isn't he adorable?'

'If he was any more adorable we would do nothing else but stand around and admire him.'

'Thank you for staying with me.'

'Are you still mad that I brought you here?'

Paula is puzzled. 'I like this hospital, but why did you bring me here?'

I lean forward. 'I'd like to answer that question honestly because I lied to you before, and I think you know it. I'll tell you in a few minutes. But before I do, may I ask about this child's father?'

Paula appears troubled. 'Why do you ask?'

'Because of your precise reaction right now. The day I met you, you reacted in the same way when I asked about the father.' I pause. 'I really would like to hear how you got pregnant.'

Paula tries to brush me off. 'Oh, I think it was in the usual way.'

'Was it?'

Paula studies me. Even though she is feeding her baby, her gaze is shrewd. It is ironic that she pays me precisely the same compliment.

'You're perceptive, Alisa,' she says. 'I noticed that the day we met. You miss nothing. Have you always been this way?'

'For a long time.'

Paula sighs and looks out the window at the city lights. 'This is called the City of Angels. It would take an angel to believe what I have to say next. The priest at St Andrews didn't believe me. I told him my whole story one day, in confession. He ordered me to do ten Hail Marys.' She adds, 'That's a huge penance.'

'It must be a great story.'

Paula shakes her head. 'It's a confusing story. I

hardly know where to begin.'

'At the beginning. That's always easiest.'

Paula continues to stare out the window, while her child suckles her breast. 'I grew up in an orphanage – I told you that – and was alone most of my life, even when I was surrounded by people. I purposely lived in my own world because my whole environment seemed harsh to me. But I wasn't what you would call unhappy. I often experienced moments of unusual joy and happiness. I could see a flower or a butterfly, or even just a tree, and become joyful. Sometimes the joy would become so strong I would swoon. A few times I lost track of where I was, what I was doing. When that happened I was taken to the doctor by the woman who ran my orphanage. They did all kinds of tests and I was given a grim diagnosis.'

'Epilepsy,' I say.

Paula is surprised. 'How did you know?'

I shrug. 'Saint Paul and Joan of Arc have since been diagnosed as epileptic because they had visions and heard voices. It's the current fad diagnosis for mystics – past and present. I'm sorry, please continue.'

'I didn't know that. I just knew that at the moments I was most alive, I had trouble maintaining normal consciousness. But when I swooned it wasn't like I passed out. The opposite – I felt as if I was transported to a vast realm of beauty and light. Only it was all inside me. I couldn't share it with anyone. These experiences went on throughout my childhood and teens. They invoked in me a sense of . . . This is hard to explain.'

'When you swooned you felt close to God,' I say.

'Yes, exactly. I felt a sacred presence. And I found, as I got older, that if I prayed for long periods the trances would come over me. But I didn't pray for them to happen. I prayed because I wanted to pray. I wanted to think of God, nothing else. It was the only thing that completely satisfied me.' She paused. 'Does that sound silly?'

'No. I often think of God. Go on.'

'It gets bizarre now. You have to forgive me ahead of time.' She pauses. 'I love the desert. I love to drive deep into it all by myself. Especially Joshua National Park – I love those tall trees. They stand out there in the middle of nowhere like guards, their arms up, so patient. I feel like they're protecting the rest of us somehow. Anyway I was out there nine months ago, by myself, near sunset. I was sitting on a bluff watching the sun go down and it was incredibly beautiful – the colours, the clouds shot through with red and orange and purple. It looked like a rainbow made out of sand and sun. The air was so silent I thought I could hear an ant walking. I had been there all day and as soon as it was dark I was going to head back to town. But as the sun vanished beneath the horizon I lost track of time, as I had done often before.'

'But this time was different?' I ask.

'Yes. It was as if I just blinked and then it became pitch-black. The sky was filled with a million stars. They were so bright! I could have been in outer space. I can't exaggerate this – they were so bright they weren't normal. It was almost as if I had been transported to another world, inside a huge star cluster, and was looking up at its night-time sky.'

'You were completely awake all this time?'

'Yes. I was happy but I hadn't lost awareness of my surroundings. I could still see the Joshua trees.'

'But you had lost awareness of a big chunk of time?'

'It was more like the time lost me. Anyway, something else started to happen. While I marveled over the stars, the blue one directly above me began to glow extremely bright. It was as if it were moving closer to the earth, toward me, and I felt afraid. It got so bright I was blinded. I had to close my eyes. But I could still feel it coming. I could feel its heat. It was roasting me alive!'

'Were you in pain?'

Paula struggled for words. 'I was overwhelmed is a better way to put it. A high-pitched sound started to vibrate the area. Remember, I had my eyes closed but I could still see the light and knew that it was growing more intense. The rays of the star pierced my eyelids. The sound pierced my ears. I wanted to scream – maybe I was screaming. But I don't think I was in actual physical pain. It was more as if I were being transformed.'

'Transformed? Into what?'

'I don't know. That's just the impression I had at the time. That somehow this light and heat and sound were changing me.'

'What happened next?'

'I blacked out.'

'That's it?'

'There's more. The next thing I knew it was morning and I was lying on the bluff with the sun shining in my eyes. My whole body ached and I was incredibly thirsty. Also, my exposed skin was slightly red, as if I had been burned.' She stopped.

'What is it?'

'You won't believe this.'

'I'll believe anything if I believe what you just told me. Tell me'

Paula glanced at me. 'Do you believe me?'

'Yes. But tell me what you wanted to say.'

'The Joshua trees around me – they were all taller.'

'Are you sure?'

'Quite sure. Some were twice the size they had been the evening before.'

'Interesting. Could you take me to this spot someday?'

'Sure. But I haven't been back to it since.'

'Why not?' I ask, although I know why.

Paula takes a deep breath and looks down at her son. 'Because six weeks after this happened I learned I was pregnant.' She chuckled to herself. 'Pretty weird, huh?'

'Only if you weren't having sex with someone at the time.'

'I wasn't.'

'Are you a virgin?' I ask.

'No. But I didn't have a boyfriend at that time. Not even around that time. You must think I'm mad.'

'I don't know,' I say. 'A few times in my life aliens

have swooped down and tried to get me to go to bed with them.'

'I didn't see a flying saucer,' Paula says quickly.

'I was joking. I know you didn't.' I am thoughtful.

'Did you have any other unusual symptoms after this incident? Besides being pregnant?'

Paula considers. 'I've had colourful dreams for the past few months. They're strong – they wake me up.'

'What are they about?'

'I can never remember them clearly. But there are always stars in them. Beautiful blue stars, like the ones I saw out in the desert.'

I think of the dreams I've had of Krishna.

'What do you think this all means?' I ask.

She is shy. 'I haven't the faintest idea.'

'You must have a theory?' I ask.

'No. None.'

'Do you think you were raped while you lay unconscious in the desert?'

Paula considers. 'That would be the logical explanation. But even though I was sore when I woke up, I wasn't sore down there.'

'But is it possible you were raped?'

'Yes. I was out cold. Anything could have happened to me during that time.'

'Were your clothes disturbed in any way?'

'They were – They felt different on me.'

'What do you mean?'

Paula hesitates. 'My belt felt tighter.'

'Like it had been removed, and then put back on, only a notch tighter?'

Paula lowers her head. 'Yes. But I honestly don't think I was raped.'

'Do you think you had an epileptic attack?'

'No. I don't think I have epilepsy. I don't believe that diagnosis anymore.'

'But you believe Joshua trees stand guard over us? Like angels?'

She smiles. 'Yeah. I am a born believer.'

Her smile is so kind, so gentle. It reminds me of Radha's, Krishna's friend. I make my decision right then. Leaning forward and speaking seriously, I make Paula jump by the change in my tone.

'I have some bad news for you, Paula. I want you to brace yourself and I want you to listen to me with as open a mind as I have listened to you. Can you do this?'

'Sure. What's wrong?'

'There are two people I know who – for reasons I do not fully understand yet – want your baby.'

Paula is stunned. 'What do they want it for?'

'I don't know. But I do know that one of these people – the young woman – is a killer.' My eyes burn and I have trouble keeping my voice steady. 'She killed a friend of mine two hours ago.'

'Alisa! This can't be true. Who is this woman?'

I shake my head. 'She is someone so powerful, so brilliant, so cruel – that there is no point in going to the police and explaining what happened.'

'But you have to go to the police. If a murder has been committed, they must be told.'

'The police cannot stop her. I cannot stop her. She wants your baby. She is looking for him now and when she comes here for him you won't be able to stop her.' I pause. 'You are my friend, Paula. We haven't known each other long but I believe friendship is not based on time. I think you know I'm your friend and that I would do anything for you.'

Paula nods. 'I know that.'

'Then you must do something for me now. You must leave this hospital tonight, with your son. I have money, lots of money I can give you. You must go to a place far from here, and not even tell *me* where it is.'

I am talking too fast for Paula. 'Is this the reason you took me to this hospital?'

'Yes. They thought you were going to the local one. But they know you've given birth to a baby somewhere in this city. They're clever – they'll check all the hospitals in the city to see where you're registered. Eventually they'll locate you.'

'You spoke of a young woman. Who is the other person?'

I am stricken with grief. 'My boyfriend.'

'Ray?'

'Yes. But he's not the Ray I once knew.' I lower my head. 'I can't talk about him now. It is the girl who's the danger – she's only twenty. Her name is Kalika. Please believe me when I tell you there is literally no one who can stop her when she sets her mind on something.'

'But how can she be so powerful?' Paula protests.

I stare at her. 'She was just born that way. You see, she wasn't born under normal circumstances. Like your son, there's a mystery surrounding her birth, her conception even.'

'Tell me about it.'

'I can't. You wouldn't believe me if I did.'

'But I would. You believed me.'

'Only because I have gone through strange times in my life. But Kalika transcends anything I've ever encountered. Her psyche *burns* through all obstacles. She could be on her way here now. I swear to you, if she gets here before you get away, your child will die.'

Paula doesn't protest. She is strangely silent. 'I was warned,' she says.

It is my turn to be stunned. 'Who warned you?'

'It came in a dream.'

'But you said you didn't remember any of your dreams.'

'I remember this one. I was standing on a wide field and this old man with white hair and a crooked grin walked up to me and said something that didn't make sense. Until right now.'

'What was it?' I ask.

'He said, "Herod was an evil king who didn't get what he wanted. But he knew where the danger lay." Then the old man paused and asked me, "Do you know where the danger lies, Paula?"' She stops and looks once more at her child, we both look at him. 'It was an odd dream.'

'Yes.' My heart is heavy with anxiety. 'Will you leave?'

Paula nods. 'Yes. I trust you. But why can't I tell you where I'm going?'

'This girl, this Kalika – I fear she could rip the information from my mind.'

Paula cringes. 'But I must have a way to get hold of you.'

'I will give you a special number. You call it a month from now and leave your name and number. But don't tell me where you are. Wait until you talk to me – until you are certain it is me – to tell me that. That is very important.'

Paula is worried for me. 'Are you in danger?'

I lean back and momentarily close my eyes. My greatest task is still before me and I am exhausted. If only I had my old powers. *If* – the most annoying word in the English language.

But what if I was powerful again?

Powerful as a vampire?

Seymour would not have to die, nor would I.

But my daughter would die. Perhaps.

'Don't worry, I have a protector,' I tell Paula. 'This wonderful man I once met – he promised to protect me if I did what he said. And he was someone capable of keeping his promises.'

Of course I don't tell her that I have disobeyed Krishna many times.

17 ～～

Arturo's alchemy of transformation works by having the substance of what one wishes to become vibrate at a high level in one's aura. To become human, I took Seymour's blood and placed it – above my head – in a clear vial the sun shone through while I lay on a copper plate surrounded by specially arranged magnets and crystals. Only Arturo knew how to use these tools fully. The New Age is still centuries behind his knowledge. The proponents of New Age mysticism hold quartz crystals or amethysts and relax some, but Arturo could use these minerals to attain enlightenment, or even immortality. His only weakness was that he strove for immortality with a vampire for a girlfriend. He was a priest and erroneously thought I could give him the equivalent of the blood of Jesus. His blasphemy was his sin, and his eventual ruin. He tried to use me, betrayed me. But he is dead now and I mourn him.

To become a vampire again, I need a source of vampire blood.

I lied to Seymour, naturally. There is one possible source – Yaksha. Yet I have sunk Yaksha's body in the sea and will never be able to locate it, not without the powers of a vampire. Still, there is one other possible source of his blood, besides that in his body. Eddie Fender kept Yaksha captive in an ice-cream truck for several weeks, kept him cold and weak. It was from this very ice-cream truck that I eventually rescued Yaksha, who had no legs and hardly any lower torso. He bled in that truck and his blood must still be there, frozen and preserved.

But that truck was parked on the street in the vicinity of a warehouse I burned down to kill Eddie and his crew of vampires. That was approximately two months ago. The chances that the truck will still be there are slim. The police will almost certainly have confiscated it, towed it off to some forsaken lot. Yet I hurry to the dirty street in the poor part of town on the off chance that I can uncover a bloody Popsicle. Desperate people do desperate things.

And the ice truck is still there. Wow.

A homeless man with white hair and a grimy face sits in his rags near the driver's door. He has a shopping cart loaded with aluminium cans and blankets that look as if they were woven during the Depression. He is thin and bent but he looks up at me with bright eyes as I approach. He sits on the curb, nursing a small carton of milk. I immediately reach for my money. It is his lucky night. I will give him a hundred and tell him to hit the road. But something in his voice gives me reason to pause. His greeting is peculiar.

'You look very nice tonight,' he says. 'But I know you're in a hurry.'

I stand above him and glance around. There is no one visible, but it is the middle of the night and this ghetto is a wonderful place to get raped or killed. Last time I was here I had to rough up a couple of cops. They thought I was a hooker, and one of them wanted to arrest me. I study the homeless man.

'How do you know I'm in a hurry?' I ask.

He grins and his smile is much brighter than I would have anticipated. Bright like his eyes even though he is covered in dirt.

'I know a few things,' he says. 'You want this truck I suppose. I've been guarding it for you.'

I laugh softly. 'I appreciate that. I have a horrible craving for an ice-cream bar right now.'

He nods. 'The refrigerator unit still works. I've kept it serviced.'

I'm impressed. 'You're handy with tools?'

'I have fixed a thing or two in my day.' He offers me his hand. 'Please help me up. My bones are old and sore, and I have been waiting here for you for such a long time.'

I help him – I don't mind a little dirt. 'How long have you been here?'

He brushes himself off, but ends up making a worse mess of his torn clothes. He blinks at my question as if I have confused him, although he does not smell of alcohol. He finishes his carton of milk and sets the empty container in his shopping cart.

'I don't rightly know,' he says finally. 'I think I've been here since you were last here.'

I pause, feeling an odd sensation coursing through my body. But I dismiss it. I have too much on my mind to waste precious minutes with an old man in the middle of the night.

'I haven't been here in a couple of months,' I say, reaching in my pocket. 'Look, can I give you . . .'

'Then I must have been here that long,' he interrupts. 'I knew you'd come back.'

I stop with my hand wrapped around a few twenties. 'I don't know what you're talking about,' I say quietly.

He grins a crooked grin. 'I don't need your money.' He turns and shuffles up the street. 'You do what you have to do. No one can blame you for not trying hard.'

I stare at him as he fades into the night.

Such a strange old guy. He left his shopping cart behind.

I wonder what his name was.

The rear compartment of the truck is locked, but I break it with a loose brick. Actually, I could have sworn that I broke the lock the last time I entered it. The interior is ice cold as I squeeze inside, a flashlight in my hand.

Just inside the door is a puddle of frozen blood.

I slip a nail under it and pull up the whole red wafer at once. Shining my flashlight through the frosted glass, I feel a surge of tremendous power. I hold in my hands immortality, and I feel as if Krishna saved this blood just so I'd find it. Back in my own car, I break the ice into small pieces and let them melt in a stainless-steel thermos.

Now I must return to Las Vegas. If it were not the middle of the night, I would fly, but driving it will have to be – at least four hours of pushing the speed limit. Also, I have to worry that Arturo's house is being watched by government agents. From reading the papers, I know the dust has not settled from the nuclear explosion in the desert. They must think I am dead, but will not assume that I am. There is an important difference.

The rays of the sun will power my transformation. What is crucial is that I have most of the day to complete the transformation back to becoming a vampire, if it is possible. There is a chance I will end up like Ralphe, a bloodthirsty ghoul. But I have no choice except to risk the alchemist's ancient experiment. To give up my hard-sought humanity will be bitter, yet I have to admit a part of me craves my old power. It will be nice to confront my daughter one on one and not tremble in my shoes.

Yet I intend to tremble, especially if I am a vampire. She will not know until too late who it is she faces.

18 ～

The drive to Las Vegas is more pleasant than I anticipated. There is something about roaring along a dark empty road that relaxes me. Keeping an eye out for police, I set the cruise control at an even eighty. It seems only a short while before the horizon begins to glow with the polluted lake of coloured neon that is the gambling capital of the world. I will roll the red dice today, I think, and pray for a successful combination of DNA. The eastern sky is already warm with light. The sun will rise soon.

I park a block down the street from Arturo's house and scan the area for FBI agents, cops, or army personnel. But the place appears quiet, forgotten in the fallout of the incinerated army base. Slipping over

Arturo's back fence, I am through an open window and into the house in less than a minute. An eight-and-a-half-by-eleven photograph stands in a cheap frame on the kitchen table – Arturo and me, taken one night while we were out on the Strip together. When I believed he was a down-on-his-luck government employee and he thought I was a sucker. The picture gives me reason to pause. I pick it up and study Arturo's features. They remind me so much of someone I know.

'You are Kalika's father,' I whisper, stunned.

Everything makes sense in an instant. Vampires are sterile, with one another, with human partners. But Arturo was neither a vampire nor a human. He was a hybrid, forged in the Middle Ages, a combination of the two, and I slept with him in a Las Vegas hotel room just before he betrayed me to the government. I was pregnant from before the transformation. In other words, I was still a vampire when Kalika was conceived. Yet she is partially human, and that no doubt explains her lack of sensitivity to the sun. She is the result of a queer toss of the genetic dice, and perhaps that's what it took for a soul of her dark origin to incarnate on earth.

And I assumed Ray was her father.

I'm aware of him at my back even before he speaks.

'I'm surprised you didn't guess earlier,' he says.

I turn, still holding the photograph. Ray remains hidden in the shadows, appropriately enough. It is not just Kalika's birth that I suddenly understand. But my new insights, which are not entirely clear to me yet, are ill-defined ghosts that refuse to enter the living body of logical reason. Despair and denial engulf me. I feel as if I stand in a steaming graveyard with a tombstone at my back. The death date of the corpse is carved in the future, the name scribbled in blood that will never dry. I know the truth but refuse to look at it.

And there is a mirror on this tombstone.

Covered with a faint film of black dust.

'You could have told me,' I say.

'I could only tell you what you wanted to hear.'

The weakness of grief spreads through my limbs. Ray has become a travesty to me, someone I cannot bear to look at, yet I don't want him to go away. He is all I have left. The graveyard in my mind is littered with hidden mines. I fear that if I move or speak to him, one might explode and toss a skeleton in my lap.

'How did you get here?' I ask.

'You brought me here.'

'Does Kalika know I'm here?'

'I don't think so. But she might.'

'You didn't tell her?'

'No.'

Putting down the photograph, I take a moment to collect myself. My imagined graveyard falls away beneath me as the tombstone collapses. Yet I am forced to remain standing in this house where Arturo once lived.

'Can I ask you a question?' I say finally.

He remains in the shadows. 'Don't ask anything you don't want answered.'

'But I do want answers.'

He shakes his head. 'Few really want the complete truth. It doesn't matter if you're a vampire or a human. The truth is overrrated, and too often painful.' He adds, 'Let it be, Sita.'

There is emotion in my voice. 'I need to know just one thing.'

'No,' he warns me. 'Don't do this to yourself.'

'Just one little thing. I understand how you found me in Las Vegas. You explained that and it made sense to me, but you never explained how you picked up my trail again in Los Angeles. While I was driving here, you should have been in the basement in this house, changing back into a human.'

'It was dark that night,' he says.

His answer confuses me. 'It's dark every night.'

'It would have been dark in the basement.'

The confusion passes. 'You need the sun to power the alchemy.'

'Yes.'

'You must still be a vampire?'

'No.'

'You must have followed us to L.A.?'

'No.'

'Who are you? What did Eddie's blood do to you?'

'Nothing. Eddie's blood never touched me.'

'But you said –'

'I lied,' he interrupts. 'You asked me to lie to you. You do not want the truth. You swear to yourself that you do but you swear at the altar of false gods. Let it be, Sita. We can leave this place together. It can be as it once was between us, if you will just let it. It is all up to you.'

'You are not ready to hear.'

'When will I be ready to hear?'

'Soon.'

'You know this?'

'I know many things, Mother.'

'Why is it all up to me?' I ask. 'You're as responsible for what happened to us as I am.'

'No.'

'Stop saying no! Stop saying yes! Explain yourself!'

He is a long time answering. 'What do you want me to say?'

I place my hands on the sides of my head. 'Just tell me who you are. Why you are not like the old Ray. How you found me in the coffee shop.' I feel so weak. 'Why you knocked at my door.'

'When did I knock at your door?'

'Here.' I point. 'You knocked at that door right there. You said it was you.'

'When did I knock at your door?' he repeats.

Of course I have not answered his question. He is asking about time, and I am talking about place. I have to force my next words into the air where they can be heard and understood.

345

'You appeared right after I changed into a human,' I say.

'Yes.'

'You're saying that's a remarkable coincidence.'

'I am saying you should stop now.'

I nod to myself, speak to myself. 'You are saying the two events are related; the transformation and your reappearance. That you only re-entered my life because I had become human.'

'Close.'

I pause. 'What am I missing?'

'Everything.'

'But you just said I was close!'

'When you roll the dice, close does not count. You either win or you lose.'

'What did I lose when you returned?'

'*What* is not important. *Why* is all that matters.'

'*Now listen to my song. It dispels all illusions . . . When you feel lost remember me, and you will see that the things you desire most are the very things that bring you the greatest sorrow.*'

'I have always desired two things,' I say, remembering the Lord's words. 'For five thousand years I have desired them. They were the two things that were taken from me the night Yaksha came for me and made me a vampire. The night he stole my daughter and husband. I never saw either of them again.'

Ray is sympathetic. 'I know.'

I hang my head and it is now me who stands in

shadows. 'But when you came into my life I felt as if Rama had been returned to me. And when I became human and thought I was pregnant with your baby, I felt as if Krishna had returned Lalita to me.' There is a tear on my face, maybe two, and I have to stop and take a deep breath. 'But it didn't work that way. The things I craved so long were my greatest illusions. And they have brought me the greatest sorrow.'

'Yes.'

I lift my head and stare at him.

'They are not real,' I say.

'Yes.'

'As a vampire, I could see through my illusions, and that kept me going all these years, but as a human I couldn't see what was real and what wasn't. I was too weak.'

You create what you want. You always have. If you don't like it, you can always leave.

He speaks with gentle passion. 'Don't say it, Sita.'

But I have to. I feel as if I can see through him. Now I understand why he never went out. Why he never met my friends or spoke to anyone besides Kalika and me. Why I had to do everything with my own hands. Between us, they were the only pair of hands. Between us, they were the only pair of hands we had.

'You're not real,' I say.

He steps out of the shadows. His face is so beautiful.

'It doesn't matter, Sita. We can pretend it doesn't matter. I don't want to leave you.'

My body is a chalice of misery. 'But you're dead,' I moan.

He comes close enough to touch me. 'It doesn't matter.'

No tears fall from my face. Dry sobs rack my body. They are worse than moist tears, worse because they are the evidence of evaporated grief, and I have only these to show to this silhouette of a boyfriend who stands before me now. This lover who can only love me as I deem myself worthy. No wonder he turned against me when I turned against him. He is a mirror on the tombstone. The film of black dust clears, and I see in the mirror that I have slowly been burying myself since I first came up the stairs of this house and heard the knock at the front door.

Who is it? Your darling. Open the door.

'I can't keep this door open,' I whisper.

He touches my lower lip. 'Sita.'

I turn my head away from his hand. 'No. You must go back.'

'To where?'

'To where you came from.'

'That is the abyss. There is nothing there. I am not there.'

A note of quiet hysteria enters my voice. 'You're not here. You're worse than a ghost. No one can see you! How can I possibly love you?'

He grabs my hand. 'But you feel me. You know I'm here.'

I fight to shake free of his hand but I just end up gripping it tighter. Yet I do not press it to my heart, as I used to. His hand is cold.

'No,' I say. 'I know you're not here.'

He lightly kisses my finger. 'Do you feel that?'

'No.'

'You lie.'

'You are the lie! You don't exist! How can I make you cease to exist!'

My words wound him, finally – they seem to tear the very fabric of his existence. For a moment his face shimmers, then goes out of focus. Yet he draws in a sudden breath and his warm brown eyes lock on to my eyes. He is not merely a mirror, but a hologram from a dimension where there are more choices than time and space. He is the ultimate *maya,* the complete illusion. The perfect love dressed in my own grief. No wonder when I met him in the coffee shop he was wearing the clothes he died in. He is nothing but a memory shouted back down the tunnel all mortals pass through when they leave this world. Yes, Ray is dead but I have let him become my own death as well.

He seems to read my thoughts.

His hope fades. He answers my last question.

'I died a vampire,' he says. 'You must kill me the way you would kill a vampire.' He grabs a knife from the nearby table and presses it into my hand. 'My heart beats only for you.'

He wants me to cut his heart out. I try to push him

away, but he holds me close. I can feel his breath on my face, like the brush of a winter wind. Yet now, here at the end, his eyes burn with a strange red light, the same light I have occasionally glimpsed in my daughter's eyes. He nods again as he reads my mind.

'If I return to the abyss,' he says, 'I'll see kali there.' He squeezes the handle of the knife into my palm. 'Do it quick. You're right, the love is gone. I do want to die.'

'I should never have been born,' I whisper, addressing his last remark.

He manages a faint smile 'Goodbye, Sita.'

I stab him in the heart. I cut his flesh and his bones, and the blood gushes over my hands, onto my clothes, and over the floor. The black blood of the abyss, the empty space of Kali. But I scream as I kill him, scream to God for mercy, and the knife mysteriously falls from my hand and bounces on the dry floor. The blood evaporates.

His heart no longer beats and I'm no longer bloody.

He is gone, my ancient love is gone.

Out the window, the sun rises.

Taking Yaksha's blood, I pour it into the vial that once held Seymour's blood, the clear vial that I place above the copper and the crystals, between the cross-shaped magnets and the shiny mirror that reflects the rays of the sun directly into Arturo's hidden basement. I recline on the copper and the alchemy begins to work its dark magic on my trembling body. I have to wonder exactly *what* I will be when the sun finally sets and the process is complete. On impulse I have added to the vial a few drops of blood from Paula's child. The blood of the infant that Kalika covets above all else.

I can only hope it does me good.

19 ～～

Eight o'clock that evening I sit in the living room of Mr and Mrs Hawkins, in the very house Eric longed to return to until his throat was cut. Eric's parents are younger than I would have guessed. Mr Hawkins can be no more than forty-two and I doubt his wife has reached forty. They must have married young and had Eric when they were barely out of their teens. He is stern faced, but it is a practised expression, one he wears for his patients. But I see his intelligence and natural curiosity beneath it. She is plump and kindly, fussing with her hands as she constantly thinks of her son. She wears her heart on her face, her eyes are red from constant crying. Their address was in the phone book.

I just knocked at their door and told them I have information concerning their missing son. They invited me in because I am young and pretty and look as if I could harm no one. They sit across from me and wait for me to speak. There is no easy way to say it.

'Your son is dead,' I say. 'He was murdered last night. I thought you would want to know rather than to be left wondering. Before I leave here, I'll give you the address where his body can be found. He's in a house not far from here.' I pause. 'I'm truly sorry to have to bring you this information. It must be a great shock to both of you.'

Mrs Hawkins bursts into gasping sobs and buries her face in her hands. Mr Hawkins's nostrils flare with anger. 'How do you know this?' he demands.

'As you look at me you must see that I match the description of the young woman who picked up Eric in the park. I am, in fact, that person. But I am not the one who killed your son. On the contrary, I fought hard to save him. I'm very sorry I failed. Eric was a sweet boy. I liked him quite a lot.'

They are in turmoil, which is inevitable. 'This can't be true,' Mr Hawkins stammers.

'It is true. You will verify that for yourself when you go to the house. But I would rather you sent the police ahead of you. Eric died from a serious throat wound.' I add reluctantly, 'Just before I came here I tried to clean up, but there is still a lot of blood.'

Mrs Hawkins continues to sob. Mr Hawkins leans

forward in his chair, his skin flushed with blood, his face quivering with fury. 'Who are you?' he asks.

'My name is not important. It's true I kidnapped your son but I meant him no harm. I do understand that you won't believe me. That you must hate me. If the situation were reversed I would probably hate you. But I can give you nothing to identify me with, and after I leave here, you will never see me again. The police will never find me.'

Mr Hawkins snorts. 'You're not leaving this house, young lady. I'm calling the police as soon as I'm through with you.'

'You should call the police. I've written down the address you need on a piece of paper.' I take the scrap and hand it to him. He frowns as he glances at the slip. I continue, 'I can give you directions to the house, but I must warn you two police officers who were there yesterday were also killed. Or rather, I must assume they were killed because they were off with the same person who killed your son and they didn't come back.'

I add this last remark because I'm puzzled that no one has been to the house searching for them. When I stopped by half an hour earlier, looking for Kalika and Seymour, I could find no sign that the place had been examined by the authorities. Especially since Eric was still lying on the couch in all his gore. It was not pleasant trying to clean him up. He looked as if he had died in agony, which, of course, he had.

'You are talking a bunch of trash,' Mr Hawkins snaps.

'I am telling you the truth,' I reply simply.

Mrs Hawkins finally comes up for air. 'Why did this person kill my boy?'

'To try to force me to reveal the whereabouts of a newborn baby. The person who murdered your son is obsessed with this child. She would do anything to get to him. But I refused to give her the information she needed, so Eric was killed.' I pause. 'None of these facts are important to you. None of them will make any sense to you. But I do want you to know that when I leave this house, I am going to meet with this young woman, and I am going to do everything in my power to stop her. I know you'll want revenge for what has happened to your son, or at the very least justice. I will try to give you both tonight, and keep this person from murdering again.' I stand suddenly. 'Now I have to go.'

'You're not going anywhere!' Mr Hawkins shouts as he tries to rise. But before his bottom can leave the chair, I effortlessly hold him down with one hand. My strength startles him.

'Please,' I say gently. 'You can't keep me here. It's not possible. And you won't be able to follow me. Just know that your son was brave and that forces beyond our control conspired to end his life before it should have ended. Try to understand his death as an act of God's will. I try to see it that way.'

I leave them then quickly. They hardly have a chance to react, and later they will both wonder if my visit was a dream. But I know they will go straight to the house after they call the police. I know they will see their dead son before anyone else does. They loved him, and they should be the ones to close his eyes.

My car is around the block. Soon I am in it and driving for the ocean. There is an appointment I have with destiny and my daughter. I don't know which I trust less.

20

The transformation has worked and I am indeed a vampire again. Yet I am different, in a variety of ways, from what I was before. It was largely Yaksha's blood that filtered the sun's rays into my aura, and no doubt that is the main reason for the great increase in my strength. If I could jump fifty feet in the air before, I can leap a hundred now. If I could hear a leaf break and fall a mile away, now I can hear an ant crawl from its hole at twice that distance. My sense of smell is a wonder; the night air is an encyclopedia of fragrant information to me. And my eyes are like lasers. Not only can I see much farther than before, I feel the fire in my gaze, and I seriously doubt if even Kalika can withstand the power of it.

Yet these refinements are not confined to strength and power. There is something else that has entered my life, something that I have never known before. I don't even have a word for it. I just feel – lucky, as if good fortune will smile on me. A white star seems to shine over my head, or maybe it is blue. I have to wonder if this is the effect of what I added to Yaksha's blood.

I am confident as I race toward the pier.

Santa Monica Beach, by the pier, is deserted as I drive up. I find that fact curious; it is, after all, only ten in the evening. The night is cold, true, but I have to wonder if there is another force at work. It is almost as if a psychic cloud hangs over the area, a fog of *maya* wrapped in astral matter. I clearly sense the force and my confidence wavers. For only my daughter could create it, and it is like nothing I have ever seen before. It seems to suck up life itself, which is why people have shunned the place. As I park my car down the block from the pier, I see not a soul. They may all be in their homes, trying to explain to their children that nightmares are not real. I myself feel as if I'm moving through a dream. My newly regained powers are physically exhilarating, but my dread of confronting Kalika is a heavy burden.

I see them, the two of them, at the end of the pier.

Seymour is looking out to sea. Kalika is nearby, in a long white dress, feeding the birds crumbs of bread. I am a half mile distant yet I see their every feature. Seymour pretends to be enjoying the view but he keeps glancing at Kalika. The muscles in his neck are tight; he is scared. Yet he appears unhurt and I am grateful for that.

Kalika is a mystery. There is an almost full moon, which shines through her long black hair like silver dust blowing on a black wind. As she feeds the birds, she is fully focused on them as if nothing else has greater meaning to her. This is a quality I have noticed in Kalika before. When she is doing something, nothing else occupies her mind. No doubt when she opened Eric's throat she was with him a hundred percent. It is a sobering thought given the fact that she has a hostage beside her. Kali and her string of skulls. Will my daughter have three fresh ones to add to her necklace before the night is over?

I think of Paula, who caught a cab from the hospital. Running out into the night with twenty thousand dollars in cash and a beautiful baby boy wrapped in a hospital receiving blanket. All because a new friend told her she was in danger. Then again, she had her dreams to warn her. Odd how the old man she described in her dream looked like the guy who was guarding the ice-cream truck.

'You look very nice tonight. But I know you're in a hurry.'
Who was that guy?

It is a mystery that will have to be solved another time.

I make no effort to hide my approach. I know it would be useless to do so. Nevertheless I move as a human moves. My steps are tentative, my breathing tight. The muscles of my face are pinched with anxiety and my shoulders are slumped forward in defeat. Yet my performance goes unheeded as Kalika continues to feed the birds and doesn't glance up until I am practically on top of them. I pause twenty feet short of the end of the pier. By this time Seymour is looking at me with a mixture of hope and terror. He cannot help but notice I don't have the child with me. The sight of Eric's spurting arteries must have dug deep into his brain. He has little of his usual confidence, although he struggles to make up for it. He forces a smile.

'I'm glad you're not late,' he says, and gestures to the moon, which was full the previous night, when Paula's child was born. 'Lovely evening, isn't it?'

'I'm here,' I say to Kalika. 'Let him go.'

She stares at me now, a handful of pigeons still pecking at the crumbs beside her sandaled feet. Her long white dress – I have never seen it before – is beautiful on her flawless figure, the silky material moving in the moonlit breeze, hugging her mature curves. The birds scatter as she brushes her hands and slowly rises.

'I did not think you would bring the child,' she says calmly.

'But I came myself. Release Seymour.'

'Why should I?'

'Because I am your mother and I'm requesting this. That should be reason enough.'

'It's not.'

'He's young. He should not be brought into our affairs.'

At that Kalika smiles faintly. 'I am young as well, Mother. I should be forgiven any indiscretions I might have committed during my short life.'

'Do you need my forgiveness?'

'I suppose not.' There is one bird that continues to eat at her feet. Kalika bends back down, plucks it into her hands, and straightens. She strokes the pigeon's feathers and whispers something in its ear. Then she speaks to me. 'You should know by now that it's not a good idea to lie to me.'

'You force me to lie to you,' I say. 'Your complaint is absurd.'

'Still, it's your habit. You have lied through the ages. You see nothing wrong in it.'

'I would have told a million lies to have saved that boy's life.' I add, 'But you must know I hate to lie to those I love.'

Kalika continues to stroke the bird. 'Do you love me, Mother?'

'Yes.'

She nods in approval. 'The truth. Do you love Seymour?'

'Yes.'

'Would you be upset if I ripped off his head?'

'I hope this is not a trick question,' Seymour mutters.

'You must not hurt him,' I say. 'He's my friend, and

he's done nothing to you. Let him go now and we can talk about the child.'

Kalika is once again the master manipulator. She holds up the pigeon. 'What about this bird? Should I let it go? Just let it fly away and complete this particular birth? You should know, *Old One,* that it doesn't matter if I do or if I don't. Whenever the bird dies, the bird will simply be reborn. It is the same with humans. If you kill one, it will in time be reincarnated in another body. Perhaps Eric and Billy will both be reborn in better conditions. Eric was not in the best shape when he died.' She pauses and coos in the bird's ear again. 'What do you think, Mother?'

There is something disturbing in her question, in her examples, besides the obvious. Maybe she is honestly trying to tell me something about her inner state, who she is, what she really is. It is said many times in the Vedas that whenever a demon dies in Krishna's hands, that demon gains instant liberation. But there are fewer books written about Kali's incarnation, her many exploits; and I am not yet ready to accept that my daughter is in fact the real Kali. Of course, I could ask her directly but the mere thought of doing so fills me with apprehension. Many things do: the way she holds the bird close to her mouth; her quick glances at Seymour; the steadiness of her gaze as she studies me, missing nothing. It is impossible to gauge what she will do next, and when she will do it. I try as best I can to answer her, trying to think what Krishna would say to her. Really, I am no saint; I cannot preach morality without sounding like a hypocrite.

'There is a meaning behind each life,' I say. 'A purpose. It doesn't matter if humans or birds live thousands of lives before they return to God. Each life is valued. Each time you take one, you incur bad karma.'

'That is not so.' She brushes the bird against the side of her face. 'Karma does not touch me. Karma is for humans, and vampires.'

She reproaches me, I realize, for being exactly what I tried not to be. 'These last few centuries I have seldom killed without strong reason,' I say.

'Eric and Billy died for a reason,' she says.

'For what reason did Eric die?'

'To inspire you.'

I am disgusted. 'Do I look inspired?'

'Yes,' she says. 'But you did not answer my earlier question, about Seymour's head.' She takes a dangerous step toward him. Seymour jumps and I don't blame him. But I catch his eye; I don't want him to make any more sudden moves. Kalika continues, 'Would you be upset if I ripped it off?'

I have a choice to make and I must make it quickly. Before she can move any closer to Seymour, I can attack. If I leap forward, I can kick her in the nose and send her nasal cartilage into her brain and kill her. Seymour wouldn't even see my blow. Kalika would simply be dead. But I am still twenty feet from my daughter, not an ideal distance. She could react in time and deflect my blow. Then, before I could recover, Seymour would die.

I decide to wait. To be patient.

I wonder if my patience is grounded in my attachment to Kalika.

She is my daughter. How can I kill her?

'Yes,' I say. 'You know I would be upset.'

Kalika squeezes the pigeon gently. 'Would you be upset if I ripped this bird's head off?'

I am annoyed. 'Why do you ask these silly questions?'

'To hear your answers.'

'This sounds like a trick question,' Seymour warns.

I hesitate. He's right. 'If there is no reason to kill it, I would say you should leave it alone.'

'Answer my question,' she says.

'I would not be upset if you killed the bird.'

Kalika rips the bird's head off. The tearing bone and tissue make a faint nauseating sound. Blood splashes over the front of my daughter's pretty white dress. Seymour almost faints. Casually, while still watching me, Kalika throws the remains of the bird over her shoulder and into the dark water below. It is only then I catch a glimmer of red light deep inside her pupils. The fire at the end of time, the Vedas call it. The smoky shadow of the final twilight. Kalika knows I see it for she smiles at me.

'You look upset, Mother,' she says.

'You are cruel,' I say. 'Cruelness without rational

thought is not far from insanity.'

'I told you, I have my reasons.' She wipes the blood on the left side of her face. 'Tell me where Paula Ramirez's child is.'

I glance at Seymour. 'I can't,' I say.

'Damn,' he whispers, and he's not being funny.

'Why do you assume I am going to harm this child?' she asks.

'Because of your previous erratic behavior,' I reply.

'If I had not killed Billy, you would not be here tonight. If I had not killed Eric, you would also not be here tonight.'

'I didn't need Eric's death to survive the last twenty-four hours.'

Kalika teases without inflection. 'Really?'

She may be hinting at the fact that I am now a vampire, that I would never have gone through with the transformation without the motivation Eric's horrible murder gave me. She would be right on that point, if it is what she is hinting at. But I continue to hope she thinks I'm helpless. I feel I must attack soon, favourable position or not. The bird's death has not increased my faith in her non-violent nature. She waits for me to respond.

'I cannot trust you around Paula's baby,' I say, taking a step closer. 'Surely you must understand that.' When she doesn't answer right away, I ask, 'What did you do to the police?'

'I fulfilled their karma.'

'That's no answer.'

Kalika moves closer to Seymour, standing now five feet from his left side. He can't even look at her. Only at me, the creature who saved him from AIDS, who inspires his stories, his savior and his muse. His eyes beg me for a miracle.

'What if I promise you that I will not hurt the child,' Kalika says. 'Will you take me to him?'

'No. I can't.'

She acts mildly surprised. But there is no real emotion in her voice or on her face. Human expressions are merely tools to her. I doubt she feels anything at all, while eating or reading, walking or killing.

'No?' Kalika says. 'Have I ever lied to you before?' She moves her arms as if stretching them. Blood drips from her sharp fingernails. In a microsecond, I know, she can reach out and grab Seymour and then it will all be over. She adds, 'I am your daughter, but I do not have your habit of lying.'

'Kalika,' I plead. 'Be reasonable. You refuse to tell me why you want to see this child. I can only conclude that you intend to harm it.' I pause. 'Is that not true?'

'Your question is meaningless to me.'

I take another step forward. She is now only twelve feet away, but I want to be closer still. 'What is so special about this child?' I ask. 'You can at least tell me that.'

'No.'

'Why not?'

She is subtly amused. 'It's forbidden.'

'Oh, and killing innocent people isn't? Forbidden by whom?'

'You wouldn't understand.' She pauses. 'Where's Ray?'

I freeze in midstep. 'He's gone.'

She seems to understand. 'He was forbidden.' She glances at Seymour, smiles at him actually as a pretty girl might while flirting. But the words that come out of her mouth next are far from nice. They sound like a warning. She says. 'Certain things, once broken, are better left unfixed.'

The decision is made for me. Something in her tone tells me she is going to reach for Seymour and that his head will go over the railing as the bird's did – and with the same emotional impact on Kalika. I attack.

My reclaimed vampiric body is no stranger to me. I have not needed time to readapt to it. Indeed it feels almost more natural than it used to. But I definitely decide to stick with an old technique of killing – the nose into the brain thrust. It is straightforward and effective. My only trouble – as I tense my muscles to respond – is that I still love her.

Kalika begins to reach out with her right arm.

I leap up and forward. My lift off the ground is effortless. If I were taped and the video later slowed down for viewing, the human eye would assume that gravity had no effect on me. Of course this is not true – I cannot fly. Only strength is responsible for the illusion. I whip toward Kalika, my right foot the hammer of Thor. I cock it back – it will soon be over.

But somewhere in the air I hesitate. Just slightly.

Probably it makes no difference, but I will never know.

The red flames smoulder deep in Kalika's eyes.

My divine hammer is forged of crude iron ore. My daughter grabs my foot before it can reach her face. Real time returns, and I begin a slow horizontal fall, helpless as she grips my foot tighter. Seymour cries in horror and my own cry is one of excruciating pain. She has twisted my ankle almost to the breaking point. I hit the asphalt with the flat of my back and the back of my skull. Kalika towers over me, still holding onto my boot. Her expression is surprisingly gentle.

'Does it hurt?' she asks.

I grimace. 'Yes.'

Kalika breaks my ankle. I hear the bones snap like kindling wood in a fire, and a wave of red agony slams up my leg and into my brain. As I writhe on the ground, she takes a step back and patiently watches me, never far from Seymour's side. She knows vampires. The pain is intense but it doesn't take long before I begin to heal. The effect of Yaksha's blood on my system no doubt speeds up the process. In two minutes I am able to stand and put weight on the ankle. But I will not be kicking her again in the next few minutes, and she knows it.

Kalika grabs Seymour by the left arm.

His mouth goes wide in shock.

'I will not ask you again what I want to know,' she says.

I try to stand straight. Insolence enters my tone. 'You know what bugs me most about you? You always hide behind a human shield. I'm here and you're there. Why don't we just settle this between us? That is, if you've got the guts, girl.'

Kalika seems to approve of my challenge. She smile and this particular smile seems genuine. But I'm not sure if it is good to push her into too happy a mood for she suddenly reaches over, picks Seymour up with one hand by grabbing his shirt, and throws him over the side of the pier. The move is so unexpected that I stand stunned for a second. I hurry to the railing in time to see Seymour strike the water. She threw him hard and high – he takes a long time to return to the surface. He coughs as he does so and flays about in the dark but he seems to be all right. I hope he is not like Joel who couldn't swim.

'Seymour!' I call.

He responds with something unintelligible, but sounds OK.

Kalika stands beside me. 'He has a sense of humour,' she says.

'Thank you for sparing him.' The pier is long and the water is cold. I hope he is able to make it to shore. I add, 'Thanks for giving him a chance.'

'Gratitude means nothing to me,' she says.

I am curious. 'What does have meaning to you?'

'The essence of all things. The essence does not

judge. It is not impressed by actions, nor does it reward inaction.' She shrugs. 'It just is, as I am.'

'I can't tell you where the baby is. I deliberately told Paula not to tell me where she was going. They could be in Canada by now or in Mexico.'

Kalika is not disturbed by my revelations. 'I know there is something you are not telling me. It relates to future contact with the child. You told Paula one other thing besides what you just said. What was it?'

'There was nothing else.'

'You are lying,' she says.

'So I lie? What are you going to do about it? I'm not going to tell you anything. And if you kill me you still won't get the information you want.' I pause. 'But I can't believe that even you would kill your own mother.'

She reaches out and touches my long blond hair with her bloody hand. 'You are beautiful, Sita. You have lived through an entire age. You have out smarted men and women of all nationalities, in all countries and times. You even tricked your creator into releasing you from his vow to Krishna.'

'I did not trick Yaksha. I saved him.'

She continues to play with my hair. 'As you say, Mother. You have faith in what you know and what you remember. But my memory is older, far older, and death or the threat of death is not the only means of persuasion I have at my disposal.' She tugs lightly on my hair. 'You must know by now that I am not simply a vampire.'

'What are you then?'

She takes my chin in her hand. 'Look into my eyes and you will see.'

'No. Wait!'

'Look, Mother.' She twists my head around and catches my eyes. There is no question of my looking away. It is not an option. The blue-black of her eyes have the pull of a black hole, the grip of the primordial seed that gave birth to the universe. The power that emanates from them is cosmic. They shine with colours the spectrum has forgotten. Yet they are such beautiful eyes, really, those of an innocent girl, and I fall in love with them all over again. From far away I hear my daughter's voice, and it is the voice of thunder echoing and also the mere whisper of a baby falling asleep in my lap in the middle of the night. 'Behold your child,' she says.

I look; I must look.

There are planets, stars, galaxies, and they are seemingly endless. Yet beyond them all, beyond the backbone of the sky, as the Vedas say, is the funeral pyre. There sits Mother Kali with her Lord Kala, who destroys time itself. As each of the planets slowly dies and each sun gradually expands into a red dwarf, the flames that signal the end of creation begin to burn. They lick the frozen asteroids and melt the lost comets. And there in that absolute space Kali collects the ash of the dead creation and the skulls of forgotten souls. She saves them for another time, when the worlds will breathe again, and people will once again look up at the sky and wonder what lies beyond the stars. But none of these people will know that it was Kali who remembered them when they were ash. None of them will know who buried them when there was no one left to cover their graves. Even if they did remember, none of them would worship the great Kali because they would be too afraid of her.

I feel afraid as I remember her.

As she asks me to remember.

There is another voice in the sky.

I think it is my own. The shock breaks the vision.

I stumble back from my daughter. 'You are Kali!' I gasp.

She just looks at me. 'You have told me the phone number Paula will call in one month.' She turns away. 'That's all I wanted to know.'

It is hard to throw off the power of the vision.

'Wait. Please? Kalika!'

She glances over her shoulder. 'Yes, Mother?'

'Who was the child?'

'Do you really need to know?'

'Yes.'

'The knowledge will cost you.'

'I need to know!' I cry.

In response Kalika steps to the end of the pier. There she kneels and pulls a board free. It is an old board, long and narrow, but as she works it in her powerful fingers it begins to resemble something I know all too well from more superstitious eras. Too late I realize she has fashioned a stake. She raises the tiny spear over her head and lets fly with it.

The stake goes into the water.

Into Seymour's back. He cries out and sinks.

'No!' I scream.

Kalika stares at me a moment. 'I told you it would cost you.' She turns away. 'I don't lie, Mother.'

My ankle is not fully recovered but I am still a strong vampire. Leaping over the side of the pier, I hit the cold salt water not far from where Seymour flounders two feet below the surface. Pulling him up for air, I hear him gasp in pain. My eyes see as well in the dark as in the daylight. The stake has pierced his lower spine. The tip protrudes from where his belly button should be. His blood flows like water from a broken faucet.

'This hurts,' he says.

'Seymour,' I cry as I struggle to keep him afloat, 'you have to stay with me. If I can get you to shore, I can save you.'

He reaches for the stake and moans in pain. 'Pull it out.'

'No. You'll bleed to death in seconds. I can take it out only when we reach the beach. You must hold on to me so that I can swim as fast as possible. Listen to me, Seymour!'

But he is already going into shock. 'Help me, Sita,' he chokes.

'No!' I slap him. 'Stay with me. I'll get you to shore.'

Then, wrapping my right arm around him, I begin to swim as fast as I can with one free arm and two boot-clad feet. But speed in the water is not Seymour's friend. As I kick toward the beach, the pressure of the passing water on the stake makes him swoon in agony. The rushing water also increases his loss of blood. Yet I feel I have no choice but to hurry.

'Stop, Sita,' he gasps as he starts to faint. 'I can't stand it.'

'You can stand it. This time you're the hero in my story. You can write it all down later. This pain will not last and you will laugh about it in a few days. Because tonight you're going to get what you've always wanted. You're going to become a vampire.'

He is interested, although he is clearly dying. The beach is still two hundred yards away. 'Really?' he mumbles. 'A real vampire?'

'Yes! You'll be able to stay out all night and party and you won't ever get old and ugly. We'll travel the world and we'll have more fun than you can imagine. Seymour?'

'Party,' he says faintly, his face sagging into the water. Having to hold his mouth up slows me down even more but I keep kicking. I imagine an observer on the pier would think a power boat were about to ram the beach. The sand is only a hundred yards away now.

'Hang in there,' I tell him.

Finally, when we are in five feet of water, I am able to put my feet down. I carry him to the beach and carefully lay him on his right side. There is no one around to help us. His blood continues to gush out around the edges of the wooden stake, at the front as well as at the back. He is the colour of refined flour. He hardly breathes, and though I yell in his ear I have to wonder if he is not already beyond hearing. Already beyond even the power of my blood. The situation is worse than it was with Ray and Joel. Neither of them had an object implanted in them. Even vampire flesh cannot heal around such an object, and yet I fear I cannot simply pull it out. I feel his life will spill out with it and be lost on the cold sand.

'Seymour!' I cry. 'Come back to me!'

A minute later, when all seems lost, when he isn't even breathing, my prayer is mysteriously answered. He opens his eyes and looks up at me. He even grins his old Seymour grin, which usually makes me want to laugh and hit him at the same time. Yet this time I choke back the tears. The chill on his flesh, I know, is from the touch of the Grim Reaper. Death stands between us and it will not step aside even for a vampire.

'Seymour,' I say, 'how are you?'

'Fine. The pain has stopped.'

'Good.'

'But I feel cold.' A tremor shakes his body. Dark blood spills over his lips. 'Is this normal?'

'Yes. It is perfectly normal.' He does not feel the stake now, or even recognize how grave his condition is. He thinks I gave him my blood while he was unconscious. He tries to squeeze my hand but he is too weak. Somehow he manages to keep talking.

'Will I live forever now?' he asks.

'Yes.' I bury my face in his. 'Forever and ever.'

His eyes close. 'I will love you that long, Sita.'

'Me, too,' I whisper. 'Me, too.'

We speak no more, Seymour and I.

He dies a minute later, in my arms.

Epilogue

His body I take to a place high in the mountains where I often walked when I lived in Los Angeles. On a bluff, with a view of the desert on one side and the city on the other, I build a funeral pyre from wood I am able to gather in the immediate area. Seymour rests comfortably on top of my construction. At the beach I had removed the bloody stake and thrown it away. He is able to lie on his back and I fold his hands over his big heart.

'You,' I say. 'You were the best.'

There is a wooden match in my right hand, but somehow I am unable to light it. His face looks so peaceful I can't stop staring at him. But I realize the day is moving on, and that the wind will soon pick up. The flames should finish their work before then. Seymour always loved the woods, and wouldn't have wanted them harmed by a raging forest fire. He loved so many things, and I was happy to be one of them.

I strike the match on the bark of a tree.

It burns bright red, and I can't help but think of Kali.

Many things pass through my mind right then.

Many questions and so few answers.

Yet I let the flame burn down to my fingertips.

There is pain, a little smoke. The match dies.

And from my pocket I withdraw the vial of blood.

Number seven. *Ramirez.* I look up.

'What is the cost, Kalika?' I ask the sky.

After opening the vial, I pour half the blood over Seymour's wound, and the other half down his throat. Then I close my eyes and walk away and stand silently behind a tall tree for five minutes. Some mysteries are best left unexplained. My hope refuses to be crushed. I have found love and lost love, but perhaps what I have finally rediscovered is my faith in love. I stand and pray – not for bliss or miracles – I simply pray and that is enough.

Finally I walk back to the funeral pyre.

Seymour is sitting up on the wood and looking at me. His fatal wound has healed.

'How did we get here?' he asks.

Of course I have to laugh. 'It's a long story,' I say.

But I wonder how to finish the story for him.

I still wonder who the child is.

More, I wonder who he *was.*

The Last Vampire

EVIL THIRST
CREATURES OF FOREVER

Kalika has transformed into a bloodthirsty killer with powers far greater than her mother's. So, Alisa faces a heartbreaking decision – to save her daughter or the rest of the world. But perhaps things are not quite as they appear to be and the lines between good and evil seem blurred – can Alisa decide the right path in time?

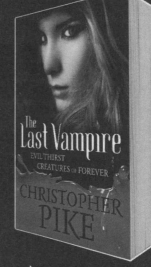

Sisters Red

'The wolf opened its long jaws, rows of teeth stretching for her. A thought locked itself in Scarlett's mind: I am the only one left to fight, so now, I must kill you ...'

An action-packed, paranormal thriller in a gritty urban setting, with a charming love story and unexpected twist that leaves you wanting more!

DARK HEART FOREVER

When Jane Jonas develops a friendship with an enigmatic stranger in town, it's exciting, it's new, and Jane wants him more than she's ever wanted anybody – until her mystery dream boy gets in the way.

Now Jane is caught between two worlds: one familiar, but tinged with romance and excitement; the other dark and dangerous, where angels, werewolves, and an irresistible stranger are trying to seduce her …

A WITCH in WINTER

When love is tangled up in magic, how can you be sure what's real?

Anna Winterson doesn't know she's a witch and would probably mock you for believing in magic, but after moving to the small town of Winter with her father, she learns more than she ever wanted to about power.

When Anna meets Seth, she is smitten, but when she enchants him to love her, she unwittingly amplifies a deadly conflict between two witch clans and splits her own heart in two …

www.ruthwarburton.com
www.hodderchildrens.co.uk

THE SECRET CIRCLE

THE INITIATION AND THE CAPTIVE PART I

Cassie is not happy about moving from sunny California to gloomy New England. She longs for her old life, her old friends … But when she starts to form a bond with a clique of terrifying but seductive teenagers at her new school, she thinks maybe she could fit in after all …

Initiated into the Secret Circle, she is pulled along by the deadly and intoxicating thrill of this powerful and gifted coven. But then she falls in love, and has a daunting choice to make. She must resist temptation or risk dark forces to get what she wants.

www.bookswithbite.co.uk

Sign up to the mailing list to find out about the latest releases from L. J. Smith

THE SECRET CIRCLE

THE CAPTIVE PART II AND THE POWER

Now that Cassie is part of the most alluring and deadly clique imaginable, she is starting to realise that power comes with a price – more dangerous than she knows. Torn between the opposing desires of the two leaders of the Secret Circle, Cassie is struggling again. Does she use her considerable supernatural power to save lives, or does she put all her energy into keeping Adam, the boy she loves.

Cassie's relationship with Adam is threatening to tear the circle apart, so where does Cassie's loyalty and strength, truly lie?

the Vampire Diaries
The Fury & The Reunion
Faced with an ancient evil, Stefan and Damon must stop their feuding and join forces with Elena to confront it. But in so doing, they are unwittingly sealing her fate …
itv 2 Now a major itv2 series
the Vampire Diaries
L. J. SMITH
itv 2 Now a major itv2 series
www.bookswithbite.co.uk
Sign up to the mailing list to find out about the latest releases from L. J. Smith

NIGHT WORLD

Volume 1
Books 1-3
OUT NOW

Secret Vampire

Poppy is dying, and it seems that James is her only chance of survival ... but is the price too high?

Daughters of Darkness

Mary Lynette has just met three mysterious sisters – on the run from their cruel brother. But can she protect them or herself with another threat lurking nearby?

Enchantress

Blaise is irresistible ... and deadly, but the Night World has rules, and Blaise is breaking them all ...

www.bookswithbite.co.uk

NIGHT WORLD

Volume 2
Books 4-6
OUT NOW

Dark Angel

Angel saves Gillian from death in the icy wilderness and then
offers to make her the most popular girl in school. But what does
he want in return?

The Chosen

Vampire killer Rashel is torn between her feelings for her
soulmate, Quinn, and her loathing for his thirst for human blood.
She loves him, but is that enough?

Soulmate

Hannah's true love – Lord of the Night World, has come back into
her life and reignited her passion. But her joy is threatened by the
return of an ancient enemy ...

NIGHT WORLD

Volume 3
Books 7-9
OUT NOW

Huntress

In *Huntress,* Jez Redfern is leader of the Night World vampires, yet she has an instinct to protect innocent mortals from her former friends … But can she resist her own desire for blood?

Black Dawn

In *Black Dawn*, Maggie's brother, Miles, goes missing. Her search for him leads Maggie to the vampire, Delos. Whilst strangely attracted to him she knows it's him or her brother.

Witchlight

In *Witchlight*, Keller is a shapeshifter. She is seaching for a new Wild Power and battling her attraction to the dashing Galen. But it seems he can never be her soulmate…

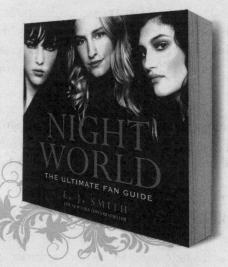